BLOOD KIN

By the same author

A Position of Trust
Seascape With Dead Figures
A Pretty Place For A Murder
A Fox in The Night
Remains to be Seen
Robbed Blind
Breach of Promise

BLOOD KIN

ROY HART

St. Martin's Press
New York

Library of Congress Cataloging-in-Publication Data

Hart, Roy.
    Blood kin / Roy Hart.
       p.   cm.
    ISBN 0-312-06909-X
    I. Title.
    PR6058.A694857B58   1992
    823'.914—dc20   91-35973
                                                CIP

First published in Great Britain by Scribners, a division of Macdonald & Company (Publishers) Limited.

First U.S. Edition: January 1992
10 9 8 7 6 5 4 3 2 1

BLOOD KIN

ONE

THE SURLY FACED MAN LOOMED larger out of the mist, his eyes like two tiny black buttons behind a pair of pebble-lensed spectacles.

'Name of Lindsey?' he grunted.

'Kate Lindsey,' she volunteered cheerfully, putting out her brightest smile and a friendly hand. In the station behind her the last carriage door was slammed shut, a whistle blew and vacuum brakes hissed off.

The proffered hand was clearly her first mistake. She took it back, feeling foolish. It was a grey, grouchy world and the train down from Waterloo had been full of grey, grouchy people. The same contagion obviously pervaded Dorchester.

'These your bags, Miss?'

'Yes,' she said, 'thank you.' She moved back a pace so that he could step between her two suitcases, one with her portable typewriter standing beside it. The typewriter was trapped under one arm, the two suitcases swung up with scarcely any effort, and she followed him along the forecourt past the drawn up rank of taxis. Rita Cavallo's car was an elderly Jaguar, very white, very sleek.

'Anything breakable, Miss?' he asked curtly, as he lifted the boot lid.

'The smaller one's got some camera gear in it. Thank you.'

The cases were stowed, the typewriter laid beside them, the boot lid slammed down and locked.

He skirted her and opened the nearside door. She stepped into the car's warm interior. A walnut panel with a privacy window above it separated passengers from the

1

driver. Which was perhaps no bad thing in the circumstances. Miss Cavallo's chauffeur did not look like a man given to deep and meaningful conversation.

As befitted the car's grandeur, he drove at a stately and unhurried progress south out of Dorchester. The early afternoon traffic was light, so that the town was soon left behind. There was little to see then but the mist-shrouded countryside, trees and hedgerows, autumn bare, huddles of ghostly cottages, some of them thatched, looming then swallowed up again in the all-enveloping murk that seemed to go on for ever and ever.

The Jaguar gently rose and fell over a humpbacked bridge spanning a still, grey watercourse. Since she had only ever seen one film with Rita Cavallo in it – and then it had been on mid-afternoon television, and Kate had only stuck with it because she had been struck low with influenza at the time and had felt too groggy to get up and switch it off – she had deemed it wise to do some advance research on her subject in the movie section of the studio's reference library. Miss Cavallo's age appeared to be some kind of national secret. One encyclopaedia had stated that she had been born in *1915*(?), another *1913*(?) and the third had been honest enough to venture nothing beyond a bracketted dash. Miss Cavallo's youthful star had begun to rocket in the early thirties, peaked in the late forties during a brief spell in Hollywood after the war, then plummetted – more or less out of sight to all but her most loyal fans – in the fifties. Nowadays, Rita Cavallo was only a legend, a name occasionally uttered by nostalgic movie-buffs. Rumour had it, however, that she was planning a comeback.

The grey sombre daylight felt like an early dusk, but a glance at her wristwatch showed that it was still only one o'clock in the afternoon.

The room was huge. In the summer it would be bright and airy, today it was as drab as the weather outside. An old electric fire with a single bar gave out a small warmth and the windows wept with condensation.

'The key, Miss.'

2

'Thank you.' She held out her hand and he dropped the key into her palm. 'Am I allowed to know what to call you – Mr ...?'

'Shaw, Miss,' he said. 'Madam will be down in the drawing-room at two o'clock, Miss.'

'Thank you,' she said. 'There's just a question of the nearest bathroom ...?'

'That door over there, Miss.' He nodded brusquely towards the corner between the fireplace and window wall. 'And if you need anything,' his tone implied that she'd better not dare, 'the bell-push is beside the bed. It rings down to the kitchen. Only not after ten p.m., Miss, if you wouldn't mind. It sets the dogs barking.'

'I'll remember that,' she said. 'Thank you.'

The dark eyes narrowed behind their pebble lenses. Perhaps he'd read some unintended sarcasm in her voice. Mr Shaw was going to be a very contrary man to get on with. She wondered if she dared to ask for a cup of tea ...

'Will that be all, Miss?'

Her courage failed her. 'Yes, Mr Shaw. Thank you.'

'Just Shaw, Miss,' he said stiffly. 'I'm quite happy with that. Leave the door open, shall I, Miss?'

'No,' she said. 'Thank you.'

And he was gone, the door closed behind him and his footfalls creaking away down the narrow passage to the landing. She usually withheld her judgements on folk until she got to know them, but Mr Shaw had made his impression quickly. She could still feel his disagreeable presence in the room now.

She decided not to tempt providence by unpacking too much too soon. Just her night things, her washbag and towel, a discreet black dress that was smart enough to wear for dinner tonight – if she was invited. The bathroom was spartanly Victorian, the lavatory pan a marvellous old relic that was willow-patterned within and without. The porcelain cistern matched. Except that it thundered like Niagara Falls when she pulled the chain and hissed away like a leaking steam engine for several minutes afterwards, and was clearly going to be a source of great embarrassment if anyone were sleeping next door. Everything else functioned and the hot water really was hot. A final dash of cold water took her breath away, a brisk rub with a towel brought it back again.

The room smelled faintly of dogs. The bed was a double, not too soft. Crisply laundered white sheets, cosy-looking patchwork quilt that smelled of moth-balls. The wardrobe looked like something picked up third-hand in a junk-shop, but it was scrupulously clean inside and all the drawers were lined with fresh white paper. There was a full length mirror behind the door. It could have been worse. And it had been decent of Rita Cavallo to offer to put her up for the week.

The dressing-table, set between the windows, was a spindle-legged twenties affair, a touch battered, with tilting mirrors and a glass top. Plenty of drawers, again, all freshly lined.

She drew a net curtain aside, and swept an arc clear of condensation with the edge of her hand. There was a flagged and balustraded terrace immediately beneath her, the start of a path, the tops of several trees floating above the mist. Then a movement near the terrace. The spectral shadow of a man wielding a shovel, the mist parting and closing about him so that she had to look twice to make sure that he was there at all.

The top of the dressing-table looked marginally less desolate with a few of her make-up bits and pieces spread out on it. The grey suit she was wearing would do for the two o'clock meeting in the sitting room; Rita Cavallo might just have seen her getting out of the car, and it might not do to give the impression that she already had one foot under the table as it were.

And only then, as she uncapped a lipstick, did she realise the reason for the sensation of disquiet in the pit of her stomach.

It was the oppressive silence. Even the man with the shovel had made not a sound.

The two upper floors of the house were a maze of small

dark passages, two of them with locked doors at their ends so that she had had to retrace her steps, go back up one flight of stairs and come down another further along. The staircase she was descending now was wide and airy, and led down to the cathedrally proportioned entrance hall at the front of the house, where a blazing coal fire crackled away in a marble fireplace on the left and a huge oak table stood four-square across the middle. She could hear voices, one of them a man's – not Shaw's, because the voice was laughing. If Shaw ever laughed, his jaw would drop off ...

Four oak doors led off the hall, one of them ajar and with a glimmer of electric light showing from it. Tentatively, she pushed it wider open. Yet another passage, and framed by the open doorway at the other end the talking man was hunched over a mug of tea at the side of a table in what looked like the kitchen. He wore no shoes and the bottoms of his jeans were tucked into a pair of long, red woollen socks. When he laughed again an unseen woman chuckled with him. His face turned towards the passage as a floorboard creaked under Kate's right foot.

'Excuse me,' she said hesitantly, at the doorway, to the buxomly comfortable-looking woman rolling out pastry on the other side of the table. The man took her in with a glance of passing interest, long enough to be flattering, short enough not to be unpleasant.

'Yes, dear,' the woman said cheerfully, pausing briefly. 'Come in. You're the television-lady, aren't you?'

'Yes, that's right,' said Kate. The woman's bright smile was like a shaft of sunlight after the mean and moody Shaw. 'I'm looking for the drawing-room.'

'Back up the passage, dear, and it's the door on the right. Bang opposite the fireplace in the hall.'

'Thank you.'

The man smiled. She smiled back, already pivoting on a heel.

'Would you like a cup of tea, dear?'

She turned quickly about again, she still had a few spare

minutes. 'Oh, yes,' she said earnestly. 'Love one. Thank you.'

It was the man who rose, and padded across to a dresser in his bright red socks. He took down a cup and saucer. A black donkey-jacket hung over the back of his chair.

'With everything?' he said.

'Please,' she said.

'Why don't you take a pew, dear,' the woman invited. 'Take the weight off your feet for a tick.'

Kate drew out a wooden chair from under the table. The kitchen was warm. She glanced at her watch.

'There's no rush, dear,' the woman said, deftly rolling up her pastry on a wooden pin then unrolling it as deftly to cover an oval dish full of apples and blackberries that made Kate's saliva glands run riot. 'She won't be down till two o'clock. Regular as clockwork, she is. You enjoy your tea.'

It was set in front of her. A sugar bowl followed it.

'Thank you,' she said. His clothes smelled earthy.

'Bill Erskine,' he said, by way of introduction. 'Hi.'

'Kate Lindsey,' she said. 'Hello.'

'And I'm Mrs Shaw,' the woman said, to Kate's mild surprise at that unlikely match. 'Or Ellen, if you like.'

'Good journey down?' the man asked. He had resumed his chair and spoke over his mug of tea.

'Not bad,' she said. He was about mid-thirties, dark and pleasantly weathered, and with a particularly nice line in dark-brown voices. His faded green pullover was riddled with moth-holes.

It was evidently him whom she had glimpsed working down in the garden. He was building an ornamental lake, he explained. A bridge over it, water lilies, goldfish, all that sort of thing. He was a landscape gardener. He had another five acres out there still to see to. About another four months' work. Miss Cavallo wanted it all up and running by spring next year.

'What's she like?' Kate dared to ask. Rule One, that was: get to know thine enemy well beforehand.

'So-so,' he said – the kind of 'so-so' that is hedged with

doubt like barbed-wire. 'She can't always make up her mind what she wants, but she pays up on the dot, and you can't say fairer than that.'

'A bit tart when she wants to be, too,' added Mrs Shaw more scathingly. 'And if you hear her rowing with Mr Sheridan, you'd best keep well out of her way for the next half hour. She's actressy, you see, dear. Up and down like a yo-yo, she is.'

'How about Mr Sheridan?'

'Just the way he is on the telly,' said Bill Erskine more warmly. 'He's not acting. He *really* is like that.'

'He's a *lovely* man,' Mrs Shaw broke in. 'Always a "please", and a "thank you". A gentleman the way they used to be, you know.'

'Time's up,' said Bill Erskine apologetically, pulling up one frayed cuff and tilting his wristwatch towards her. 'It's two to two.'

And so it was. She gulped down the last of her tea, rose and pushed her chair back under the table. Bill Erskine wished her luck.

'Don't worry about a thing, dear,' advised Mrs Shaw. 'She'll be on her best behaviour. Charm you out of the trees, she will. You'll see.'

The drawing-room was another barn of a room, with three large green leather settees ranged about a marble fireplace big enough to be the entrance to a mausoleum. A white Steinway grand piano, photographs of a dozen long-familiar faces, paintings on the walls, in the baroque gilt frames, and more pieces of collectable porcelain than she had ever seen outside an antique shop. On a winter's night, with the curtains closed and the fire alight, it could easily be cosy and the camera-crew were going to love it. But what it looked more like, on this miserable autumn afternoon, was the last outpost of a decadent empire, hastily evacuated and only waiting for the restless natives to storm in and repossess it.

Yesterday in London the sun had been shining. Kate warmed her hands on the ugly, cast-iron radiator under the window. She swivelled quickly, bracing herself, as the door knob turned softly behind her. Not Rita Cavallo, though. A man, tall and stooped and hugely built and instantly recognisable, with the rumpled hair and the sad baggy face that had endeared him to at least two generations of movie and television watchers. And plainly caught as much by surprise as she was.

'Ah – m'dear,' he said diffidently, 'Sorry. Left a book in here. Paperback. Chap on the front brandishing a couple of six-shooters. Haven't seen it lying about, by any chance?'

'No,' she said, slightly awed. 'Sorry.'

His bemused gaze went all about. He settled for one of the settees, rooting, not very methodically, around and under its silk cushions. Bill Erskine had been right. George Sheridan had no need to act. He really was that endearing old bumbler.

He moved towards a tall cabinet beside the fireplace. 'Have a look in the piano stool, would you, m'dear? Most kind.'

She skirted the piano and lifted the seat of the stool. Nothing in it but a stack of sheet music. From somewhere behind her a door catch clicked, and she distinctly heard the dull clink of one full bottle knocked against another. Tactfully keeping her back to him, until she heard the catch click softly again, she let a few sheets of music riffle through her fingers before closing the embroidered seat on them. 'No,' she said. 'It's not here. Sorry.'

He was already back by the door, one hand and half an arm behind him and looking about as subtly innocent as a small boy caught in someone else's orchard with a shirtful of apples.

'Ah, well, no matter. Must be somewhere else. See you at dinner, I expect. You're very pretty, by the way.' He tapped the wing of his nose. A secret sign. It made them conspirators. 'See you later.'

A dexterous conjuring trick behind his back had the bottle transferred from one hand to the other, so that she never did actually see it, as he turned and crept out again in his carpet slippers, and closed the door softly behind him.

His shave was a narrow one – a matter of only seconds, and she was still wearing the smile she had shared with him when the brisk tattoo of a woman's heels sounded across the marble tiles of the hall, and the door knob was turned again.

This time it really was Rita Cavallo.

TWO

TWO HAIRY PEKINGESE DOGS SCURRIED in ahead of her to reconnoitre Kate's ankles.

'My dear, I'm a few minutes late. Do forgive me.'

'Yes, of course,' said Kate, as one of Miss Cavallo's plump warm hands curled around hers and squeezed it. The years had not been kind to Rita Cavallo. Everything about her was overfleshed, overblown, luxuriant, faintly tropical. You had to look hard to realise that she had once been beautiful.

'We'll talk over a pot of tea. More informal. Did you have lunch?'

'Yes,' lied Kate. 'On the train. Thank you.' Something cold and wet snuffling over her foot was Mr Wu. The other Pekingese was Mr Chen. From the way Mr Shaw had warned her about the dogs, she had expected them to be Alsatians at the very least. But she had never particularly cared for toy dogs either.

She was led towards the green settees that surrounded the fireplace. Rita Cavallo had drenched herself in some kind of perfume that trailed in the air behind her. It smelled expensive.

'You there. Me over here. So that we can see each other. Yes?'

Kate sat gingerly, until the green leather stopped sinking beneath her. Rita Cavallo lowered herself to the settee on the other side of the vast expanse of Chinese hearthrug, settled herself and leaned back amongst the cushions with one arm and a handful of rings along the back of it. Her huge breasts were divided and hoisted into two quite separate entities.

'I may call you Katherine?'

'Please,' said Kate.

She was measured across the Chinese rug. Two smiling little eyes set in slits of heavily powdered fat surveyed her. Miss Cavallo was definitely going to be a subject for the soft-focus lens – and a lot of work for the make-up department.

'And you've come down to prepare the ground?'

'Yes,' said Kate, 'but I'll try not to be intrusive. If there are any questions you and Mr Sheridan don't like, then you only have to say.'

Rita Cavallo made an airy flourish with the handful of rings. 'My dear, George and I have *nothing* to hide. Absolutely nothing. I told Mr Welsh that over lunch – oh, *poor* Woosie-Wu, does 'oo want to come up? Come on, den ...' The lapse into pouting baby talk was addressed to the begging Mr Wu, who jumped up and arranged himself across her lap, panting noisily and with his wet pink tongue lolling out. 'You were saying, my dear?'

'I was going to say that *Partners* isn't intended to be an investigative programme. It's scheduled for a slot between two and three in the afternoon, so the audience will be predominantly female. We're looking for human interest, but I expect Mr Welsh told you that.'

'Yes, he did.' The heavily beringed hand caressed Mr Wu's head. Had it not been for the rings and the scarlet nail varnish, it could easily have been a man's hand.

The door was opened after a discreet rap, and Shaw backed in with a brass and glass tea-trolley with china rattling on it. It was patently a regular routine. Without a word, he came between the settees, switched on the two electric sconces either side of the fireplace, then crouched in front of the hearth and struck a match. There was a soft thud of lit gas, and flames flickered up around the fake wooden logs. The room was already warm enough, which was more than could be said for Kate's own. Miss Cavallo was plainly fond of her creature comforts.

'Would you like me to pour, Madam?'

'No, Shaw, thank you, I'll see to it.'

11

The tea trolley was wheeled closer. Shaw pussy-footed out without a sound, not even a click of the door catch. Kate wondered if George Sheridan had made his escape safely with his loot. It had been momentarily disconcerting to find out that the man who did the voice-overs for Montmorency Marvelmouse was a secret drinker.

Rita Cavallo, with some effort and so as not to disturb Mr Wu too much, wriggled further forward in order to pour. Her legs, like the rest of her, were thick and heavy. The flowing red tent was dramatically flamboyant, the matching chiffon scarf loosely tied around her throat probably hid a multitude of sins. But there was still something about her, something that she still managed to convey, a hint of the Mediterranean ... sensuality, was it? Certainly something.

Kate rose for the cup and saucer and the little Chelsea biscuit plate that were extended to her. The selection of biscuits was arranged on a two-tiered silver rack. Most of them were thick with black chocolate. But drool over those as she might, she settled for two plain digestive. Sitting down again, with something in each hand, and the unresisting cushions not helping, required infinite balance.

'The programme will be going out when?' asked Miss Cavallo – or did she prefer to be called Mrs Sheridan? – around a chocolate biscuit. She had taken up several, Kate observed, one already in her mouth, two more waiting to be devoured on her plate, although one of those was broken in half and shared with Mr Wu. The red chiffon bobbed as she swallowed.

'It's scheduled for autumn next year,' said Kate. Filming would be done in May. The programme would be one in a series of six, all of them featuring a married couple with a mutual claim to fame. All she would require for the coming week was a couple of hours each day with Miss Cavallo and Mr Sheridan, and permission to wander around the house and the gardens with her camera in order to give the director some idea of suitable rooms and vantage points so that he could work out the best

12

disposition of the cameras. She would be quite happy to work from her room. But that wasn't necessary, Miss Cavallo told her. There was a study downstairs at the back of the house. She was more than welcome to use that. And in the study was a *host* of scrapbooks. They went back over thirty years.

'Perhaps a browse through those might provide some ideas?'

'Yes,' said Kate. 'They'd be a great help. Thank you.'

With the exception of Monday, Rita Cavallo could spare Kate two or three hours every day. And George Sheridan might have problems with Monday, too. He would be working. In London. Rehearsals. And Sunday might be just a *little* difficult because her daughter and son-in-law would be coming down. The son-in-law, Julius Worboys was a barrister. Perhaps Kate could spend the weekend taking her photographs and looking through the scrapbooks ...

For the next two hours, Rita Cavallo waxed garrulous, about the house – it had been built in 1805, the year of Trafalgar – and about the work going on in the garden – by the time Mr Welsh and the film crew arrived it would look absolutely *splendid*. Mr Wu and Mr Chen were twins. Had Kate noticed all the photographs? Yes, the one on the piano was of *dear* Noel. The signature was genuine. It had been taken in 1935. Was her room comfortable? If she needed anything she had only to ask.

It was clear that Mike Welsh wasn't going to find it difficult to get Rita Cavallo talking, the greater problem looked like being getting her to shut up again.

'I'd like us to be friends, Katherine. I'm *sure* we shall be, aren't you?'

'I hope so, Miss Cavallo.'

'We shall, dear.' Kate was left with the distinct impression that her knee had just been patted. 'And Rita, please. I'm really *quite* ordinary.'

Total recovery came after leisurely unpacking and putting away, ten minutes of yoga, and an hour-long slow soak in the bath with several replenishments of hot water. A more detached view of the black dress revealed that it needed a press here and there. She plugged in her travelling iron, snatched her hand quickly away from the plug and waited for the bang, she and electricity never had struck up an amiable working relationship. No explosion came. The last time she had ironed anything on the floor had been in her college days. Mrs Shaw would doubtless have an ironing-board, but Kate shrank from the thought of having Shaw fetch it up for her. Mr Shaw was definitely on her blacklist. Although Rita Cavallo had certainly been friendly enough, and chatty enough, which boded well.

The dress on, she debated then whether or not it was the right one. It looked *too* smart, and she wondered if it was wise to look too smart too soon, and risk having Rita Cavello get the idea that Kate was setting up in competition with her in the fashion stakes. With her hair dragged back, the dress looked a little more severe. Nothing too aggressive by way of paint, nor too much. Black shoes, quite plain. No jewellery except her wristwatch and her mother's engagement ring, she never went anywhere without that.

Tights and today's underwear left to soak in the handbasin in the bathroom, she was still running the water on those when a metallic resonance boomed from somewhere downstairs and it was six o'clock and time for dinner. It seemed an unusual hour to eat, but from what she had seen of it so far it appeared to be an unusual household.

She was lost again. Whoever had designed the house had either suffered from architectural schizophrenia or had merely been perverse. She was sure she had come up this way with Shaw the first time. Another passage, a murmur of voices at the end of it. Except at the end of it there was a door and it was locked.

She turned and retraced her steps, but only two of them before she stopped short and took a tighter grip of her handbag. The burly silhouette that filled the opening of the passage, almost from side to side, was Shaw's, his

14

square face and spiteful mouth lit palely by a nearby wall-lamp and his spectacles twinkling.

'It's private up here, Miss,' he said, making the chide plainer still by moving back and standing pointedly aside just beyond the arch. 'This way, please, Miss.'

'I'm lost,' she said, feeling fatuous and angry both at once.

Close to, he smelled of soap and too much aftershave. He said firmly, 'That way, please, Miss. Left, then right, then down the stairs.' A peremptory hand gestured. It brooked no argument.

He stalked her all the way, making the hairs prickle at the nape of her neck, left, then right. And then a flight of carpeted stairs, but not the ones she had used this afternoon. She must have crossed the house from one side to the other. These stairs were at the back of it. At Shaw's further muttered instruction, she then turned left again, along a broad, brightly lit passage with linen-fold panelling on the walls. Civilisation came at last with the familiar reception hall and the blazing fire.

The dark little eyes fixed her. 'You always use *those* stairs, Miss,' he said nodding towards the ones she had come down by this afternoon.

'I see,' she said, smiling a smile that was hewn in stone. 'Thank you, Mr Shaw. I'll remember next time.'

And just make sure you do, the dark little eyes said.

'You'll find Mr Sheridan in the drawing-room, Miss. Behind you.'

'Thank you.'

Each waited for the other to go. Shaw won. Infuriated, she turned her back on him and stalked off stiffly to the drawing-room, still feeling those cold expressionless eyes boring into her back.

George Sheridan, a cow-lick of wayward hair over one eye, but togged out dashingly in a black dinner-jacket, stood with his back to the lit gas-fire. The other man, less formally attired in a new grey suit with a black pullover underneath it, and presently making himself free with a decanter and glasses at the sideboard was Bill Erskine. She

15

observed him with some relief, because his presence made her feel less of an outsider.

George Sheridan thrust out a hand towards her. 'Ah, m'dear,' he said. 'Come and join us. Miss Lindsey, isn't it?'

'Kate Lindsey.' Her hand was pumped enthusiastically.

'I'm George,' he said. 'And the acting barman's Bill – whom, so he tells me, you've already met.'

'What'll you have, Miss Lindsey?' asked Bill Erskine, from the sideboard, as the stopper rattled back into the neck of the decanter.

'Nothing for me, thank you.'

'Must have something m'dear,' insisted George Sheridan. 'If it's only a tonic with a slice of lemon.'

She settled for that, although the last thing she needed just now was something to stimulate her taste buds. The last decent meal she had had was breakfast, and that had paled into history.

Bill Erskine came over with two tumblers, and a stemmed glass with a sliver of lemon floating in it. One tumbler was handed to George Sheridan. It was a gesture made with easy familiarity.

'A long and happy life, George,' Erskine said, raising his glass. 'Happy birthday.'

'Many happy returns,' said Kate. 'I didn't know.'

'The old villain's trying to tell us all he's seventy,' said Bill Erskine.

'True, alas, m'dear,' George Sheridan said. 'Remember seeing old King Ted the Seventh's funeral. The Kaiser was there on a white horse. Had a withered arm, you know.'

'The horse?' said Bill Erskine, plainly teasing.

'Ignore him, m'dear,' advised George Sheridan lugubriously. 'Fellow's an intellectual thug. Only put up with him because he plays a decent game of snooker. Don't suppose you play, perchance?' he asked hopefully.

'No,' she said. 'I don't. Sorry.'

'No,' he said gloomily. 'Thought not. Still don't give gels the full benefits of a liberal education do they? Damned unfair.' But then all the bumbling vagueness dissolved in a

16

flash and he cocked his head alertly. 'Ah,' he murmured. 'M'lady cometh. Me thinketh.'

'Ah, you're *here*.' The dramatic entrance was all for Kate, the outstretched hands, the whisper of blue silk tent, the teetering rush, the two Pekingese bringing up the rear like pageboys. 'My dear, *how* lovely.' For one awful moment Kate thought Rita Cavallo was going to embrace her and smother her in all that bosom. As it was, the two hot hands turned her upper arms to gooseflesh and made her shrink with embarrassment, more so when in more or less the same breath Rita Cavallo purred over her shoulder, 'Don't you think so, Bill?'

'Why – yes,' agreed poor 'Bill', who was scarcely able to say much else in the circumstances.

Dinner went on in much the same vein, Rita Cavallo doing most of the talking and everyone else listening, the rare pauses filled in by one or other of the two men. Bill Erskine ate methodically, George Sheridan slowly and fastidiously, Rita Cavallo as if a famine was likely to be declared nationally at midnight. The meal was unexpectedly ordinary – beef, Yorkshire pudding, roast potatoes, carrots and Brussels sprouts – but whatever could be said of Mrs Shaw she could certainly cook. The wine, however, was heady stuff, and when George Sheridan tilted the bottle again, she quickly shook her head. He didn't press, only continued with his interested probing.

'Your father's an army chap, then. Still serving?'

'Yes,' she said. 'He's based in Brussels. NATO.'

'I did a stint in Brussels, m'self. During the war, of course. How about your Ma?' George Sheridan topped up his own glass and the bottle was passed on to Bill Erskine.

'She died. Three years ago.'

'Oh, m'dear. Stupid question. Shouldn't pry. Sorry.'

'You'll have to forgive George,' came sweetly along the table. 'He's always putting his foot into something or another, aren't you, George.'

He picked up his knife and fork again. 'Yes, m'dear,' he murmured dutifully. 'I'm sure I do, if you say so.'

Kate made a mental note. Beside their mutual claim to

17

fame, the other prerequisite for the participants of *Partners* was an easy-going relationship. Rita Cavallo gathered them all in again with her slitty little eyes.

'I've had Shaw set up the projector for afterwards. I thought we might all enjoy that. Mm?'

George Sheridan stiffened. 'It's my birthday, dammit,' he growled. 'And young Bill's traipsed all the way over here to give me a game of snooker. That's the reason I asked Mrs Shaw for an early dinner, for God's sake.'

'But Bill *likes* old movies,' she twittered on relentlessly. 'Don't you, Bill?'

'I really don't mind,' said Erskine, taking cover behind his wineglass.

'And Katherine?'

'Yes, of course,' said Kate, picking up hers.

George Sheridan lowered his knife and fork. 'You are placing these two nice young people in an invidious position, my dear. Miss Lindsey *might* even prefer an early night.'

'No, really,' Kate protested, in an effort to cool a situation that looked like boiling over. 'I enjoy old movies.'

George Sheridan plied his knife and fork again. 'You may do whatever you wish, m'dear,' he said, with quiet authority. 'But Bill and I intend to play snooker, I trust you'll excuse us.'

The remainder of the course was eaten in frosty silence, until Mrs Shaw wheeled in the apple and blackberry pie that Kate had seen her making that afternoon. George Sheridan ogled it shamelessly and kept growling '... bigger bit, bigger bit ...', guiding her wrist until she sliced a portion that suited him.

'Cream, dear?' asked Mrs Shaw.

'Please,' said Kate.

'Miss Lindsey would *probably* prefer to be called by her name, Mrs Shaw. You might remember that.'

'Yes, Madam,' mumbled Mrs Shaw, her knuckles suddenly whitening around the jug handle as she poured cream over Kate's pie.

'You seem to forget we pay that woman wages, George,'

Rita Cavallo said, as the door closed behind Mrs Shaw and the trolley. 'You *don't* have to suck up to her in that *disgusting* way. She's *not* family. She *works* here.'

'For God's sake, woman,' George Sheridan retorted, his eyes blazing angrily. 'It's nineteen seventy-bloody-six; servants went out with the bloody war. Sorry, m'dear.' The apology, and the brief glance that went with it, were solely for Kate. 'And *I*, as I recall, pay her wages. All right?'

The black and white images came and went in the flickering half-dark of the projection room. Another chocolate wrapper rustled.

'Nineteen thirty-two, this one,' whispered Rita Cavallo, leaning close, her breath laced with brandy. 'My third film. I was seventeen.'

Or not, thought Kate, as the case might well be. She looked more like seventeen going on twenty-one.

The scene dissolved into another, a youthful Rita Cavallo with tightly-tonged blonde curls and scantily clad in a short white petticoat, dabbing on lipstick at a dressing shelf in a rocking ship's cabin, then scampering back to the bunk and snatching up a dress to cover herself as a knock came at the door.

'Come in,' she squeaked, amidst a sound track that sounded like frying bacon.

Enter, stage right and staggering, a swarthy and heavily brilliantined ship's officer – the wireless operator, because he was clutching a telegram. Outside the wind was blowing a gale that crashed the door shut behind him.

'Chester Barclay,' whispered Rita Cavallo, again at Kate's ear so that she felt another hot and unpleasant waft of alcohol. 'Dead now. God, he was an *animal*, that man.' But it was not so much a complaint as a thrill of lecherous approbation. 'An absolute *animal*. Another chocolate, my dear. *Go on*.'

'No, thank you. Really.'

The projection room was a lavishly appointed cinema in miniature – twelve red plush seats, tiered in rows of four, fading house lights and velvet curtains that had opened to the soft buzz of an electric motor. The projector's cone of light came from a slit in the wall above and behind them. Shaw was working the projector.

The telegram was read. Shock and horror. Dress falls to floor, hand flies to mouth. Ship rocks, cabin light dims, then brightens again, foreshadowing the inevitable disaster still to come. That steamer is *never* going to reach Java in one piece. The only people who don't seem to know it are the cast.

'God, what a ham,' chuckled Rita Cavallo. 'But the audiences *loved* it.' She had leaned loathsomely closer again. 'Ah, but that figure: I wish I had it now. I could have had *anybody*. *Any* man I ever wanted.' Kate's flesh, every inch of it, shrank, as a hot heavy hand was laid on her knee and crushed it in a grip of iron; then Rita Cavallo whispered at her ear, 'Youth, Katherine, *how* I envy it,' and the hand went away and the moment was over.

'And that one's Virginia Dawson,' confided Rita Cavallo huskily. 'Went to America and turned alcoholic. They found her dead in Central Park. With a bottle. Naked, under a mink coat. They say she looked fifty years old. She was only twenty-three, poor child. And pregnant – of course.'

'Lost again, Miss?'

The sneering voice had come from behind her.

'Yes, I am,' she snapped. It was close to midnight, she was starting a headache, and he'd practically frightened her out of her skin, creeping up behind her like that.

'The end of the passage, Miss. Then left. You can't miss it.'

'Thank you,' she said.

'Goodnight, Miss.'

'Goodnight,' she said, with a look that should have struck him dead where he stood. But of course it did not.

This time he didn't follow her, instead, he must have doubled back somewhere along another passage and got in front of her because she heard a floorboard creak around the next corner. She prepared herself for battle because this time she was ready for him.

But it was only George Sheridan, glazed of eye and weaving majestically, a glass in one hand, his dinner jacket over the other arm. A cautioning finger went to his lips.

'Sorry, m'dear,' he whispered hoarsely. 'Got m'self a bit hat-racked. Sleep well.'

She drew back against the wall to give him room. 'Goodnight,' she whispered.

'Night, m'dear,' he whispered back. 'God bless.'

THREE

HER OUTWARD BREATHS TURNED TO strands of vapour. The cold damp morning felt like winter and, although the mist had lifted during the night, its moisture still glistened on the grass and trees.

The house that yesterday had been obscured by the mist stood sharply stamped against the sky this morning, slate-roofed over mellow old bricks, white-painted sashed windows. A touch gloomy. Last summer's leafless creeper clinging to the walls like a lacework fungus. It did not require a lot of imagination to conceive of a mad Mrs Rochester being locked away somewhere in an attic. Her keeper, of course, would have to be Shaw. Kate's own room was over on the right, on the second floor. The three gable-rooms set among the slates had probably been servants' quarters in the house's halcyon days. On her way down this morning, a woman she had not seen before had been running a vacuum cleaner over the stairs.

She shivered inside her coat. It was the sort of morning to keep on the move. The path she took was bordered by empty, freshly turned flower beds. Little white plastic labels sprouted here and there, heralding what was planned for the spring blooming. A bed on the right was probably the one she had seen Bill Erskine digging over yesterday, its newly turned soil still lay in moist black slabs waiting for the frosts to break them up. A huge stack of boughs and twigs had once been rhododendrons; all they were now was bonfire kindling.

She had been a long time getting off to sleep last night, her mind a mosaic of broken images, bits and pieces of that awful film, Shaw's sinister face half lit by a wall-lamp, the flash of anger in George Sheridan's eyes when he'd more or less told his wife to shut up along the length of the dinner table, Rita Cavallo stuffing a chocolate biscuit into her mouth and greedily chewing it to extinction. And lying there in the cold room Kate had come to the conclusion that Rita Cavallo was eminently dislikeable, and that what she had tried to recognise in her face the previous afternoon was simply studiedly disguised nastiness. She was a revolting woman, and it was little wonder that dear old George sought solace in his bottles. And first thing on Monday Kate was going to have to phone Mike Welsh and warn him that one episode of *Partners* would have to be very carefully worked – or even abandoned.

She climbed three flagged steps between stone balustrades, surmounted by two funereal urns where the ground levelled off again. Trees then, and slippery dead leaves underfoot, the path gravelled, and her nostrils flaring at the smell of woodsmoke.

Where the trees thinned, parked on the grass, there was an old white truck, with *Erskine Landscapes* written on its side and its tailgate hanging open. Its owner was a crouched, backward shuffling figure unrolling a huge cylinder of polythene sheeting that overlapped another sheet already dressed out across the middle of the new lake bed, she presumed to make it watertight. Every couple of yards, he stopped and rose and collected a house brick from a nearby metal barrow and used it to weight down the overlap. A blazing bonfire crackled a few yards away, the welcome warmth of it striking her face.

'Morning,' he called cheerfully, glimpsing her and flourishing a brick by way of greeting. 'Doing a bit of exploring?'

'Just getting my bearings,' she called. 'Seems to be miles of it.'

'Twenty acres,' he said. 'Quite modest for these parts.' The brick was laid and he straightened and started towards her, gumbooted and leather-gloved, glimpses of old khaki shirt showing through the holes in his museum-piece of a pullover, and mud on the knees of his jeans.

'Tea-break,' he said, stepping up on to the bank beside her. 'Fancy a cup?'

'No, thanks. I didn't mean to stop you working.'

'You didn't,' he said. He went to the cab of the white truck and took a vacuum flask down from the passenger seat. The bonfire drew her like a magnet. She took her hands from her pockets and stretched them towards the crackling twigs.

'How are you getting on with her ladyship?' He was sitting on the running board of the truck and unscrewing the top of the flask, his distance making an easier ambience between them than if he had joined her by the fire.

'Oh, not bad. Haven't had much of a chance yet.'

'How about old George?'

'I think I'm in love,' she said.

'Everybody is,' he said, sipping from his plastic cup. 'He's a hell of an old guy, our George.'

'Think you got him wrong, though,' she said. 'About his not acting. I think he's iron underneath all that waffling.'

'Only with Rita,' he said. 'And only when she pushes him hard enough.'

Bright red sparks spat upward and the middle of the bonfire suddenly subsided in a rush of heat.

'Not working today?' he said.

'I'm working now,' she said.

'Cushy job.'

'It pays the rent. I was hoping to have a chat with Rita and George, but I think they're still in bed.'

'Rita's not,' he said. 'Saw Shaw driving her out on my way in.'

'She's back then. I saw the Jaguar tucked up in the garage.'

'They were using George's – he's got one, too.'

'Oh, I see.' From the tail of her eye she saw him toss the dregs of his tea across the grass beside him. It was time to move on. 'Thanks for the warm.'

'You're welcome,' he said. 'If you walk a couple of hundred yards on up that path you'll get a view all the way

24

back to Dorchester. If you've got a soul, it'll take your breath away.'

'How was it?' Bill Erskine asked, on her way back again.

'Grand,' she said. He was unrolling yet another run of polythene sheeting. 'I noticed a bus-stop outside yesterday, can I get to Dorchester from it?'

'Weekend service,' he said. 'Every hour, on the hour. Reliable though.' Another brick was lifted from the metal wheelbarrow. 'I'm going in myself this afternoon to pick up glass for some cloches. I'll give you a lift if you like.'

'I thought I'd have lunch there,' she said. 'But thanks all the same.'

She was back at two in the afternoon. The house was quieter than ever, and a glance down into the garden showed that both Bill Erskine and his white truck had gone, and a glance the other way showed the doors to the coachhouse-cum-garage still open and only the one Jaguar standing in its shadows.

At three o'clock, with the house to herself, she loaded a film into her Nikon, checked that her flashgun was working and set off downstairs to take a few photographs of the reception rooms and anything on the way which might provide a talking point.

By daylight the passages were less of a maze, and, sure in the knowledge that Shaw was not likely to leap out and ambush her, she took the route by which she had come upstairs with Rita Cavallo late last night. She was equally sure that the door that lay ahead of her led to the first floor landing where they had parted company and bade each other goodnight, and that beyond the door was a small vestibule that had once been a dressing cubicle for one of the bedrooms but was now no more than an extension of the passage she was presently in. She turned the brass knob exactly as she had last night, but from the other side, and stepped through.

And stepped quickly back, briefly frozen to the spot before she drew the door shut again, gathered her wits and launched herself back up the passage on tiptoe.

She was not, after all, alone in the house.

She was tilting the boiling kettle over a mug as the brisk click of high heels faltered momentarily – in surprise, probably, in the second before they took their last full stride into the kitchen behind her.

Kate almost forgot to smile in her astonishment. Mrs Shaw, when the cat was away, clearly underwent an apotheosis. 'I was just making myself a cup of coffee,' Kate said. 'I hope that's all right.'

'Yes, dear, feel free,' said Mrs Shaw, swiftly recovering her aplomb. 'Been back long?'

'About twenty minutes,' lied Kate. It was nearer three hours in fact. 'I took the bus into Dorchester.'

Mrs Shaw switched on the kettle again and reached for the tea-caddy on the shelf beside the cooker. She was wearing crimson nail varnish, a grey jersey dress that clung, and black high heels.

'Yes,' she said. 'Mr Erskine said you'd gone out for the afternoon. Buses running to time, were they?'

'Yes,' said Kate, hoping they had been, tipping milk into her coffee. 'Fine.'

'So you got back about five, then?' It was meant to sound inconsequential, but that was not the way Kate heard it. Mrs Shaw was at the pantry now, taking out a new packet of biscuits and breaking the seal on it.

'A bit afterwards,' said Kate. 'You're looking very swish,' she added, because when a plump and ordinary Mrs Shaw suddenly becomes a statuesque and glamorous Brünhilde it was likely to cause less suspicion by commenting upon it than not.

'I've been out with a gentleman-friend, dear,' confided Mrs Shaw, now collecting a tray and a cup and saucer from the dresser. 'Over at Wareham. I see him every Saturday afternoon.' She returned to the bubbling kettle. The teapot was filled, cosied, set on the tray. She was also wearing a potent perfume and her face was lavishly but artistically painted. Mrs Shaw, to Kate's eyes at least, was never going to seem quite the same again. 'Gordon doesn't know, of course,' Mrs Shaw added, in the manner of a woman who wanted to set the records straight from the very beginning. 'So that's just between you and me, dear. A little secret. You know.'

'Gordon?' said Kate, sipping at her coffee, and generally giving the impression that she was only listening out of common courtesy; while, inside, her stock-in-trade of an all-consuming curiosity was seething to know more.

'My son, dear,' said Mrs Shaw. 'He drove you down from Dorchester yesterday.'

'Oh,' said Kate, as realisation dawned and a slightly different perspective was put upon the events of the earlier afternoon. 'I thought he was your husband.'

'Oh, no, dear.' Mrs Shaw seemed at last reassured that her other secret was safe; and, as people do when they find that their moment of alarm is unjustified, Mrs Shaw's tension found its release in loquacity. 'Not Gordon. I was never a Mrs anything. Gordon's my son, dear. A little accident, he was. I was only thirteen. His dad was a soldier-boy over at Aldershot. Both of us were too young to get married, you see, and my old Dad put his foot down. Sent me up to Scarborough, to his sister, until I was eighteen. Like being in prison on hard labour, that was. She was one of those mealy-mouthed Christians – made my young life purgatory, and ruled Gordon with a rod of iron, she did. I think that's why he's the way he is now. I look at him sometimes and can't believe him and me's the same flesh. But it's all down to her, my old Aunt Sophie. Dead now, she is, of course, and I can't say I'm sorry. George, his name is, just like Mr Sheridan.'

'George?' said Kate.

'My gentleman friend. The one in Wareham.'

'Oh,' said Kate. 'I see.'

George Sheridan knocked on her bedroom door, round about eight o'clock.

'Not eating, m'dear?' he asked anxiously. 'Gave the gong a bash several minutes ago.'

'I ate earlier,' she said. 'I told Mrs Shaw I wouldn't be down.'

'But you missed lunch too.'

'I went out,' she said. 'I had lunch in Dorchester. Really.'

'Oh, yes,' he said, as if he had just remembered. 'So Bill said. So there's nothing wrong?'

'No,' she said, not quite truthfully. 'Of course not.'

Like Mrs Shaw, he seemed immensely relieved to be reassured that Kate really had spent the afternoon in Dorchester.

'I won't disturb you then. Goodnight m'dear.'

'Goodnight, Mr Sheridan.'

She turned in early and slept the sleep of the dead, recalling only the creaking of the central heating system that had disturbed her briefly, and a particularly vivid dream wherein a plumply naked Mrs Shaw had beckoned her in a mirror and said 'Why don't you come and join us, dear?'

She woke as the first of the daylight was showing through the curtains, straightened the bed and took a bath. She finally opened the curtains at a quarter to eight. The day had made little advance, but Shaw was already up and about, going hell for leather with a skipping rope, down by the coachhouse-cum-garage. A pale ghostly figure stripped down to a singlet and a pair of gymnast's white stretch trousers that fitted him like another skin, his teeth gritted and his outward breaths exploding in bursts of steam.

Intrigued, she watched him for several minutes during which the skipping rope was looped and put aside on the lid of the garage water butt and he went briskly into the knees full bend, arms outward stretch routine that she remembered from her schooldays.

Then press-ups. He did twenty-five – she counted them, his chin and his chest almost touching the frost-rimed concrete each time, then he shot to his feet again, bolt upright, back braced, high stepping on the spot, before suddenly breaking away across the front of the terrace and sprinting off towards Bill Erskine's new lake, until his bobbing white shape went from sight among the trees.

Aunt Sophie's holy-roller influence, perhaps, a pure mind in a healthy body and all that stuff. Or the man was simply a masochist. It was freezing out there this morning. This place, she decided, was certainly a rum old do all round.

Between the dream and the substance, Mrs Shaw had reverted to her pinkly scrubbed and nylon-overalled self. Even the nail varnish was gone this morning.

'Who are the people in the dining room?' asked Kate, as Mrs Shaw scooped up two sizzling sausages with the fish-slice and slipped them on to her plate beside a fried egg. There had been three, or there might have been four, new faces taking breakfast in the dining room with George Sheridan as she had passed its open door.

'The man in the grey cardigan, that's Mr Worboys,' said Mrs Shaw. 'And the lady in the red pullover, that's his wife – Madam's daughter – used to be Greta Manders, the actress. And the unwashed hippie with the pony-tail, that's their son, Joel. He's just come across here to make a nuisance of himself, I expect – they don't get on. And the girl in the black dress, she's his singing partner. Mr Sheridan calls her the 'Walking Dead'; they're a pop group, least, that's what they tell everybody.' The Worboys were spending the week here. Mr Worboys was some kind of lawyer. 'And they're a funny old lot, dear. I'd keep well out of the way if I were you.'

'I'll smuggle all this upstairs, then,' said Kate. 'And bring the plate back later.'

It was almost ten o'clock when she managed to waylay Rita Cavallo in the hall.

'I thought I'd make a start on the scrapbooks, Miss Cavallo.'

'Rita, dear, please. Yes, do. You'll find them in the study, in the filing cabinet that's unlocked. I've had Shaw tidy it up in there for you. Lunch is at two today.'

'Thank you,' said Kate. 'The study is …?'

'That way,' said Miss Cavallo, pointing across the hall in

the direction of the passage at the bottom of the main staircase.

The study was a dark but comfortable little room, with a narrow, mullioned bay window, at the downstairs back of the house. The window gave on to a pleasant vista of the garden – or, rather, it would when spring came. In the distance, she could just see the top of Bill Erskine's white truck – he and another man were lowering some prefabricated wooden frames from it. From here, the terrace lay to the right, and the coachhouse to the left, with Shaw in it rubbing another layer of polish over an already glittering black Jaguar, George Sheridan's she presumed.

The two rust-flecked green steel filing cabinets stood by the door, and the one nearest to it, the unlocked cabinet, was the first one she tried to open. The top drawer was crammed with old correspondence, masses of envelopes bundled together with string, the second drawer similarly. Not until she stooped to open the third drawer did she find a cheap, child's scrapbook with fairies and toadstools on the cover; that was the only one, and it was wedged upright against the front of the drawer by yet more bundles of letters.

She tugged it out, stood upright and opened it, her back to the window, wondering if the scrapbook was one of Rita Cavallo's childhood relics; it certainly looked, and smelled, old enough to be. She flipped through the thick grey paper – only the right hand pages had pictures pasted to them, the left hand ones were all blank. She riffled through it backwards, half-heartedly, the way she scanned magazines while she waited for the dreaded call in the dentist's waiting-room. Rita and George Sheridan had been married at Caxton Hall as recently as 1970. Rita was George's second wife, he her fourth husband.

Rita Cavallo, pictured as a fur-coated Mrs Gerald Schwarz, leaving a New York clinic with her new baby in the snowy winter of 1947. A brother, as the caption stated, for Greta, aged ten at the time of the clipping's dateline. Mr Schwarz had been a wealthy New York stockbroker, and already in the past tense when his son had been born:

'perished tragically in the fire that destroyed his summer home in Maine last July ...'

Rita Cavallo had not had a great deal of luck with her husbands. An earlier, faded clipping, dated August 1935, showed her leaving a church in Westbourne Grove after a memorial service to another spouse. 'The inquest on Mr Manders concluded that the balance of his mind had become disturbed ...' Which sounded to Kate as if the very late Mr Manders, as the pithy phrase had it, had done himself in.

Her attention was momentarily diverted by a clack of footsteps outside on the terrace, and she half-turned to watch a dark and emaciated young woman come into view and go to stand against the stone balustrade that overlooked the garden.

The Walking Dead, as George Sheridan called her, for it could only be her, tall and gaunt and wearing a long black cotton dress down to her ankles. Kate could not see her feet but it had sounded as if she were wearing wooden clogs. Black, unkempt hair hung all the way down her back and the only one of her hands that Kate could see was tipped with purple talons.

Then another figure appeared, Joel Warboys, Rita Cavallo's grandson, short and stocky, black leather-clad and leather-booted, a lurid stylised tiger's head stencilled across the back of his fringed jacket. His blond hair was dragged back in a pony-tail. As he joined the Walking Dead, she turned away. Shoulder joined shoulder, so that they looked like a pair of conspirators. Joel Warboys little more than eighteen or nineteen, surely no older, drew something that might have been a piece of paper from the pocket of his leather jacket. It passed from one to the other of them. The Walking Dead's expression became one of unconcealed glee. The piece of paper, which looked like a cheque, briefly reappeared as it was stuffed back into his pocket and a zip was closed over it.

Kate turned her attention to the far more interesting scrapbook. A yellowing picture of an incredibly beautiful man in evening clothes – Angus Kilcullen the aviator, so the caption read – and a doll-like blonde, in a skimpy white satin dress, dangling from his arm was 'the promising young actress Rita Cavallo'. The flashlit picture had been taken outside a London nightclub. The clipping had been hacked out with pinking shears from an old *Tatler*; it had been cut from the top right hand corner of the page and included the publication date, June 12th, 1930.

Immediately beneath the picture was a stop-press clipping cut from an old *Evening Standard*. 'Mr Angus Kilcullen,' Kate read, 'the aviator, was found dead by his valet at his home in Portman Square late last night. Mr Kilcullen's service revolver was lying on the carpet near his right hand. Police are investigating ...'

And there was more of that on the next page, and the next. And Kate, recognising dynamite when she saw it, flipped more interestedly from the front to the back again. A woman, heavily veiled, descending a ship's gangplank, a sombre man walking down behind her with a small box on his shoulder. Then, as Kate turned away to take the book to the desk and the better light, she realised that the left hand pages were not blank at all. They were solid with pencilled annotations and slashed with exclamation marks.

The backs of her legs found the chair. She started to lower herself and felt a momentary draught as the study door was opened.

'I came to see if ...' Rita Cavallo's voice said. She had been smiling. But even as Kate's head lifted the smile withered on Rita Cavallo's face as her gaze fell to the open scrapbook on Kate's knees. 'Where did you get *that?*'

'The drawer. You told me ...'

With bewildering speed – Kate thought momentarily that she was going to be attacked – Rita Cavallo shot forward and snatched the book from her hands. 'I said the *unlocked* cabinet!'

'But it *was!*'

Rita Cavallo stood over her, breathing heavily after her moment of exertion, her face flushed and already beginning to sweat, her eyes narrow and venomous. 'You broke it open,' she raged. '*Did* you break it open?'

'No, of course I didn't,' protested Kate. 'I ...'

'I don't like prying! You understand?'

'I *wasn't* prying,' protested Kate, dangerously close to anger herself. 'The cabinet was unlocked.'

'*This* one, Katherine. Do you see?' Rita Cavallo stormed and demonstrated the two top drawers of the other cabinet, which slid open easily on their runners. She spoke to Kate as she might to a witless child, her teeth bared in a death's head smile. '*This* one, dear. You see?'

'Yes,' said Kate, still gritting her teeth. 'I'm desperately sorry. But the other one was the first one I tried. I never thought to try that one.'

Rita Cavallo, with some considerable effort, managed to regain a steely self control. 'Well, forgiven and forgotten,' she said. 'I'm sorry I shouted at you. I'm sure you meant no harm.' She turned away, the offending scrapbook was stuffed back whence it had come, the drawer slammed shut and given a firm tug. It stayed shut.

'There,' said Rita Cavallo. She was still trembling and her awful smile looked as if it was held in place with sticking plaster. 'That's made sure it can't happen again, hasn't it? I couldn't have shut the drawer properly the last time I used it. Silly me. Forgiven? Mm?' She was offering her hand. 'Please?'

The hand was hot and clammy. 'Yes,' said Kate, really she could have struck the wretched woman. 'Of course. No harm done.'

'When do you start filling it?' she asked.

'Tomorrow morning,' said Bill Erskine. The lake bed was now completely lined with polythene sheeting. The wooden frames she had glimpsed being unloaded that morning were the skeleton of a little footbridge. He was presently in the throes of bolting them together. It was afternoon and the sun had come out sufficiently for her to take several decent photographs of the gardens and the outside of the house.

'How long will it take to fill?'

'A couple of days,' he said. 'Or with any luck it might

rain.' He threaded another washer and nut on to a galvanised bolt. 'How's your job going?'

'Badly,' she said, with some considerable feeling.

She had lunched with the Sheridans and met the Worboys. Neither of the latter had been exactly likeable. Their son and the Walking Dead had not been in attendance, so she presumed that they had left in the racketty car she had heard soon after the incident with Rita Cavallo in the study. Neither of them had been mentioned during the meal. Greta Worboys, brittle and nervous, had talked incessantly, while her supercilious, frosty and overweight husband had been the kind of man who would much prefer to be breathing the rarer air of Olympus. Rita Cavallo, for once, had uttered hardly a word.

'Are you working tonight?' Bill Erskine asked, giving a final downward wrench on his spanner.

'No,' she said, hopefully, sensing an invitation. She was fast getting the impression that Bill Erskine was the only normal person around these parts, and almost anything was better than spending the evening alone in her room. 'I hadn't intended to.'

'Wondered if you'd fancy a meal,' he said, threading another washer and nut on another bolt. He knew a quiet little restaurant that opened on Sunday evenings on the road to Yeovil, oldy worldy, and the food was always reliable.

'Can I pay my whack?'

'Yes,' he said. 'If you like.' The nut was spun on and tightened with a couple of turns of the wrench. 'Pick you up about seven-thirty?'

'Yes,' she said, nodding. 'I'd like that. Thank you.'

She walked on and completed her circuit of the garden. It was as she approached the house again, along the sunken path by the wall, that she saw feathery black ashes floating up from one of the chimneys at the far right of the house. At the time she took little notice of them. But then, soon after four o'clock, she returned to the study, or rather she crept to the study, and, as she had this morning,

34

she gave a tug to the top drawer of the green filing cabinet nearest the door. It didn't open the first time, but it did the second, there was clearly a knack to it. She stooped to the third drawer. That opened easily, too, but the child's scrapbook was gone.

Monday began much like Sunday, except that it had rained a torrent around about five o'clock in the morning which probably augured well for Bill Erskine's lake-filling. The puddles, however, did not deter Shaw from his daily bout of callisthenics, but in shortened form this morning because when she came back from the bathroom he had gone. Bill Erskine's white truck was parked on the path near the lake, and she caught a brief glimpse of Rita Cavallo, fur-coated and booted, and with a scarf over her head, walking her two Pekingese on a leash near the garden wall over on the left. And Kate would remember the time – it was seven forty-five – because she had forgotten to cancel her alarm clock, and it suddenly started buzzing so that she had to rush from the dressing table to the bedside cabinet and stab her thumb on the button to switch it off.

When she went down to breakfast at eight o'clock, there was a hose connected to the standpipe outside the garage and snaking away into the distance towards the lake.

Yesterday evening had been decidedly pleasant. She had half-expected him to turn up in the old white truck, but he had arrived in a new red Mini, wearing a smart set of sports-clothes and a shiny pair of brogues. The meal had been excellent, the restaurant a comfortable little lair of high-backed oak settles and bottle-bottomed windows, his company easy-going and undemanding. They had talked the hind legs off several donkeys; she had gleaned from him that he had done a three-year stint in the army on a short service commission, decided he didn't like being ordered about, resigned and had done a complete about-turn by taking a degree in horticulture. He was presently contemplating the purchase of several acres of gardening centre up in Harrow – if his bank manager could see it in his way to come up with the cash. He had also come clean and confessed that he was divorced, which came as a great relief to her because, when a personable man hits thirty-five, either some smart woman has securely handcuffed herself to him or there has to be something wrong with him. Kate had then explained her own and similar position. With the air thus mutually cleared, they had returned to less stilted conversation. At the beginning of the evening he had been simply another man to whom she had taken a mild – and probably passing – fancy. By ten o'clock last night, however, she had found herself warming towards him more than somewhat. And when she had covertly slid a five-pound note across the tablecloth, he had asked only once 'if she was sure?' and she had said that she was and he had taken it without argument. She had approved of that, she had never liked pushy men. These were early days yet, but Mr Erskine seemed an all-round nice guy, with both his feet firmly planted on the ground.

The morning stayed gloomy, with intermittent rain-showers, and she spent it taking flashlit photographs of the downstairs rooms – which she had intended to do on Saturday afternoon but never had after she had walked through that wrong door. And, as it had been on Saturday, the house was very quiet. The Worboys had driven off, presumably to Dorchester, soon after nine o'clock, and Shaw had driven away with George Sheridan some half-an-hour afterwards. Shaw had come back, on his own, and garaged the black Jaguar soon after ten. From then until lunchtime Kate caught occasional sight of him going from one room to another with a stepladder and a bucket and she presumed that he was cleaning the insides of the windows. The howl and rumble of a distant vacuum cleaner probably meant that Mrs Shaw was about somewhere too, although Kate didn't see her again until lunchtime, and then only her back, and briefly, as she went out with a shopping trolley, presumably to the village.

The first portent of ominous things to come manifested itself in the kitchen soon after one o'clock, when she contrived to place herself in Bill Erskine's way when he came in to fill his vacuum flask and found her putting a sandwich together. They bandied the weather about, a little guarded with each other again. But then, out of the blue and apropos of absolutely nothing, as he filled his flask from the steaming kettle, he said, with heartwarming coyness, 'Look, I'm not very good at this, but if you're not doing anything tonight ...'

'I'm not,' she said promptly, reasoning that she might as well be hanged for a hussy as a lamb, licking a blob of butter from her thumb.

Nothing ambitious, he was careful to explain. A meal at his cottage, he was a passable cook, then a trip down to the local pub.

'Yes,' she said. 'I'll look forward to that. Thank you.'

That business out of the way, he was in no hurry to get back to work. The rainstorm early that morning had put nearly half an inch of water into the lake before he had arrived; water from the hose had raised the level another half inch. By Friday, given the further rain that the forecasters were promising, the hosepipe could be disconnected and the rest left to Nature. It was at that point that their conversational thread was broken by a scratching and a thin, distressed whine at the door to the garden.

'Sounds like one of the dogs,' he said, sliding back his chair and padding across to open the door. She saw him drop quickly to a crouch and scoop up something that tried to slip past him. It was Mr Wu, according to the silver tag on his harness, sopping wet, mudsplashed and pitiably bedraggled. He was planted on the draining-board beside the sink and held there while Kate briskly towelled off the worst of the mess.

'Odd, that,' Bill Erskine said, still wrestling to hold the wriggling mass down.

'What is?' said Kate, drying the dog's elusive ears.

'They're like bookends,' he said. 'It's the first time I've ever seen one without the other. And they never go out of the house, except on a lead. Seen the other one about anywhere?'

37

'No,' said Kate. 'Not since before breakfast. I thought they'd gone out for the day with Rita.'

'I presume she *has* gone out?'

'I thought so,' said Kate, and there the matter was left to rest. It was not until midnight, when she arrived back from her date with Bill Erskine and found the local bobby in the hall with Shaw, that she realised anything was amiss.

'You are who, Miss?' the policeman asked, and at once cruelly snatched away the nice warm comfortable feeling that had been building up inside her all evening, scarcely before Shaw had closed the door behind her.

'Lindsey,' she said, caught momentarily wrong-footed. 'Katherine. Why?' she added, catching a glimpse now of a black plastic rubbish sack on the floor near the coat-stand. It was Sellotaped at the neck, low down. And her stomach churned because whatever was inside it looked just about the right size for a dead Pekingese.

Which, the policeman, a burly young sergeant with a ginger beard, was quick to explain, it was. He had found it himself, about a mile up the road to Dorchester. A traffic accident, most likely, although the driver had not reported it.

'Thing is, Miss,' the policeman said, 'it's stone cold, so its been dead a good few hours. Mr Shaw here tells me that its twin came back here alone at lunchtime and Mrs Sheridan's usually home by now, and she isn't. Got any ideas, have you, Miss?'

'No,' said Kate. 'I haven't.' And nor had Shaw. Nor had Mrs Shaw when she came down a few minutes afterwards in her dressing gown.

And when the policeman left at half-past midnight, and after Shaw and his mother had scoured the house, Rita Cavallo had still not come home.

FOUR

'THE WOMAN'S ALMOST A NATIONAL monument, Douglas,' said Superintendent Mower, dour of outlook and hawkish of nose, flipping open his snuff box. 'It's like waking up one morning and finding Nelson's been nicked from his bloody column.' A pinch of snuff was nipped up between finger and thumb, the box snapped shut, the savage stuff inhaled, one nostril dilated, then the other.

'Perhaps she wants to go missing,' said Chief Inspector Roper. Mower was a Dorset man to his very marrow, Roper a lapsed Londoner, ex-Met. Lean of frame and sharply dressed, he was a man who, despite twenty-odd years in the Force, still continued to seek the best in humankind even when faced with the worst. Patient by nature and thorough by calculation, he could think of better things to do this chill autumn morning than playing pat-a-cake with a missing ex-film star. 'Could be she's after the publicity. It's been done before.'

Mower's nostrils started to twitch, and Roper waited for the inevitable explosion. 'Signs aren't right,' said Mower, his nostrils flaring, 'and there's the business with the dogs. Story has it they went everywhere with her.' His eyes began to water. 'She was last seen walking them in her garden round about a quarter to eight yesterday morning. On a lead. One dog came back on its own at lunchtime, and the local beat officer came across the other one on the road between Milton St. Philip's and Dorchester late last night while he was doing his round.' Mower could contain himself no longer. He broke off to fumble hastily for his khaki handkerchief, and was too late, but then he always was. His sneeze shattered the silence while the handkerchief was still six inches short of its destination. 'Dead,' he just managed to add before another splutter overwhelmed him; Roper assumed he was referring to the second dog.

'Just a courtesy call, Douglas. Have a sniff around and talk to George Sheridan.' Mower dabbed his tear-filled eyes and tucked his handkerchief back in his pocket. 'Put on a bit of a show, let him know we're available. You know the form.'

Roper arrived in Milton St. Philip's in the rainswept dullness of the afternoon. The village itself looked as if the twentieth century was passing it by – a grocer's shop, a pub, a newsagent's, a scattering of cottages, no sooner glimpsed than passed.

The Sheridan's house was a half mile or so further on, a great grey slab of a place saved from being depressing only by the electric lights glowing in several of the downstairs windows. The driveway was carpeted with wet dead leaves, the trees half-naked, the flower beds stripped bare so that the immediate impression was one of desolation but, closer to, he saw that all the window frames were newly painted, the curtains behind them tastefully draped, and expensive, the flower beds freshly turned over.

The face that answered the door to him was immediately familiar, although the body beneath it was several inches taller than he had imagined it was going to be.

'Roper, Mr Sheridan,' he said, holding out his warrant card. 'Chief Inspector. County CID. My superintendent made an appointment.'

'Yes,' Sheridan said vaguely as he held the door aside. 'Yes. Do come in, old chap.'

Roper wiped his shoes on the several acres of coconut matting just inside the door. The huge, panelled hall was marble floored, a flight of beautifully crafted oak stairs over on the left, a narrower flight on the right. The centre piece, a Jacobean refectory table, black with age and with a copper vase on it, was the kind of thing auctioneers slavered over.

Sheridan took Roper's raincoat and hung it on a mirrored Victorian coatstand near the fireplace. The fire was laid ready, but unlit. A smell of beeswax, the real old-fashioned sort, hung tantalisingly.

'Somewhere we can talk privately, sir?'

'Yes, of course.' Sheridan led the way across the tesselated marble to a room opposite the fireplace, opened its door and stood aside courteously to usher Roper in ahead of him. 'Can I get you something? Tea, perhaps?'

'Yes,' Roper said. 'Be most welcome, sir. Thank you.'

Sheridan padded out again in his carpet slippers and left Roper alone. The room was a drawing-room, vast enough to contain three massive settees, a theatrically ostentatious white grand piano and still leave space enough to walk around freely among all the little tables full of knick-knacks and silver-framed photographs. A glass-fronted cabinet held a collection of porcelain figures, several of them in pairs, any pair of which would fetch four or five hundred pounds at auction if they were the Derbyware he thought they were.

He drew away from the cabinet and went to stand by the fireplace as the sound of flapping slippers slapped across the hall.

'Do sit, Inspector.'

'Thank you, sir.' The luxurious green leather was cold. Sheridan sat opposite, his frayed old woolly cardigan strangely at odds with his sharply pressed and elegant twill trousers and his crisp, pink shirt.

'Tea won't be a moment.'

'No rush, sir,' said Roper. Sheridan was a far, far bigger man than he had expected, loose fleshed rather than fat, very tall. And what would he be? Seventy, or thereabouts? He seemed to be wearing exceedingly well.

'No sign of Mrs Sheridan yet, sir?'

'No. Afraid not.' Sheridan sat with his broad shoulders hunched, the palms of his big hands rubbing together worriedly and staring at nothing in particular between his slippers. 'Your man, Mr ...?'

'Superintendent Mower, sir?' ventured Roper.

41

'Yes, that's the chap. Decent sort, most helpful – he was saying your people couldn't do a great deal as yet.'

'That's right, sir. But we are taking your wife's disappearance seriously. It's just that we'd like a little longer to be certain that she isn't with a friend, or something of that sort. When did you last see her, sir?'

'The night before last,' said Sheridan. 'Sunday. We don't see each other much in the mornings, as a rule. And yesterday I had to go up to London. Rehearsals. So we didn't meet yesterday at all. Mrs Shaw, she's our cook and housekeeper,' he explained, as Roper shot a questioning eyebrow, 'rang me in London soon after one o'clock this morning and told me my wife hadn't come home last night – and that one of the dogs had wandered back here on its own yesterday lunchtime, and the other one had been found dead last evening on the road to Dorchester. I didn't like the sound of that, so I came back here early this morning.' The palms stopped rubbing together and Sheridan dragged back a woollen cuff to look at his wristwatch. 'And now it's two o'clock in the afternoon and there's still no sign of her.'

'Any idea where she intended to go yesterday, sir?'

'No, I haven't.' George Sheridan's hands were together again, but loosely clasped now and hanging between his knees. 'I hadn't even been aware that she'd intended to go out – although Mrs Shaw apparently knew.'

'And she would have taken the dogs with her, would she, sir?'

'Always,' said Sheridan.

He seemed certain. The dogs wouldn't even go out into the grounds around the house on their own, and they slept in baskets in his wife's bedroom. What equally concerned him was that the dogs always went out on a leash. And neither the one that came home alone yesterday lunchtime nor the one that Sergeant Morrison had come upon late last night had had a leash attached to their harnesses.

'How about relatives, sir? Could Mrs Sheridan be with one of them?'

'She has only two. Her daughter – who's staying here at

the moment – and a grandson.'

'You checked with the grandson, sir?'

'I can't,' said Sheridan. 'From what I've heard, he seems to live in what I believe is called a squat, somewhere in Portsmouth. I don't have an address.'

'He's this daughter's son, is he, sir? The lady who's staying with you?'

'Yes,' said Sheridan. 'But I doubt she has his address, either. They're estranged. The boy's a musician, which these days means he can strum a few chords on a guitar, if you know what I mean.'

'I see, sir,' said Roper, registering Sheridan's stoney disapproval of his wife's grandson. 'How about friends?'

They were few, and mostly of the kind with whom his wife only exchanged Christmas and birthday cards. Theatrical people mostly. So far as Sheridan knew she had only seen three or four of them in the last couple of years. She was hardly likely to be with any of them.

'You're welcome to look at her address book.'

'Yes, sir,' said Roper. 'That'd be useful. Thank you. Tell me about yesterday, sir. Did anyone hear or see your wife leave the property?'

'Not leaving the property exactly,' said Sheridan. Mrs Shaw, the cook, had heard the side door to the garden open and close – and the scuffling of dogs' paws – at about quarter to eight yesterday morning, and both her son, who was the Sheridans' chauffeur and handyman, and Miss Lindsey had glimpsed Mrs Sheridan, very briefly, walking along the sunken path that bordered the left hand side of the grounds, at roughly the same time. No one was certain that she had come back into the house, but merely supposed that she had.

'This Miss Lindsey, sir ...?'

'A television researcher,' said Sheridan. 'She's down here for a few days. They want to do a programme about us.'

The only other person in or about the house on a regular basis was a landscape gardener, by name Erskine. A local man. He had been reorganising the gardens since the end of the previous August. But he had not seen Mrs Sheridan at all on Monday.

Roper made formal notes of the names in his pocket book, although there was still no reason to suspect that this was police business. The only anomaly so far seemed to be the behaviour of the two dogs, which was not of itself sufficient to start an expensive hue and cry for a woman who was old enough and sensible enough to come and go as she pleased.

After a discreet rap at the door a woman came in with two cups of tea on a wooden tray. She was the housekeeper Sheridan had mentioned, Mrs Shaw. She repeated what she had told Sheridan, that she thought she had heard Mrs Sheridan and the two dogs going out through the side door to the garden at a few minutes before eight o'clock yesterday morning. And that her son had seen Mrs Sheridan out there at about the same time.

'But you didn't see Mrs Sheridan after that?' asked Roper.

'No, sir,' she said. She looked a reliable sort, a full-figured, handsome woman, early fifties perhaps.

Roper pressed her a little harder. Had she heard Mrs Sheridan go out later on in the morning?

No, she had not. And Mrs Sheridan never took breakfast so Mrs Shaw had had no need to go and look for her for any reason. The first sign that something was wrong was when she had come back from the village yesterday afternoon and found that one of the dogs had come home on its own. According to Miss Lindsey and Mr Erskine, the dog had put in its appearance at about one o'clock. They had let it in at the kitchen door. It had been covered with mud, and Miss Lindsey and Mr Erskine had cleaned it up. Mrs Shaw had taken charge of it immediately upon her return. More anxious when Sergeant Morrison had brought back the other dog, dead, in a bag, late last night, she had taken it upon herself to telephone Mr Sheridan at his London hotel in the early hours of this morning.

'You knew Mrs Sheridan had intended to go out yesterday, Mrs Shaw?'

'Yes, sir.' But Mrs Sheridan had given no indication of where she might have been going.

'Did she mention anything to your son? About driving her somewhere?'

No, she had not, at least, not so far as Mrs Shaw was aware. 'But the last time she went out on her own for the day, sir, it was in a hire-car. I heard her telephoning for it the night before. I think she's done that several times.'

'You don't know if Mrs Sheridan phoned for a car on Sunday night?'

'No, sir,' said Mrs Shaw. 'I really couldn't say.'

The chintz and lace bedroom smelled of perfume, overlaid with the mustier odour of dogs. There was no sign anywhere of male habitation – which probably signified something or other ...

'That's the handbag you saw Mrs Sheridan using last, is it, Mrs Shaw?'

'Yes, sir,' said Mrs Shaw. 'It's the one she uses most of the time.'

It was a handbag of quality. Genuine brown hide, with lacquered brass fittings.

Roper took the bag from Mrs Shaw, unclipped the catch and one by one removed its contents and laid them out on the yellow silk quilt that covered the bed. A wallet; an old-fashioned enamel-inlaid powder compact, gold-plated, with a fancy clip at the side that held a matching lipstick cylinder. A tiny phial of Yves St Laurent perfume. A cheque book in a blue plastic slip-holder, a key-ring with several Yale keys on it and a couple of others which might have been for a desk or a filing-cabinet; one folded, lace-edged white handkerchief. A leather purse heavy with coins. An unopened cellophane pack of paper handkerchiefs. A small diary, black leatherette-covered – there was no engagement noted in it for yesterday – a gold-plated ballpoint pen and a matching propelling pencil, both well used. From Roper's limited experience of women it seemed a modest enough collection.

45

'Can we look inside that, sir?' asked Roper, passing the wallet to Sheridan.

Sheridan came up beside him and stripped out the wallet on the quilt. Six £1 notes and two £5 notes. Again, a modest enough sum for the kind of lifestyle Mrs Sheridan enjoyed. A credit card and two of Mrs Sheridan's own deckle-edged visiting-cards emptied the wallet completely.

'Do you mind if I look in here, sir?' asked Roper, picking up the cheque book.

'No, old chap, you carry on.'

The book was down to the last two cheques. Roper worked forward through the stubs. Mrs Sheridan had lately written two cheques of £500 each, which she had drawn as cash, one two months ago and one four weeks ago. Another, for £180, had been written to pay her dressmaker, that had been three weeks ago. Two cheques then, again drawn as cash, for £50, then a stub with last Friday's date written on it but otherwise blank, and then the last stub. The amount recorded was £250, the date last Sunday's. All that was missing from the stub was the name of the payee – or any indication that Mrs Sheridan had intended to draw the money as cash …

'Any ideas, sir?' asked Roper.

Sheridan shook his head. 'No,' he said. 'None.' Nor was it likely to have been written to cover a household bill. Sheridan himself wrote the cheques for all those, even the grocery bills. What was in his wife's cheque book was merely her pin money.

But what seemed fairly certain, had that cheque been written in order to draw cash for herself, was that £250 would not have kept her head above water for very long. A couple of weeks in a smart hotel, four in a modest one. Besides which she would need a change of clothes. And a handbag, and a cheque book, and a credit card, and all the other paraphernalia that women toted about with them and that were presently scattered on the bed. And if Mrs Sheridan had intended to vanish it would have been more sensible to wind up her bank account altogether and open a new one under another name somewhere else.

Roper made a note of the Sunday cheque and Mrs Sheridan's account number. Cheques were easily traceable, once they had been presented. It would be interesting to find out who had drawn on that one, and where, and when.

'Any of your wife's suitcases missing, sir?'

Sheridan looked vaguely at Mrs Shaw. She went to them at once. They stood upright in a shallow cupboard let into the bedroom wall, four of them stowed one inside the other when Roper drew them out and opened them. Like the handbag they were quality goods, real hide, with brass catches and heavyweight locks. One of the keys from the ring in the handbag fitted all of them. According to Mrs Shaw, Mrs Sheridan had no other cases. These had been purchased last Christmas, all the old ones put out for the dustmen.

'Did your wife have her own passport, sir?'

Again, it was Mrs Shaw who knew where it was, in a black tin deed-box in the cupboard of the bedside cabinet, and again it was one of the keys from the handbag that unlocked it. The passport was tucked under a couple of insurance policies and a stiff manilla envelope that probably contained a will. The passport, renewed three years ago, in 1973, had only been used twice since, and that it was still in the house made it fairly certain that Mrs Sheridan had at least not gone abroad.

Nor had she taken much jewellery, if any. The leatherette-covered casket, stowed, somewhat cavalierly in Roper's opinion, under some underwear in the top drawer of a chest of drawers where any self-respecting housebreaker could not fail to find it, was brimming. Some of the contents were merely expensive gewgaws, some of them the real McCoy that no woman would ever have left behind if she had intended to do a runner. Neither Sheridan nor Mrs Shaw was able to say positively if anything was missing.

More easily established were the outer clothes that Mrs Sheridan was probably wearing. According to Mrs Shaw, there was a fur coat missing, Canadian squirrel, very old and very worn, but something that Mrs Sheridan slipped on when the weather was chilly and she wasn't going any further than the garden. The old black boots she usually wore for the same purpose were also missing. What she might have been wearing underneath the coat was less certain – Mrs Sheridan seemed to go in, almost entirely, for voluminous and colourful tubes that were made especially for her – and so far as Mrs Shaw could ascertain they all seemed to be there on their hangers, several dozen of them.

Another small but important detail was added by the television researcher, a dark, lean and strikingly attractive young woman with bright clever eyes. She was certain that Mrs Sheridan, of whom she had clearly seen the back view yesterday morning, had also been wearing a white scarf around her head and with one end of it trailing down her back. She also confirmed the fur coat and the black boots. She was also certain of the time, because her alarm clock had gone off at that same moment and she'd turned away from the window to cancel it. It had been a quarter to eight, give or take a couple of minutes.

'You didn't go back to the window afterwards, Miss Lindsey?'

'No, I didn't. That was the last I saw of her.'

From her bedroom window, she pointed out to Roper the exact spot of her sighting of Mrs Sheridan and the two dogs. It was a few yards short of a green wooden gate set into the garden wall, partially obscured, from this angle, by an overgrown box hedge. Mrs Sheridan had been walking towards it from the direction of the house.

'Could she have gone out through the gate, d'you think?'

But on this point Miss Lindsey was honest enough not to commit herself.

Shaw, the chauffeur, knew very little more. Roper tracked him down to the garage where he was polishing several pairs of men's shoes at his workbench. Wearing a canvas apron, he stood rigidly at attention, broad-shouldered, stomach drawn in, an ex-soldier, probably, and one who refused absolutely to succumb to the folly of a civilian haircut. For no particular reason he also made Roper feel just a touch uneasy.

He agreed that, yes, he had seen Madam's head and shoulders bobbing above the sunken path on the left-hand side of the garden yesterday morning at a quarter to eight.

'Before the gate, relative to the house, Mr Shaw, or after it?'

'Before it, sir, as I recall. But I could not be absolutely certain.'

'You didn't see her go through it?'

'No, sir,' said Shaw.

'Is she in the habit of going through it when she walks the dogs?'

'Never, sir,' said Shaw. 'Certainly not since I've been here.'

'Thank you, Mr Shaw,' said Roper, his unease still lingering, until, at the garage doorway, he simply had to stop and turn and size up Shaw again.

The man hadn't moved. Roper took him in slowly, head to feet and back again.

'Have we ever met before, Mr Shaw?' he said, frowning.

'No, sir,' said Shaw. 'I wouldn't have thought so, sir.'

Roper turned away again, still frowning. Somewhere ... some time ...

Erskine the landscape gardener was of even less help. He had arrived yesterday morning soon after half-past seven and got straight down to work. At about eight o'clock, he had been connecting a hose to the standpipe by the garage in order to fill the lake beside which he and Roper were presently standing. From then on, he had worked alone on the footbridge. He had not seen Mrs Sheridan at all.

'All I know is that I let in one of the dogs through the kitchen door at lunchtime. Sorry.'

'So how do we stand, Douglas?' asked Superintendent

49

Mower, over ten miles of crackling telephone line from County. 'Is the good lady missing in suspicious circumstances or not?'

'Reckon she might be,' said Roper, perched on a corner of the desk in George Sheridan's study and looking out towards the darkening garden. It was coming up for four-thirty in the afternoon and raining heavily again. 'She didn't even have a purse on her.'

'Her bed slept in on Sunday night, was it?'

'So the housekeeper says.'

'How about her passport?'

'It's still here in the house.'

'And nobody actually saw her leave the property?'

'Nary a one,' said Roper. He gave Mower a quick précis of the few notes he had made in his pocket book during the course of the afternoon.

'So she could have gone out through this gate,' suggested Mower. 'Taken a walk outside and met with an accident – or had a heart attack or something. Could even be she's lying dead in a ditch. Unhappy thought, of course.'

Roper agreed. Nothing was impossible.

'What's the weather like down there?'

'Stair-rods,' said Roper. 'But I think we ought to start looking around the immediate vicinity pretty soon. A few of the lads with torches. Just the roads and ditches for half a mile round the house, say. I doubt she'd have wandered much further than that. They've only got little legs, Pekingese.'

Mower mulled that over. 'Tonight, you mean?'

'Right now, I'd say,' said Roper. 'A dozen bobbies and a couple of cars. And if they don't come up with anything, we'll have a proper ground search tomorrow.'

'All right, Douglas,' agreed Mower eventually. 'I'll send a posse out. But if she's mucking us about for the sake of publicity, I'll have her guts for bloody garters.'

FIVE

BY WEDNESDAY MORNING, RITA CAVALLO was famous again. The news of her disappearance had been slotted into all the bulletins on television and radio late the previous night, and made the headlines in most of the daily newspapers. One of the more strident tabloids was already hinting darkly that she had been kidnapped for ransom and wild though that suggestion was it might yet prove to have substance. But whatever the truth was, enough noise had been made for Mrs Sheridan – most of the newspapers had chosen to call her Rita Cavallo – to have heard of it. But quite obviously she had not, or for some reason was not responding to it.

The hastily organised search of the nearby roads and ditches by torchlight had turned up nothing, which might be good news or might be bad, and a more thorough scouring of the surrounding highways and byways had begun at daybreak. In the meantime, Detective Sergeant Morgan, Roper's leg man, was closeted back at County with Mrs Sheridan's address book and a telephone and trying to track down anyone who might have some idea of her whereabouts, while a couple of detective constables were touting Mrs Sheridan's photograph around a few likely railway stations, bus depots and car-hire firms.

'I have to ask, sir,' said Roper. 'Did you and your wife quarrel at all over the weekend?'

'No,' said Sheridan. 'A snap or two, perhaps, but nothing serious.'

The drawing-room was chilly. It was ten o'clock in the morning. The rain that had started an hour ago had passed over and a pale watery sun was shining from time to time.

'How about lapses of memory, sir?'

'Rita?' said Sheridan, as if that were the most preposterous thing he had ever heard. 'God, no! She remembers everything.'

'How about her health?'

'Strong as an ox,' said Sheridan. 'Hardly had a day's illness since I've known her.'

It was easy to say, but, as Mower had suggested yesterday, it wasn't impossible that she could have had a heart attack out on a lonely road somewhere and fallen into a ditch. She might even have unclipped the two Pekingese from their leashes in the few moments before she had been overcome, in the hope that they would find their way home and thus signal some kind of SOS. And if that had been the case and she had been on foot, Mrs Sheridan, or her body, could be no further away than a Pekingese dog could walk in half the time between eight o'clock in the morning and one o'clock in the afternoon, namely two and a half hours. Or she could be even closer if the dogs had stayed with her, or her body, for some time after whatever had happened to her had occurred.

Roper got Sheridan to backtrack again over the events of the previous weekend in more detail, but none of it seemed particularly relevant. Miss Lindsey had arrived on Friday afternoon. It had been Sheridan's birthday and Erskine, the gardener, had come across in the evening for a celebratory dinner and a couple of frames of snooker. Mrs Sheridan had gone out with Shaw on Saturday morning, soon after nine o'clock. She had returned some time around eleven on Saturday night. Her daughter and son-in-law, the Worboys, had arrived shortly afterwards from London, later than expected because they had volunteered themselves as witnesses to a serious traffic accident on the A31, just outside Ringwood. The son-in-law was defending in a fraud case at Dorchester County Court and he and his wife were staying the week here.

The only other visitors had been Mrs Sheridan's grandson, Joel Worboys, and his girl-friend. They had turned up at breakfast time on Sunday but left a couple of hours afterwards. And Mrs Sheridan had still been very much alive on Monday morning.

'And this is where you found it, is it, Sergeant?'

'Yes, sir,' said the ginger-bearded Morrison. He and Roper stood on the footpath of the road to Dorchester. The path itself was flagged, and between the flagstones and the kerb was a yard width of muddy grass verge. Nearby was a telegraph pole. It was here, late on Monday night, that Morrison's headlights had picked out the furry wet bundle stretched out on a kerbstone.

Like most rural beat-officers, Morrison knew the whims and habits of almost everyone on his patch. With the exception of Mrs Sheridan. She was not exactly reclusive, but she was seen about the village only rarely, and when she was it was only ever in a car, with Shaw in close attendance. And, of course, the two dogs. It was Morrison's impression that Mrs Sheridan did not walk far if she could help it.

'The dog had still got its harness on?'

'Yes, sir.'

'But there was no lead?'

'No, sir. No lead.'

Roper took a long look about. It was a desolate stretch of road, bleak empty farmland at each side and not a dwelling in sight – at this time of year, a cold, windswept place. It was an unlikely area for a woman to walk two toy dogs, especially when she had several acres of land for her own back yard.

'Got a local map?'

'Yes, sir.' Morrison went back to his white Escort and took an Ordnance Survey map from the glove compartment.

'Not many places she could go, is there?' said Roper, scanning it.

'No, sir,' said Morrison. 'Not a lot.'

The road went uninterrupted all the way to the outskirts of Dorchester. Most of the side roads off it were private and only provided access to a few farmhouses. Habitation was sparse, a few clusters of cottages, a pub, a filling station.

'What about this river? Near this bridge.'

It was not so much a river as a stream. At this time of year it was too shallow to hide a body, and Morrison had already had the nous to go and look up there just in case, even though it was unlikely that Mrs Sheridan would have walked that far from home. If Morrison was right, she was not a woman given to a great deal to physical exertion.

What she would not have done, in Roper's considered opinion, was to have left the road and traipsed about in the mud of the fields either side. It had rained heavily early on Monday morning and anywhere off the road would have been a morass.

'I suppose she could have been kidnapped,' ventured Morrison. 'From what I've seen and heard, old George isn't short of a few bob.'

But Roper had begun to doubt that now. The pattern was wrong for a kidnap. With the victim secure, kidnappers didn't hang about for several days. Their ransom demands followed swiftly, and certainly before the police were likely to get wind of their villainy. When it came to kidnapping, the police, like a wife with a wayward husband, were frequently the last to know.

'Looks like a lot of legwork, Sergeant.'

'Yes, sir,' agreed Morrison. 'I'll start knocking on a few more doors, shall I?'

'Yes,' said Roper. 'Do that.'

While Roper was out with Sergeant Morrison, Katherine Lindsey had walked up to the telephone box outside the Crown and Compass in the village, which is where she was now, a column of tenpence pieces stacked on the coin-box, the receiver huddled between her ear and her shoulder, and her handbag between her feet while she juggled with her notebook to keep it open.

'I can hardly hear you,' she shouted.

'I can hardly hear you either. What's going on down there?'

'Not a lot. Except the whole place is absolutely swarming with bobbies.'

A trill of female laughter came, 'So who's a lucky girl then?'

'This is serious, Mags. I need a favour.'

'Speak,' said Mags.

'I want you to do a newspaper search for me. Nineteen-thirty. From early June onward. Some flyer called Angus Kilcullen. He shot himself. It'll be in the London papers, so it shouldn't take too long. Anything you can find. Okay?' She fed in more coins as the pips went.

'Okay. I'll ring you back.'

'There's more,' said Kate. A lengthy sigh came loudly at her ear. 'Somebody called Manders. He committed suicide, I think, some time in 'thirty-five. Probably July or August.' She broke off to turn another page of her notebook, almost dropped it, caught it again. 'And see if you can get hold of Di Gruber ...'

'That's New York, for Pete's sake,' wailed down the line. 'Who's going to *pay* for all this?'

'I'll make it right when I get back. Promise,' said Kate, feeding in two more coins. 'A man called Schwarz. He was a stockbroker, and he died in a fire in Maine. 'Forty-six. July. You got all that?'

There was a brief silence. 'This is all very vague, old love. What's the point exactly?'

'I don't know myself yet,' said Kate. '*You* might even be able to tell me once you've sniffed around a bit. And Mags —'

'What?'

'Whatever you find, it's just between you and me. For now. Okay?'

'Okay,' said Mags. 'If you say so.'

'I say so,' said Kate. 'Or I'll skin you alive.'

Mrs Worboys had returned to the house while Roper had

been out with Morrison. She had again driven her husband to the courthouse in Dorchester that morning. She was somewhere around forty, a well-dressed, bony woman with the brightly protuberant eyes of the hyperthyroid, and restless hands that were continually clasping and unclasping on her tweeded lap. She had last seen her mother on Sunday evening. 'After dinner. About ten o'clock, I suppose it was.'

'Not on Monday, Mrs Worboys?' asked Roper. 'At all?'

No, she had not. At nine o'clock on Monday morning she had driven her husband to Dorchester, as she had yesterday and today. On Monday, she had spent the entire day shopping in Dorchester. Her husband's court case had been adjourned at four-thirty in the afternoon and after returning to the house, briefly, to change, they had spent the evening with a barrister colleague of her husband in Salisbury. They had arrived back at the house at eleven-thirty and gone straight to bed. She had not been told that her mother was missing until George Sheridan had returned post-haste from London yesterday morning. It was he who had broken the news to her which had made her a little angry at the time, because Mrs Shaw had known something was wrong since the night before.

'But apparently she didn't want to worry me. I've telephoned most of Mother's friends since then – at least the ones I know of. She isn't with *any* of them.' A choke came into her voice and her huge eyes began to brim with tears. 'I really am becoming desperately worried. She could be dead, couldn't she? I mean that's not impossible, is it? Just *lying* somewhere.' She plucked a handkerchief from a pocket in her skirt and dabbed at her eyes with it. 'I'm so sorry,' she said, sniffing, then blowing her nose and generally making an effort to recover her composure. 'Crying won't help anything, will it?'

'Has your mother ever gone off before like this, Mrs Worboys?' asked Roper sympathetically.

She shook her head.

'Did she tell you she might be going out on Monday?'

'Yes,' she said, nodding, 'but not where. I assumed it

might have been a shopping expedition.'

'Is it likely she could be with your son?'

She shook her head again. 'Hardly,' she said. 'He lives with his awful friends in a derelict house in Portsmouth. None of us have much to do with him.'

'But I understand from Mr Sheridan that the lad was here on Sunday morning,' said Roper.

'Oh, yes, he was. Briefly.' Her tone now was one of sneering disparagement. 'He came for money. And to embarrass us.'

'So he must have known you were coming down here.'

'He phoned Julius last week in his chambers. Julius is my husband,' she explained. 'My second husband. Joel's step-father. Joel needed money. Julius told him that he wouldn't let him have it. Then foolishly told Joel that we were coming down here for the week. He turned up here on Sunday morning, just as we'd sat down to breakfast.' Mrs Worboys had spoken bitterly and at some unnecessary length. There was plainly little love lost between her and her son.

'Do you know if anybody gave your son this money he wanted?' asked Roper, recalling the £250 stub, dated last Sunday, at the back of Mrs Sheridan's cheque book.

'Yes,' she said, with a wryly angry twist to her mouth. 'Mother. To get rid of him – *and* that wretched girl he brought with him.'

'How much, Mrs Worboys? D'you know?'

She shrugged. 'I have absolutely no idea. She only told me she'd written him a cheque. I left it at that. Julius was disgusted.' Her mouth twisted bitterly again. 'And so was I.'

So if that cheque had been written for young Joel, then Mrs Sheridan had probably left the house not only without a penny but also without the means of acquiring any.

'Your son calls himself Worboys, does he?'

'Yes,' she said. 'When we married Julius had Joel's surname changed by deed poll.'

Roper took out his pocket-book and scribbled a note to himself. The sole fact that Joel Worboys lived in a squat in

57

Portsmouth didn't make him impossible to trace. With the upsurge in drug-dealing and general youthful villainy, most police divisions kept a very close eye on their local squats these days. And despite the fact that the lad had left before lunchtime on Sunday, he was still a possible witness to something or other.

A rap came at the drawing-room door as he tucked his notebook away again. It was Shaw, this morning wearing a brown overall, and with a yellow duster in his hand.

'For you, sir,' he said to Roper. 'The telephone in the hall. A Sergeant Morgan, sir.'

Roper rose from the settee, thanked Mrs Worboys for her time, and followed him out. Shaw accompanied him as far as the hall, then went off in the direction of the kitchen.

'Yes, Dan?' said Roper, at the telephone table beside the fireplace.

'Got a possible lead,' said Morgan. 'A minicab driver. He saw Mrs Sheridan's picture on the telly last night, and reckons she might be the lady he's taken over to East Choately a couple of times. She told him her name was Manders, but what put him on to her was the two dogs. He's pretty certain now she was Mrs Sheridan.'

'How handy is he?' asked Roper.

'On his way here to County. I asked him to call in. He'll be about ten minutes.'

'Bring him over here with you,' said Roper. 'I'll expect you in half an hour.'

Roper sat beside the bald, swag-bellied and talkative minicab driver, by name Buckle, in the back of Morgan's car. It was coming up for eleven o'clock in the morning and the air was filled with a fine drizzle.

'I've done the trip twice with her,' said Buckle. 'And each time she's rung me on the night before – Sunday night, as I remember. Except last week she 'phoned on Friday afternoon, but cancelled on Sunday afternoon. 'Bout four o'clock. The missus took the call.'

'When she booked you on Friday, that was for Monday, was it?'

58

'Right,' said Buckle. 'But she cancelled. Sunday. Like I said. The two times I did pick her up it was at that bus stop.' He pointed past Morgan's shoulder, through the windscreen, towards the bus stop some thirty yards beyond the gateway of the Sheridan's house. It was the stop for the Dorchester route. 'Nine o'clock the next morning,' he said, 'both times. With the dogs. She left 'em with me in the cab. Don't like dogs in the cab as a rule – smelly bloody things – but she tipped good so I let it go. I always like people to tell me if they want me to carry dogs. I have to hoover it out afterwards. All the hairs, see. And they were *bloody* hairy, those two dogs she had.'

'Pekingese, Mr Buckle?' said Roper, breaking in before Buckle got too carried away on the subject of dogs in his cab. 'Those dogs?'

'Right,' said Buckle. 'Moulting they were. All over the seats ...'

'And both times you took her to East Choately?'

'Right,' said Buckle. Morgan passed his cigarette packet over the back of his seat. Buckle plucked one out and Roper lit it for him.

'Same place each time?' asked Roper.

'Right,' said Buckle, around the cigarette, as it glowed.

'So you'd know the address she went to?'

'Well, no,' said Buckle, sitting back again and exhaling smoke. 'Not the address exactly. I dropped her off at the end of a road each time.'

'The same road both times?'

'Both times,' said Buckle. 'She was gone about an hour. She came back to the car, and I dropped her off in Dorchester on the way back.'

'And she told you her name was Manders?'

'Right,' said Buckle, reaching for the ashtray on the back of Morgan's seat.

'Remember the name of the road?' asked Roper.

Buckle shook his head. 'I'd recognise it, though. If that's any help.'

'Got an hour to spare, have you, Mr Buckle?' said Roper.

*

59

Morgan drew the car in by a telephone box on the outskirts of East Choately, although it could have been anywhere. The only signpost Roper could see, a few yards beyond the telephone box, proclaimed only that this road was the A30 and that it was only four miles from here to Yeovil – which meant that East Choately was rammed hard up against the boundary with the adjacent county of Somerset, and twenty miles or more from Milton St Philip's.

'This is where you dropped her off, is it, Mr Buckle?'

'Just here,' said Buckle. 'Both times.'

Roper climbed out on to the soggy grass verge. Morgan and Buckle joined him. The busy road was broad, hedged on this side, a large pub and a row of small shops and a sub-post office opposite the telephone box. A mail van outside the post office was picking up the morning collection.

Roper turned towards the T-junction which they had passed some fifty yards back along the road and which Buckle had pointed out to him as they had driven by.

'And she went up there, did she?'

'Definite,' said Buckle. 'Saw her in the mirror. She came back from there too.'

'Remember what she was wearing?'

'Yeah. Fur coat. A black, shiny one. The last time.'

Roper stepped on to the flagged footway and started walking. It seemed to him that Mrs Sheridan's request to be dropped off outside the telephone box so far from the junction, to which she returned, had simply been a piece of business to make sure that Buckle didn't see exactly where she went. Which probably signified something or other that it might be possible to find out if he looked hard enough.

The lane leading off the junction was a little cul-de-sac and lined along each side with a row of terraced Edwardian cottages. Across its far end were the open entrance gates of a tractor repair works with the faint sounds of hammering echoing inside it. A more likely venue was one of the cottages closer to hand. There were only a dozen or so of them, so it shouldn't take long.

Roper sent Buckle back to wait in the car while he and

Morgan knocked on a few cottage doors, Roper on one side of the lane and Morgan on the other. It was Morgan who had the greater luck. Roper received no response at the first two cottages he knocked at and, at the third, a bent and grey-haired old lady with a deaf-aid refused to open her door and shooed him off from behind her net curtain, vociferous in her conviction that he was a Jehovah's Witness, despite the warrant card he pressed against the glass of her window.

The fourth front door was opened by a woman with a small child perched on one hip and a feeding bottle in her free hand. She explained apologetically that she had only moved in last week and barely even knew her next-door neighbours as yet.

'A lady – so tall.' He demonstrated Mrs Sheridan's height with the flat of his hand. 'Stockily built. Wearing a fur coat.'

'No,' she said, shaking her head, already backing away and closing the door. 'Sorry.'

Roper trod back along the front path. DS Morgan was only just turning away from his first front door where he had been in deep and deedy conversation with an elderly lady for several minutes, together with much gesticulating towards the cottage opposite her own.

Morgan came hurrying across the road as Roper reached the gate.

'Think we've found it,' said Morgan, still putting his pocket-book away. 'The old girl I was talking to reckons she saw a fur-coated woman call at number one a while back. And she says her sister saw her that time too, *and* once before. She turned up in the morning so they say. Left about an hour afterwards. And the rest of the description fits.'

'Let's go and have a look, shall we.'

With Morgan beside him, Roper retraced his steps to the first cottage that he had knocked at, and knocked again.

'Who lives here?' he said, stepping back to look at the upstairs windows with their smart new paintwork. 'Do we know?'

'Widow,' said Morgan. 'Name of Blaney. Keeps herself to herself. They haven't seen her since Saturday.'

Roper knocked again, and this time peered through the letter box. There was an electric light switched on in the room at the end of the hall, probably the kitchen.

Morgan went around the side of the house. There came the rattle and the creak of an opening wooden gate. He was back in a moment.

'Three pints of milk on the back step,' he said.

'Perhaps she orders three pints a day,' said Roper.

'They didn't all arrive on the same day,' said Morgan. 'They've got three different codes on the caps.'

'Now there's a thing,' muttered Roper, following Morgan around the corner and through the opened side gate. Three pints of milk stood on the kitchen doorstep; the aluminium foil cap of one was embossed with a figure 2, the adjacent bottle with a 3, and the third one, set to one side in the line, with a 4, which probably represented this morning's delivery.

The windows of the door were net-curtained and running with condensation, so that they were difficult to see through; but there was a light showing in there, probably the one he had seen through the letter box. And when he shielded his eyes and put his nose closer to the cold glass he could just make out a blurred red glow across the room, lower down, near the floor, that might have been a single bar of an electric fire.

Which it was, he established, when he had tentatively tried the door knob, given the sticking door a shove with his shoulder and cautiously taken the two upward steps into Mrs Blaney's kitchen.

'Cher-rist,' muttered Morgan at Roper's shoulder, as they both saw why the two old ladies across the lane had not seen Mrs Blaney since last Saturday.

SIX

STILL AT THE KITCHEN DOORWAY, Roper took in the shambles, the broken crockery, the overturned table, the chair trapped by its back underneath it, the bloody hand-smear down the white enamelled door of the gas cooker, and lastly, although he would have preferred not to look at it at all, the mortal remains of the late Mrs Blaney, if it was that lady, huddled on its side on the lino in front of the cooker.

She had been, he guessed, somewhere in her middle forties, distinguished only by the manner of her death from the millions of other women like her who were going about their business that morning, her very ordinariness now turned into the extraordinary. She lay with her mouth open and her face turned towards the cooker, so that the left hand side of it, the side from which she had been beaten to death – she could never have sustained injuries like that in a fall – would have to remain unseen until the doctor and the pathologist arrived. She had been a thin, spare woman, her brown hair touched with grey at the temples, her plain but smart green dress, heavily bloodstained, rucked up over her knees, one sheepskin slipper on her left foot and the other one lying on its side half under the cooker.

He opened the door wider to let in some more fresh air. Morgan had gone back to the car to arrange for the necessary technical support, and transport back to the garage for the minicab driver. Mr Buckle had not driven Mrs Sheridan here last Monday, although she had booked him and then cancelled, but had some other driver? Because it seemed a coincidence of the most curious kind

63

that Mrs Blaney had been murdered and that a woman who had been known to visit her had disappeared – all in the matter of a few days. All of which led to the possibility of a whole new scenario: had Mrs Sheridan herself wreaked all this carnage, then, panic-stricken, gone into hiding somewhere? It didn't seem likely, but it wasn't impossible.

With a handkerchief pressed to his nose, despite the open door the stench of human decay in the warmth was still overpowering, Roper crouched on his heels beside the body and lightly touched its bare neck. It was chill, its pallor grey and bloodless. One hand wore, he observed, both a wedding and an engagement ring. He shuffled sideways and flicked down the hem of the green dress to restore to Mrs Blaney a little of the decorum that had been so viciously beaten from her, then, rising, he stepped over her to switch off the electric fire. Its iron casing was too hot to touch, a sure sign that it had been burning for days rather than hours, and the linoleum on the floor in front of it was already beginning to bubble and blister in the heat. And those milk bottles on the back step had to be a certain sign that Mrs Blaney had been dead for at least three days.

She had kept a tidy house. The narrow passage to the front door was newly carpeted, its wallpaper clean and bright. She took a daily newspaper, four of them lying on the doormat. The topmost one was Wednesday's – today's – Tuesday's beneath it, then some mail – a bill for rates and a circular for double glazing – and then Monday's newspaper and, finally, the fatter edition of the Sunday paper with its glossy supplement still tucked inside it: evidence, perhaps, that Mrs Blaney had been dead not for those three days but four. The front door was secured only by an old-fashioned Yale latch and a flimsy bolt top and bottom. The bolts were open.

The tiny front room was a sitting room, only large enough for two armchairs, the obligatory television set, a glass-fronted china cabinet with a twenties dinner-service in it, and a low bookcase set in the recess beside the open fireplace.

The dining room was even smaller, a dark little room,

with just sufficient space for a table pushed against the wall and three chairs at it, a tea trolley and an oak stand with a potted aspidistra on it in front of the window that overlooked the side gate. The grey carpet on the floor looked new, like the one in the hall. Clearly, Mrs Blaney had not been short of money.

Upstairs were two bedrooms, the front one in use, the back one empty apart from a couple of plywood tea chests, one crammed with motor cycle and pop music magazines, the other with scrapped motor cycle parts. Mrs Blaney had been a widow, so perhaps there had been a son, and he had moved out and left the two tea chests behind to pick up later.

Roper went back downstairs to wait for Morgan. It was only a gut-feeling as yet, but it seemed as if Mrs Blaney had died as long ago as last Saturday, some time after the paper-boy and milkman had called.

Roper stood in the doorway between the kitchen and the hallway and watched the prescribed processes being carried out on the corpse of Mrs Blaney. The police doctor had been and gone. He had thought that Mrs Blaney had been dead for several days. The little house now was a hive of quiet activity. The Coroner's Officer had been the next to arrive, and Weygood, the pathologist, and his assistant had turned up about twenty minutes ago. They had been followed shortly afterwards by a technician, from the forensic laboratory, who was presently dusting around the back door and its frame for fingerprints. In the time between there had also been a visit from the local bobby who had been alerted, somewhat belatedly, by Mrs Blaney's milkman.

Mrs Blaney had her milk delivered to her kitchen door because twice last summer she had had bottles pilfered from her front step. On Sunday morning, in accordance with a note Mrs Blaney had stuffed into an empty bottle, the milkman had left no milk. On Monday, he had left a pint. On Tuesday morning, another, despite the fact that Monday's delivery was still on the doorstep, although the milkman had not placed Tuesday's bottle himself, his small son, on half-term holiday from school, and helping the milkman on his round, had delivered that pint for him and had not mentioned that there had still been Monday's pint on Mrs Blaney's step. It was only this morning, when the milkman himself had delivered, that he realised that Mrs Blaney had not taken in her milk on Monday and Tuesday. Concerned, he had knocked on the kitchen door – he had noticed the electric light was on – and recalled hazily that it might also have been so when he had called on Monday. He had tried the door but had believed it to be locked, which is what Roper had believed until he had put his shoulder to it. He had left another pint, just in case Mrs Blaney had been poorly and unable to get downstairs for the last couple of days, then reported the matter to the local beat-officer's wife, to whom he also delivered. She had telephoned her husband at once.

According to the milkman, Mrs Blaney was a very quiet lady who settled her bill with unfailing regularity every Friday morning, and had done since he had taken over the round last July. Other than that, he knew absolutely nothing about her, and nor did the local beat-officer who knew her only by sight.

'Any idea how long she's been dead, sir?'

'Your guess is as good as mine, Chief Inspector,' said Weygood tartly, green rubber overalled, shirtsleeved and kneeling on the lino beside the body as he began to put his instruments back in his case. A red-headed, balding man of middle but otherwise indeterminate years and a thin mouth, Weygood was not Roper's favourite pathologist. On the few occasions that their paths had crossed, Roper had been left with the distinct feeling that he had only provided yet another unwarrantable incursion into Professor Weygood's already busy life.

'The Sunday newspaper's still on the doormat,' ventured Roper.

'There's your answer then,' said Weygood, snapping shut the catches of his black case at the same time for

66

added emphasis. 'I'm not a bloody magician, Chief Inspector.' He peeled off his latex gloves and dropped them into the plastic bag his young lady assistant was dutifully holding open for him. Then he relented a little. 'Post mortem this afternoon. Tell you then. Heavy weapon, might have been a hammer, can tell you that much. Struck from the left hand side as the victim viewed it. Two blows, possibly three. One powerful enough to have penetrated the bone.' He turned and unrolled his sleeves while his assistant untied the waistband of his overall and helped him off with it. 'And whoever did it must have left here covered in blood.'

'Could a woman have done it?'

'Possibly,' agreed Weygood, now fastening his gold cuff-links. 'Given the weapon had a fairly long handle. But I'm not really prepared to say more for the time being. When I know, you'll know.' He stretched out his arms behind him for the reception of his jacket, then his lightweight overcoat. His gloves he managed to tug on for himself, but then had to tug one off again in order, belatedly, to sign a chitty for the Coroner's Officer, which he did with a quick, irritable flourish as if that, too, was yet another unnecessary interruption of his tightly organised schedule.

'I suppose we ought to be thankful he doesn't deal with live ones,' confided the Coroner's Officer drily to Roper, when Weygood and his assistant were on their way back to their car and safely out of earshot. 'Crusty old sod.'

Mrs Blaney, photographed, probed and prodded to the law's satisfaction, and now with her head and hands parcelled up in plastic bags, was taken away in a temporary coffin shortly afterwards.

By half-past midday, Morgan had assembled a potted biography of Mrs Blaney. In a creased manilla envelope in the top drawer of her dressing table were two birth certificates, her own – she had been registered as Audrey Elizabeth Lawson in March 1931, born in Colwyn Bay in North Wales – and that of her son, one Peter Nigel Blaney, born December 1955, in Potter's Bar in the county of Hertfordshire. His father was one William George Blaney, a motor mechanic, deceased, according to yet another certificate, and had been since the summer of 1968. In another, smaller, envelope, Mrs Blaney's marriage lines showed that she had married Mr Blaney in January, 1952 – again in Potter's Bar. Nothing more than the ordinary landmarks in the ordinary life of an ordinary woman, or so, at the moment, they seemed.

The most useful witnesses were the Misses Murrell who lived opposite. It was the elder sister to whom Sergeant Morgan had spoken earlier.

'Not that we pry, of course,' the elder Miss Murrell hastened to assure Roper, as he sat in one of the bagged-out armchairs in her knick-knack-filled sitting room and sipped at the tea that she had just brewed for himself and Sergeant Morgan. 'But the lane's a cul-de-sac, you see. So we really can't help but notice whatever's going on. All the comings and goings.'

'Can't help it,' agreed the wheelchair-bound and younger Miss Murrell brightly. 'All the comings and goings.'

They were, the two of them, retired schoolteachers, both of them well into their late seventies, grey haired and twinkling of eye and eager to exchange what little they knew for a bit of juicy gossip about whatever had happened across at number one. Even Iris Murrell, riddled with arthritis and confined to a wheelchair, was scarcely able to contain herself. She spent most of her daylight hours by the sitting room window, which is how she had come to see Mrs Blaney last Saturday afternoon. Mrs Blaney had been shopping, 'I know because she was carrying two carrier bags. Quite full.'

'What time would that have been, Miss Murrell?' asked Roper.

'Tea time. About half-past three, quarter to four.'

'Did she go out to work?' asked Morgan.

'We don't think so, do we, Agnes?'

Agnes agreed. Mrs Blaney did not go out to work. 'We think,' she proposed, dropping her voice a pitch lest she be heard by the neighbours, 'that Mr Blaney left her *comfortable*. If you know what we mean.'

And, alas, no, they never knew *Mr* Blaney. Mrs Blaney had only moved into the cottage in the early summer, when she was already a widow.

'With her son,' added the chairbound Miss Iris.

'But he's gone,' added Miss Agnes. 'He moved out.'

'Thank Heaven.'

'Those motor cycles!'

'Lord, yes. Those motor cycles.'

'*And* that guitar.'

'We were going to complain.'

'To the council.'

'When did the son move out, exactly?' asked Roper, between sips of his tea.

'August.'

'No, dear, earlier,' insisted Miss Agnes. 'The week of your birthday, it was. The middle of July.'

After a little thought, Miss Iris agreed. Mrs Blaney's son had indeed moved out a couple of days before her birthday. Neither had seen him since, although he might have called on a Tuesday afternoon, when they had been out. On Tuesday afternoons they went to the church hall to attend the vicar's wife's literary circle. The curate came to fetch them in one of those new minibuses ...

No, they had no idea where Mrs Blaney's son lived now, although it was probably with a girl. There had been a girl who called at the house a few times, quite young. She had driven a motor cycle. They had seemed very keen on each other ...

'Did you ever see any other men call there?'

'Oh, no,' came from the horrified Miss Agnes. 'She was never *that* sort.'

'*Never*,' agreed Miss Iris, with equal passion. 'Mrs Blaney kept herself *very* much to herself. She was here for a month or more before we even knew her married name, and that was only because the postman dropped one of her letters through our letter box by mistake.'

'Her married name?' queried Roper. 'Does that mean you knew her before she was married?'

'We knew her mother.'

'Amy, Mrs Lawson,' explained Miss Agnes. 'She moved into the lane the same year we did. Nineteen fifty-five.'

'And when she died, she left the house to Mrs Blaney ...'

'That was this year ...'

'June.' Interrupted the more pedantic Miss Iris. 'Pneumonia ...'

'She fell, poor dear. Down her stairs. And she was never particularly robust ...'

'But always so cheerful.'

'She'd been something to do with the stage,' ventured Miss Iris from her wheelchair, a confidentially whispered aside, as if anything to do with the theatre was the ultimate in naughtiness.

'The stage?' Roper broke in, his interest quickening at the hint of a connection between Mrs Blaney and Mrs Sheridan, however tenuous that connection was.

'Mrs Lawson,' explained Miss Iris. 'When she was younger, of course.'

'She was in films once, too, so she told us.'

'Only as an extra,' cautioned Miss Iris. 'She didn't actually *speak*.'

'No, but still, she was in a film or two,' protested Miss Agnes crossly. 'She showed us a photograph, didn't she?'

'They call them stills,' Miss Iris asserted. 'Those photographs.'

'Well, whatever,' retorted Miss Agnes waspishly.

'How about Mrs Blaney?' Roper broke in again, before Miss Iris's airing of her knowledge of the film world's *lingua franca* started a quarrel. 'Was she on the stage?'

The Misses Murrell were at last stopped in their tracks. They didn't know. Mrs Blaney had not been the most communicative of neighbours. No, not secretive exactly, merely the kind of woman who minded her own business. Before Mrs Lawson's fall, and consequent death, Mrs Blaney had visited her mother two or three times a year, but usually only for the day, so they had never seen much of her. After Mrs Lawson's accident, while the old lady had been in hospital, Mrs Blaney had moved into the house, on a temporary basis, to be closer to her mother in order to visit her at the hospital in Dorchester. After the funeral, Mrs Blaney had returned briefly whence she had come, then moved into her mother's house, with her son, lock, stock and barrel. The son had moved out again a few weeks afterwards. More recently, the front of the house had been painted and twice, lately, the Misses Murrell had seen new carpets being delivered ...

'We think she might have come into a little money.'

'She'd started to dress more smartly ...'

'We couldn't help noticing.'

'This son of Mrs Blaney's – any idea where he might have gone to?' Morgan asked again.

They shook their heads. It was only neighbourhood gossip, and of course the Misses Murrell denied strenuously that they listened to any such thing, but the story was that Mrs Blaney and her son had quarrelled and that the boy had left the house in a huff. But there was a girl concerned, so the rumours said. And she might even have been the cause of the quarrel. But no one actually *knew* ...

'You told my sergeant that Mrs Blaney recently had a lady visitor,' said Roper, at long last getting down to the main reason for his and Morgan's visit. 'And that you saw her. Twice.'

Yes, they had. So far as they knew, the lady was the only visitor Mrs Blaney had had, although it was only the arthritic Miss Iris Murrell who had seen her twice. Her sister had only seen the woman once. Their description of the visitor was sparse, but what there was of it fitted Mrs Sheridan. Both agreed that the woman had been short and stocky and smartly dressed, but they had not seen her face because, on both occasions, she had worn her coat collar turned up, and a headscarf. On each occasion she had come on foot and been let into the house by Mrs Blaney. The last time, the lady had been wearing a dark fur coat. It had looked *very* expensive.

But exactly when the lady had called they were less certain. One day passed very much like another, although they finally agreed that the first time they had seen the woman had been about two months ago and the last occasion about four weeks ago, or it might have been five.

Which agreed, more or less, with the evidence of Mr Buckle.

Superintendent Mower made what he called a site-visit at two o'clock that same afternoon. With Roper at his side, he regarded the yellow chalked outline on the linoleum in front of the cooker in the late Mrs Blaney's kitchen.

'And nobody heard anything?'

'Not a thing,' said Roper. The immediate neighbour, widowed only a fortnight before, had been spending the time since with her son and daughter-in-law. Hearsay had it that she would be away at least another week. And the old lady next door to her, whom Roper had earlier tried vainly to dissuade that he was a Jehovah's Witness, had spent the weekend with her elderly brother along at Sherborne. The remaining few neighbours had neither heard nor seen anything untoward over the entire weekend.

'Housebreaking job, perhaps? And she caught him at it?'

'Not the usual sort,' said Roper. Mrs Blaney's handbag had been found upstairs in plain view on her dressing table. There had been over sixty pounds in notes in it and a couple of pounds in coins. 'Unless she caught him on the way in. Or her, whoever it was might have been a woman.'

'Mrs Sheridan?'

'She's been here twice before.'

'And she might have intended coming here again on Monday.'

'But she cancelled the cab,' said Roper. 'She phoned for it Friday and cancelled it on Sunday. And sometime in between, Mrs Blaney cops it. That's a hell of a coincidence.'

Mower stretched his mouth speculatively. 'Bit far-fetched though, eh, Douglas? Mrs Sheridan's what ... sixty-five-ish?'

'She's fit enough,' said Roper. 'And she's a hefty woman.

She could have put plenty of weight behind it. And it depends what her state of mind was, doesn't it?'

Mower had to agree. It was possible. Frailer and older ladies than Rita Sheridan had occasionally swung a blunt instrument to equally deadly effect. And long though the arm of coincidence often was, rarely did it stretch this far.

'I'll stay here until the lads have finished,' said Mower, fishing in his waistcoat for his snuff-box. 'And you concentrate on finding out what's happened to Mrs Sheridan. And with any luck we'll meet somewhere in the middle. One of the lads can drive you back.'

'Right,' said Roper.

He was back at Milton St. Philip's at three o'clock in the afternoon, with only an hour and a half of daylight left and rain in the air again. His first port of call was Sergeant Morrison's smart brick cottage, half of it living accommodation for Morrison and his wife and the other half a police station, its little forecourt presently the parking lot for the three coaches that brought in the search-parties at the crack of daylight that morning.

Colston, the uniformed Chief Inspector from County, who was co-ordinating the search with the help of Morrison and a large-scale Ordnance Survey map, was with Morrison in the front office, the two of them in their shirtsleeves. From the blue crayoned cross-hatching on the map spread out on the desk it looked as if a lot of ground had been covered.

'Any joy, Bob?' asked Roper.

'Could be,' said Colston. 'They found a fur coat and a dog-lead on the Dorchester road. About an hour ago.'

'Whereabouts?' asked Roper.

'In a gritting-bin, sir,' said Morrison. 'Beside the road. Just there, sir.' One of his thick forefingers bowed over a ballpointed cross on the map, about a mile north-east of the Sheridan's house on the main road to Dorchester and only a few hundred yards from where he had found the dead Pekingese on Monday night.

'Buried in the grit?' asked Roper. 'Were they?'

'No, sir, just dumped in there. The dog-lead's one of those that divides into two at the working-end and my missus reckons the coat's made of squirrel.'

Morrison brought them up from the floor beside the desk, a red leather dog-lead in a manilla envelope and a bulky fur coat in a polythene bag.

'Had them identified yet?'

'No, sir,' said Morrison. 'We thought we ought to wait for your opinion. Didn't want to go alarming Mr Sheridan unnecessarily.'

'Good thought,' said Roper. On the desk, a portable transceiver clicked to life with four more sets of map co-ordinates. Yet another square of fields and footpaths was cross-hatched by Colston.

'And one of Mr Sheridan's neighbours called in, sir,' said Morrison. 'George Watcherley. About two o'clock this afternoon, that was. He swears he saw Mrs Sheridan walking down his service road about a quarter to eight last Monday morning.'

'Swears?' Roper interrupted. 'Why swears? Somebody else saying he didn't see her?'

'Well, he's *certain* he did see her, sir. Except, if he did, Mrs Sheridan must have dropped into a hole in the ground. First she was there and then she wasn't. And there was nowhere she could have gone.'

Standing at the main gateway to his farm, the bearded, gumbooted and duffle-coated Mr Watcherley went through his testimony again for Roper's benefit. Like most witnesses he had been unaware at the time of the importance of what he might have seen.

The five-barred gateway led on to his service road, bordered on its left hand side, as they presently viewed it, by the long brick wall of the Sheridan's property with the green gate set into it – the gate which Katherine Lindsey had seen Mrs Sheridan approaching, on the garden side, that same morning – and it was here, at his own gate, sitting in his van early on Monday morning, that he had seen, or thought he had seen the back view of Mrs

Sheridan walking her dogs towards the Dorchester road. To the best of his memory, Mrs Sheridan had been wearing some kind of dark, chunky coat, and a white scarf over her head.

'It was coming up for quarter to eight,' he said, which roused Roper's interest even more, because both Watcherley's and Lindsey's spotting of Mrs Sheridan could only have been a few minutes apart. 'I got the van out of the shed, stopped just here,' Watcherley gestured at his feet with his pipe, 'and got out to open the gate. That's when I saw her first.' His pipe was lifted to point down the service road. 'She was about halfway between her side gate and the T-junction with the Dorchester road.'

At that juncture, with his gate open and about to climb back into his van, Watcherley had remembered the two letters that his wife had asked him to post and which he had left on the kitchen table. He returned to the house for them – the work of perhaps a minute – then walked back to his van. As he settled himself behind the wheel again, he happened to notice that Mrs Sheridan had almost reached the corner of her wall, where it abutted the road to Dorchester. He drove his van a few yards beyond his gate and climbed out yet again to close it behind him. 'I'm only talking a matter of seconds now,' he said, with a waggle of his pipe. 'I climbed back into the van and drove off.' The pipe was again aimed down the service road. 'Got to the junction, waited for a couple of cars to go by, then turned out – to the left, the way I could have sworn Mrs Sheridan went, towards Dorchester. And she'd gone. Only at the time I didn't think anything of it.'

'Could she have slipped in through her front gateway, Mr Watcherley?' asked Roper.

'Only if she could have sprinted fifty yards in about ten seconds,' said Watcherley, 'which I doubt.'

'Might she have turned right, and not left?'

'I'm sure she didn't,' said Watcherley, slowly shaking his head. 'She'd have to have crossed my road to have done that. I'd have seen her.'

'Much traffic about was there, sir?' asked Roper.

'No,' said Watcherley. 'Not a lot. Just a dribble. We get a sort of rush hour from about eight-fifteen to nine o'clock – folk going to work in Dorchester – but even then it isn't nose to tail.'

'Could she have been picked up? Somebody waiting for her in a car, perhaps? Down there at the junction?'

'Kidnapped, you mean?' said Watcherley, obviously a reader of the tabloid press.

'I was thinking more of someone who might have called to collect her by arrangement,' said Roper. 'A taxi perhaps.'

Watcherley shook his head doubtfully. He had seen no vehicle that might have been a taxi pulling away from the verge as he had reached the corner, but admitted that his attention had mostly been confined to his right and the flow of traffic he had been about to join; although he did agree that Mrs Sheridan had disappeared so quickly that the only solution had to be that she had stepped into a vehicle of some sort and been whisked away before he had made his left turn towards Dorchester.

'Damned funny business, though, eh?' he said.

And Roper agreed that it was, so much so that he and Sergeant Morrison re-enacted for themselves what Mr Watcherley might have seen at 7.45 on Monday morning, to establish the likelihood of Mrs Sheridan being able to vanish into thin air in so short a time.

Leaving Morrison in his Escort in front of Watcherley's gate, he started walking down the service road beside the crumbling brick wall. It was starting to rain again.

After some fifty paces he passed, on his left, the green wooden gate set in the wall – now more than likely the exit Mrs Sheridan had used on Monday morning. He heard Morrison start the engine of his Escort. Thirty more paces and Roper had reached the Dorchester road and the brick pier that formed the junction of the Sheridans' walls. He turned the corner, as Mrs Sheridan probably had, and, walking deliberately more briskly, strode out along the footpath towards the driveway to the house. He heard Morrison slip the Escort into gear.

Another twenty paces and Morrison was pulling up beside him. And Roper was still a good thirty or forty yards from the Sheridans' ball-finialled gateway.

'She could never have made it, could she?' said Morrison.

'Damn right she couldn't,' said Roper.

SEVEN

GEORGE SHERIDAN EXAMINED THE GRIT-POWDERED red leather dog-leash in its manilla envelope. He sat in the settee to the left of the fireplace, the paperback he had been reading – with a black-stetsoned gun-slinger on the front – on the cushion beside him. Roper sat on the arm of the settee opposite him, and waited, careful not to prompt.

'Yes, Inspector,' Sheridan conceded at last. 'It does *look* very like – I can't be certain, of course.'

'No, sir, quite,' agreed Roper, rising to take the package back again. Leather dog-leashes were made by the million, red ones by the thousand, and even bifurcated red ones, for those who preferred to walk their dogs in pairs, were probably turned out in their hundreds. But there could not be all that many of the latter lying around in Milton St Philip's. That would be one coincidence that was just too many.

'May I ask where you found it?' asked Sheridan, unhooking his half-moon reading spectacles. 'It looks very dirty.'

'Yes, sir, it would be,' said Roper. 'One of the search parties found it a mile or so up the road to Dorchester. It was in a roadside gritting bin.'

'And you think my wife dropped it in there?' asked Sheridan.

'No, sir,' said Roper. 'Not necessarily. Only it wouldn't have got in there on its own, if you take my point, sir.'

Sheridan swept a hand across his harassed forehead and up into his shock of hair, which made it untidier than ever. Then the hand came down again and joined the other

78

which was toying agitatedly with the reading glasses in his lap.

'We also found a fur coat, sir,' said Roper, lifting the carrier-bag from beside the settee and peeling the top open to give Sheridan a glimpse of the coat in its polythene bag.

'My wife's?'

'I was hoping you could tell me, sir.'

Sheridan shook his head. 'No,' he said. 'I'm sorry. They all look alike to me, all I ever recognise is her mink one.'

'Perhaps Mrs Shaw could help, sir.'

Sheridan rose and pressed a bell-push set into the wall beside the chimney breast. 'May I ask where it was found?' he asked, as he sat down again.

'The same place, sir,' said Roper. 'Dropped in with the dog lead.'

Sheridan looked only more baffled.

'Really,' he said, 'I don't even begin to understand.' He spent a moment in bewildered contemplation. 'If my wife *did* put those things in this bin ... it looks almost as if she'd decided to run away. Doesn't it?'

'Yes, sir,' agreed Roper. 'It certainly looks that way.'

Sheridan opened his mouth to speak, but shut it again without saying a word.

'You've got a thought, have you, sir?' asked Roper hopefully. If Mrs Sheridan had run away, she might have done so with good reason. Although he doubted very much if Sheridan knew anything about it.

'No,' said Sheridan, shrugging. 'Sorry. My mind's gone quite blank.'

After a light rap on the door Mrs Shaw joined them.

She was quicker than Sheridan in positively identifying the red leather leash – when it wasn't in use, it usually hung on a hook beside the kitchen door to the garden. But, like Sheridan, she was less sure about the coat, although it did look like Madam's, and the silk lining was certainly the right colour.

'Does the name Blaney mean anything to you, Mrs Shaw?' asked Roper. 'Mrs Audrey Blaney?'

79

'No, sir,' she said, shaking her head after a moment or two. 'Nothing.'

'Mr Sheridan?'

Sheridan thought for considerably longer. 'No,' he said eventually. 'Not a thing. Should it?'

'I think she was a friend of your wife's, sir,' said Roper, carefully phrasing that blatant overstatement. 'According to several witnesses, your wife visited Mrs Blaney from time to time.'

Sheridan and Mrs Shaw only looked at each other and shook their heads.

'How about the name of Lawson? Does that one ring any bells? Audrey Lawson? Amy Lawson?' He glanced at each of them, but their faces stayed blank.

Roper didn't press them further. Unlike Mrs Sheridan, Mrs Blaney was unlikely to make headlines in the national newspapers tomorrow, but the news of her murder would get about soon enough and Roper didn't want Sheridan or Mrs Shaw making too many connections before he himself did.

At four-thirty Roper ambled along the sunken path towards the green gate that gave egress to Watcherley's service road. He was beginning to set great store by that gate, because if Katherine Lindsey had seen Mrs Sheridan on one side of it at seven-forty-five last Monday morning and Mr Watcherley had seen her on the other side of it a few moments afterwards, the only possible conclusion was that Mrs Sheridan had gone out through it – which of course she had every right so to do. But she had passed through it unobserved, which begged the question: had she hoped to leave unobserved? Had she at some time after the murder of Mrs Blaney – or even because of it – decided to vanish without trace? Arranged to have herself spirited off by an accomplice in a car? Because that was the only way she could have vanished so suddenly, more or less under the eyes of Mr Watcherley, and hidden herself somewhere until all the furore over Mrs Blaney had died down? At which point she would reappear with a carefully scripted explanation. Kidnap or loss of memory, they were the usual yarns in these situations. They rarely worked, they were too old in the tooth, but that still didn't stop villains, or villainesses, from trying them on for size.

And the fur coat might have been worn because it would have fitted loosely enough over some other coat, perhaps a new one – one that Mrs Shaw didn't know about and therefore would not recognise as being missing from the wardrobe in Mrs Sheridan's bedroom. And perhaps she had got access to money. Perhaps somewhere she did have another bank account under another name, neither of which was illegal. But then, if she had, had she set up that account with something like this in mind? Had she really intended to kill Mrs Blaney with that much forethought? And what could possibly have been her motive ...?

He reached the green gate. It was unbolted on the inside, but when he turned the cast-iron door knob he found it securely locked. There was no key in the lock, which he established by crouching and peering through the keyhole and seeing dusky daylight on the other side. The lock had been oiled, and fairly recently because there was a runnel of a thick greenish oil still dribbling from the bottom of the keyhole. He touched a finger to it. It smelt like engine oil.

There was similar oil, too, on the three wrought iron hinges and the barrels of the two drawn bolts, applied so liberally that it was running down the woodwork.

With the bolts drawn and the lock locked, the inference had to be that whoever had used the gate last had gone from the inside to the outside, rather than outside to inside or – unless they had forgotten to do so – they would have shot the bolts after them.

If Mrs Sheridan had wanted to flit away without too much fuss there could hardly have been a better route.

He wiped his shoes on the kitchen doormat. 'I'm looking for keys, Mrs Shaw.'

She put aside her potato peeler and dried her hands on a towel draped over the rail beside the cooker.

81

'They're over there, sir,' she said. 'On the wall, beside the dresser.'

They were on an oak panel fitted with rows of brass hooks, each with a number above it in faded gold leaf. Car keys, door keys, some in bunches on rings, some hanging alone with a tattered baggage label tied to them to denote their function. Several of the larger ones looked like antiques and were probably as old as the house.

'Which one's the key to the side gate, Mrs Shaw, the one in the garden wall?'

'On the bottom row, sir.' Mrs Shaw came up beside him. 'Just there, sir …' Her hand hovered over an empty hook. 'Or it was,' she added, picking around the rest of the keys and lifting a few aside in case the gate key had got mixed up with them. Her puzzlement looked genuine.

'Not there, Mrs Shaw?'

'No, sir,' she said, still frowning. 'A big old iron thing, it is. You can't miss it.'

'When did you last see it? D'you remember?'

No, she did not. It was a sort of fixture that she's got used to seeing there, simply because it was never used. To her knowledge, the last time the gate had been opened had been when her son had painted it back in the summer. And that was the only time in several years.

'Would Mrs Sheridan have been likely to use it?'

'Oh, no, sir,' she said. 'Leastways, I've never seen her.'

'Not even to walk the dogs?'

'No, sir. Unless they go out with her in the car, they never go out of the grounds.'

'Might Mr Sheridan have the key?'

'I doubt it,' she said. 'But I'll go and ask him if you like, sir.'

'Please,' said Roper.

She was briskly back.

'No, sir,' she said. 'Mr Sheridan says he's never used it. And he wouldn't recognise it if he saw it.'

'How about Mr Shaw?'

'You can ask him yourself. He'll be back in a minute, I expect. Would you like a cup of tea while you're waiting?'

82

'Be most welcome,' said Roper, pulling out a chair from under the table and unbuttoning his raincoat. 'Thank you.'

The kettle was put on to boil, a cup and saucer were set on a tray with a jug of milk and a sugar bowl.

A little chit-chat about the weather, present and prophesied, soon had Mrs Shaw at her ease, so that by the time she had peeled her potatoes and the tea was brewing Roper had established that she had been with the Sheridans for five years and her son for nearly two – since he had come out of the army. And before becoming a cook – well, she was a housekeeper and general dogsbody really, she had been a theatrical dresser, which was how she had come to meet Mr Sheridan – and Mrs Sheridan too, of course. And the theatre was dying – well, not dying exactly but people just weren't putting a lot of money into it any more and television was the big thing now, wasn't it? So when the Sheridans had bought this big house and needed someone to work as a cook-housekeeper, Mrs Shaw had grasped the opportunity with both hands. She had always fancied living in the country ...

Only when Roper broached the subject of the Sheridans more directly did Mrs Shaw become more reticent, or perhaps guarded, or may be it was simply the good old-fashioned quality of loyalty rearing its head.

'But they rub along all right together?'

'Yes, sir. So far as I know.'

Roper decided to leave it at that. Mrs Shaw was wise enough not to bandy gossip about her employers and he could scarcely blame her. Besides which she did not look the kind who pressed her ear to keyholes. Anyway, his interest at the moment was focussed on the whereabouts of Mrs Sheridan and her possible connection with the late Audrey Elizabeth Blaney, neé Lawson. It wasn't even important now how Mrs Sheridan had slipped out of the house on Monday morning, because it was obvious that she had. What interested him more was the fresh oil on the working parts of the gate, perhaps to ensure their silence. If Mrs Sheridan had applied it herself, perhaps by dark

83

the night before, it indicated a most thorough degree of preparedness.

He heard the metallic sounds of a bicycle being leaned against the wall by the back door, and a moment later Shaw came in, lifting one knee then the other as he took off his cycle-clips. Like his mother, he did not know the present whereabouts of the key to the garden gate. Nor could he remember the last time he had seen it on the hook. So far as Shaw was aware, the gate had not been opened since late July when he himself had painted it, inside and out.

'The gate's kept locked, is it, Mr Shaw?'

'Yes, sir,' said Shaw. 'Madam insists on it.'

'And bolted?'

'Always, sir.'

'It's not bolted now. It's only locked.'

'I know nothing about that then, sir,' said Shaw. 'The last time I checked it, it was locked *and* bolted.'

'Which was when?' asked Roper.

'About a week, sir, the last time.'

'Not since?'

'No, sir. There's no need. The gate's never used, sir. It doesn't go anywhere.'

Shaw had last oiled the bolts and the hinges in July. At that time, the bolts had seized solid with rust and he had had to oil them before he could finally release them in order to open the gate to paint it.

'You haven't oiled them since?'

'No, sir,' said Shaw. 'I'm quite positive.'

At five-thirty in the evening, Roper was back at Sergeant Morrison's house. The search for Mrs Sheridan had been called off at dark. Whether or not the net was spread wider tomorrow was down to the Chief Constable, but ground-searching was a costly business and extravagant of manpower, besides which Mrs Sheridan was probably miles from here by now, and very much alive.

For an hour, while Morrison went out on his early evening rounds, Roper sat alone in the sergeant's back office with the hundred or so statements that had been collected during the door-to-door enquiries over the course of the day. Not that many of them, strictly speaking, were statements. Most consisted only of answers to the half a dozen formal questions: Do you know Mrs Rita Sheridan? When did you last see her? Where did you last see her? Did you at any time after 7.30 a.m. last Monday morning see one or two Pekingese dogs walking unattended? Have you seen anyone (e.g. a stranger), in or about Milton St Philip's, who aroused your suspicions? And ditto a vehicle of any kind which might have had a woman passenger who might have been Mrs Sheridan?

The answer to the first question was a heartening yes. Everyone in the village knew Mrs Sheridan although mostly only by sight. Few knew her on terms much more intimate than passing the time of day with her.

The answers to the second question were widely spread between last month and last week and included many 'can't remembers'. The wheres were mostly confined to the village, although two women had seen Mrs Sheridan sitting in a tea shop in Dorchester, but that had been a fortnight ago.

The answers to the remaining questions were, without exception, categorically in the negative, and, when Roper counted them, of statements there were only four, none of which had any relevance to the matter at hand, except that one local lady had seen Mrs Sheridan getting into a minicab, with her dogs, a month or so ago. Her vague description of the car fitted Buckle's cab.

Beyond that, however painstakingly Roper nit-picked at them, the questionnaires were so much waste paper. He was by nature a patient man, but he was aware of a growing sense of frustration because he wasn't even certain what he was investigating any more, and it was at eight o'clock, in desperation rather than expectation, that he was parking his car again on George Sheridan's rainswept front driveway. An earlier phone call had established that the Worboys were in the house that evening and that Mr Worboys would be available for an interview.

It was Mrs Shaw who showed him into the drawing-room to wait for Worboys who, when he finally appeared, turned out to be a big, balding, powerful man, magisterial of tread and pendulous of jowls, and plainly not the sort to apologise for keeping a mere policeman waiting for the better part of a quarter of an hour. Even sitting down, he contrived to give Roper a view up his nostrils. He was, Roper guessed, rising fifty, his crisp, lapidary style a cover for what was probably an innate shyness. Despite the firmness of his deliveries his feet and hands were continually on the move, small gestures, but Roper noticed them and thought better of him for them.

Yes, George Sheridan had already told him and his wife of the finding of the fur coat and the dog-leash. He had played the matter down with his wife, although, privately, he considered the findings gave rise to even more concern than his mother-in-law's disappearance. George thought similarly. It was all very worrying.

'Do you think your mother-in-law could have had some kind of nervous breakdown, sir?'

'I doubt it,' said Worboys.

'Anything unusual about your mother-in-law's behaviour over last weekend, sir?'

Worboys weighed that carefully, his brow beetled. 'No,' he said, after a while. 'I don't think so. She was a little quiet on Sunday, at lunch. But I have to confess that I've always found her rather more prey to her emotions than the common run. Other than that I can think of nothing extraordinary.' He had last seen Mrs Sheridan on Sunday night, although he had heard her going past his bedroom door on Monday morning, and so had his wife, who slept next door.

'What time on Monday morning, sir?'

'Seven-thirty.'

'And you're both sure it was Mrs Sheridan, sir?'

'She was talking to the dogs. From the fuss they were making I gathered they were being taken for their morning exercise.'

'And you're fairly certain of the time, sir?'

'No,' said Worboys, grudgingly conceding his fallibility on this particular point. 'Not precisely.' Pressed a little harder he agreed that it might have been later, which Roper thought far more likely. Worboys and his wife had arrived here late on Saturday night. He had spent most of Sunday reviewing the case he was defending over in Dorchester, and in the evening he and Mrs Worboys had taken a walk up to the village before the evening meal. Mrs Sheridan had been perfectly normal again at dinner. The Worboys turned in early on Sunday night and when they had driven to Dorchester on Monday morning they had done so in the belief that Mrs Sheridan was still in the house. The only remarkable happening over the entire weekend was that the central heating had come briefly to life early on Sunday morning. From the way Worboys spoke, it seemed that the chill of the bedrooms was a cross that all its visitors were forced to bear.

'But I'm sure that doesn't interest you.' He gave a little smile, and Roper, always aware how dangerous first impressions were, found himself liking the man.

'No, sir,' said Roper, smiling back. 'Not particularly. I believe your stepson was here briefly on Sunday morning – with a young woman.'

'Briefly.'

'D'you have any address for him?'

'I don't.' said Worboys. 'I'm sorry. He lives with that same young woman. At the moment I think they're along at Portsmouth. But they could have moved on since Sunday. One never knows.'

'Not to worry, sir. I'm sure we will be able to find him if we need to talk to him.' Roper tucked away his pocket-book and started to rise.

'My wife,' said Worboys, hesitantly, still sitting, his pink pate glistening in the light of the sconce beside the fireplace. 'She's beginning to feel the strain of all this. If you come up with anything ... unpleasant, I think it might be more than she can bear. I may rely, mayn't I, on you handling the matter with ... well, discretion?'

'You may, sir,' said Roper. On his feet now, he toyed

briefly with the idea of asking Worboys if the name Blaney meant anything to him, but then decided against it. If George Sheridan had never heard of it then it was even more unlikely that Worboys had.

Worboys rose and advanced, a hand extended, but Roper, who never shook hands with anybody who might, however remotely, belong to the opposition, was saved from grasping it by the sudden bowling in of George Sheridan.

'Ah, sorry. Good evening, Mr Roper. Didn't realise ...'

'It's all right, sir,' said Roper, as Sheridan started to back out again. 'We've just finished. I can see myself out. Thank you for your time, Mr Worboys.'

With one of Rita Cavallo's leather-bound scrapbooks hugged tightly under one arm, she crept stealthily down the dark staircase towards the hall. An hour ago Mags Biggs had phoned – and half a minute into the conversation there had been a click on the line. Kate had thought little of it at the time, but when she had put the receiver down again she had distinctly heard the faint tinkle of another telephone being put back somewhere else in the house, which could have meant that someone else had been listening in – not that it mattered all that much, because Mags' call had dashed her expectations at a single stroke. Whatever Rita Cavallo had been, or had done, and despite the accidents that had seemed to befall her menfolk, she could not have shot Angus Kilcullen. Stupid to have thought so in the first place. That click on the phone though, that had scared her, it was creepy ...

From lower down, she could hear the muted rumble of two male voices, one George Sheridan's, the other probably Julius Worboys'. They sounded as if they were in the drawing-room.

Three more stairs, then the bottom landing, faintly lit from a pair of sconces in the hall. Then she stilled, balanced on the edge of a stair, her breath held and the hairs standing up at the nape of her neck. The soft creak she had heard was followed by another then, as she glanced upward and backward into the darkness above her, a pale and disembodied white hand came into view, sliding down the balustrade towards her.

'Up to a bit of hanky-panky, are we, Miss?' a soft voice enquired, and Shaw came down out of the shadows, slowly and relentlessly, his spectacles glinting and looking as if he hadn't got a face but only a pair of huge glass discs for eyes.

She clutched the scrapbook closer. It was too late to hide it. She stepped down to the marble floor of the hall, backing away. 'Mind your own bloody business, Mr Shaw,' she hissed spiritedly, but for all her resolution her heart was thudding and her feet felt as if they were glued to the floor. Even though she knew the layout of the house now, Shaw still found ways and means of springing out of dark corners and catching her unawares.

'It is my business, Miss.' He continued to descend, leisurely, menacingly, the pale hand gliding over the banister rail like a hairless white spider. He extended his other arm and clicked his finger and thumb together. 'Give,' he said, padding closer until she could smell his aftershave.

'You touch me ...' she threatened.

'Touch you,' he sneered softly, scarcely above a whisper. 'I wouldn't touch you with gloves on, Miss. You're dirt, like all the others. Sneaking about, prying ...'

'I'm *not* prying,' she lied, feeling her legs turning to water because this time Shaw really meant business.

'Lying cow,' he whispered softly, pushing his face close to hers. She smelled toothpaste. 'That's what you are, Miss. A proper lying cow.' His fingers closed over the edge of the scrapbook. She snatched it away. He padded swiftly after her – he was wearing white sneakers she observed uselessly – his hand shot out again.

She opened her mouth to yell, but the voice that seemed to come out of it was a man's so that her own voice died in her throat.

'Ah, Miss Lindsey,' it said, cool, calm, composed. 'Just the lady I'd like a few words with. Good evening, Mr Shaw.'

Her mouth was still open when he joined them from somewhere in the shadowy alcove by the coatstand, a raincoat neatly draped over his arm, the detective, the one she had spoken to yesterday, either on the point of arriving or the point of leaving – although at the moment she didn't care which.

'Somewhere where we could have a little chat, is there, Miss Lindsey? Privately?'

'Well, I'm not sure …' she said, a shake in her voice, and still wary of the proximity of Shaw. She *betted* it was him on that extension …

'I'll ask Mr Sheridan if we can use the study.'

'Yes,' she said falteringly, half an eye still on Shaw. 'Yes. All right.'

'If you wouldn't mind, Mr Shaw,' the detective said. 'There's no need for you to hang about, sir. We can find our own way.'

For a second or two Shaw didn't move, the light from one of the electric sconces reflected in each of the pebble lenses of his spectacles, and his fists clenched low down by his sides.

Then, without a word, he skirted the detective and slunk away in the direction of the kitchen.

EIGHT

ROPER FOLLOWED HER INTO THE study and hung his
raincoat on the hook behind the door.

'You all right, Miss Lindsey?'

'Yes, fine,' she said, her heart still thudding. When she'd
first met him she hadn't cared for him all that much, but
like Julius Worboys he improved with acquaintance.
'Thank you for coming out of the wall just now.'

'Can I get Mrs Shaw to get you a cup of tea?'

'No,' she said. 'Really. I'm fine.' She subsided gratefully
into the swivel chair in front of the desk. He sat on the
spare chair against the wall.

'I'm surprised you're still here, Miss Lindsey. Con-
sidering the circumstances.'

'My boss has told me to stay put for as long as I can.'

'Waiting for the story to break?'

'Sort of,' she said. 'George won't let reporters into the
place.'

'And he hasn't noticed you're still lurking about?'

'Not yet.' Although privately she suspected that dear old
George, bless his heart, was keen on doing a bit of
match-making. His frequently dropped asides to her
about what a good chap Bill Erskine was had hardly been
subtle.

He stretched out his feet, crossed his ankles and
regarded her lengthily.

'Came on a bit strong, didn't he?' he said. 'Our Mr
Shaw.'

'I think it's the way he gets his jollies,' she said.

'You don't like him.'

She shook her head. 'No,' she said. 'Not a lot.'

He nodded towards the scrapbook to which she was still clinging like grim death. 'What is that, exactly?'

'A scrapbook,' she said. 'One of Rita's.'

'And you're doing a bit of research on her, so I hear.'

'Yes,' she said.

'Can I take a look?'

'Sure,' she said. He half rose, and she held out the scrapbook. He sat down again. She felt the blood tingling back into her fingers as she watched him lift and turn a few pages.

'Shaw done anything like that before?' he said, to the scrapbook.

'No,' she said, to the top of his head. 'Not quite like that. His favourite hobby's springing out from dark corners.'

'Know much about him?' he said, still turning pages on his knee.

'Hardly anything,' she said. 'Except he's spent most of the last twenty years in the army.'

He changed the subject. 'She was a pretty woman,' he said, lifting another page.

'Yes,' she said. 'She was.'

The subject was changed again. 'Turned anything up? Yet?'

'No,' she said. 'I thought I had, but I hadn't.'

Another silence. 'Care to try it on for size?' he said, still to the scrapbook.

'No,' she said. 'Not really.'

And that was his technique, although it wasn't for a good while afterwards that she realised that it was a technique and that he'd polished it into an art form. He changed the subject, she followed, he asked little questions and she answered them. She did not, his tone made it plain, have to answer any of them, and anyway most of them were in the shape of asides addressed to the scrapbook and not to her. She merely happened to be there, a sounding board for his thoughts, as it were.

'And what happened to this other scrapbook?'

'I think she burned it. Sunday afternoon. In the boiler-room. When I came back in here to look at it again,

92

it'd gone. I reckon the smoke I saw going up was it.'

'It wasn't a scrapbook like this one?'

'No,' she said. 'It was tatty. And old. *Really* old. The sort of things kids have. With fairies and toadstools on the covers.'

'And the writing in it?'

'I didn't get a chance to read it. She saw it, swooped and locked it up again.'

'Then it wasn't there any more.'

'No,' she said. 'Right.'

It was at that juncture that it occurred to her that he and she were looking each other straight in the eye and had been for some time. She wished she hadn't noticed that. It had been easier talking to the top of his head.

'I had this crazy idea, you see. That she'd had all these lovers. And none of them died naturally.'

'Reckon she did 'em in, do you, Miss?'

'Yes,' she agreed, ready at any time for his face to register mirth. 'Something like that.'

'And?'

'She hadn't. At least, not the first one. We haven't looked into the other ones yet.'

'We?' he said. 'Who's we?'

She told him about Mags Biggs, and how Mags had spent the day working her socks off, looking up old newspapers in Fleet Street for references to Angus Kilcullen. And how the idea that Rita Cavallo might have been concerned in his death had died on its feet. Rita had been called to the inquest on Angus Killcullen, as one of that gentleman's more intimate friends, to give evidence on the possible state of his mind.

Following Kilcullen's death, the police, who regarded all sudden deaths caused by a weapon as suspicious, had questioned Miss Cavallo, who was publicly known to have been a frequent visitor to the house in Portman Square. But Miss Cavallo had been several miles away, with a friend, in Earl's Court. The friend, one Amy Stole, had vouchsafed this. Miss Cavallo had arrived for tea with her that day, and stayed on to spend the entire night with her in her lodgings. Amy Stole was another actress.

'You sure the name wasn't Lawson?' he said, breaking suddenly in on her. 'Amy Lawson?'

'No,' she said. 'Definitely. Mags spelled it out and I wrote it down. And she's in there, by the way. Amy Stole. About five or six pages in.'

'Show me.'

She stood up and showed him. The glossy black and white photograph, crazed and beginning to turn yellow at the edges, was a still from one of Rita Cavallo's early movies. It showed a dimly lit nightclub sometime in the late 'twenties or early 'thirties, and five people, two tarty blondes in evening dresses and the two mean-looking men in dinner-jackets. The two men had just started to grapple with each other, one already on his feet. All the participants in the scene had signed their names on the photograph, the two women across the chests of their white, flounced dresses, the men across the fronts of their shirts; the ink had barely adhered to the shiny surface of the photograph in the first place, and the years had faded it almost to illegibility. One of the brassy young women was Rita Cavallo – she could not have been much more than eighteen, if that – but what drew Roper's interest more was the fifth face, the one that Lindsey's forefinger had circled: a cigarette-girl, standing to one side of the table, just drawing back in fright from the impending fisticuffs. Her autograph was signed across the front of the tray of cigarettes that hung from her neck on a leather strap. The name was Amy Stole.

Roper, ready to clutch at any straw, wondered if this was the photograph that the Misses Murrell had seen, because, if it was, it was a smaller world than he had ever dared to hope it was, and Amy Stole might eventually have become Amy Lawson, the recently deceased mother of the even more recently deceased Audrey Blaney.

Lindsey pointed again, eastward an inch. 'And that's Chester Barclay.'

'Something special about him too?' he said.

'He was another one of her boyfriends. *He* didn't die a natural death either.'

94

Roper picked up his change and walked back to the banquette beside the fireplace in the saloon bar of the Crown and Compass. It was coming up for half-past nine and the bar was just getting busy. Down at the far end a couple of lads were playing Russian pool.

'Cheers,' Kate said, picking up her tomato juice and sipping from it. He had driven them here in his car. 'Thank you.'

'Prosit,' he said, sampling his half of bitter.

She took another sip, then unzipped her shoulder bag, from which she took a cheap red notebook.

'I've logged it all in shorthand,' she said.

'Wise,' he said, sipping again. A chill damp draught blew around the bar floor as an elderly couple came in with an overweight bull-terrier and left the door flapping behind them.

'Where do you want me to start?' she said.

'The beginning,' he said. 'Whenever that was.'

'I don't know when the beginning was,' she said. 'But she started early. She was in a repertory company in nineteen-twenty-eight. There's a programme in the first scrapbook. She played somebody's daughter, so it was probably a juvenile part.'

'How old d'you reckon she is?'

'God knows,' she said. 'But if, say, she was sixteen in 'twenty-eight she'd be about sixty-four or five.'

'Fairly robust, is she?'

'Very,' she said. 'Then she was in a film, I think it was a silent. 'Twenty-nine, that was. It was only a bit-part, but Chester Barclay was in it. I found several snapshots of them together. They looked very buddy-buddy.'

Two more films had followed, both with Chester Barclay also appearing in them. By that time, Rita Cavallo had gone from the bottom of the cast list to somewhere near the top.

Then Angus Kilcullen had come on the scene, although she had not been able to find mention of that young gentleman in any of what she called the 'public' scrapbooks. The only sign of him had been in the child's one that had disappeared on Sunday. During the year of Angus Kilcullen's suicide, Rita Cavallo had made no film. In 1932, she had appeared in a talkie, *Last Ferry to Java*, which Lindsey had been shanghaied to watch last Friday evening.

In 1933 Chester Barclay had died in a car accident in the south of France.

'How d'you find that out?'

'George Sheridan told me,' she said. 'He knew him.'

'He didn't tell you more than that?'

'No,' she said. 'I didn't want to push my luck. I tried to make it sound casual.'

'Wise,' he said, again.

She listed a few more films that Rita Cavallo had made, then arrived at 1935. At that time, Rita Cavallo had become the wife, or rather, the widow, of a Mr Something Manders. Lindsey knew no more of him than that, his was only a quickly glimpsed name under a picture of Rita Cavallo in the scrapbook that had disappeared. But she had remembered the month and the year, and sufficient of the caption to be fairly sure that Manders had committed suicide.

'That's the usual euphemism, isn't it: the balance of his mind had become disturbed?'

'Yes,' he said. 'I'd say so.' So Mrs Sheridan had not used an entirely fictitious name to book Mr Buckle's cab. It was a name she had once used legally.

Rita Cavallo had made three more films, then had come the war during which she made only two. Immediately after the war in Europe was over she had been signed up for Hollywood. At some time during that period she had married a Mr Something Schwarz – again she could recall little more of him, except he had died in June 1946.

'How?'

'His house in Maine caught fire. I got the impression he didn't get out quickly enough.'

'Interesting,' he said, sipping.

'And the same clipping,' she said, 'had a picture of Rita

96

coming out of a New York hospital with a baby in her arms. A boy.'

'So she's got a son somewhere, has she?'

'No,' she said, leaning forward over the drink she had scarcely touched. 'That's the point. In all the other scrapbooks there's a lot of pictures of Greta Manders ...'

'Greta Manders?' he said, frowning at her, his glass of bitter stopping a couple of inches below his chin on its way to his mouth.

'She was in a few movies. I don't think they ever came to anything.'

'That's the lady who's Mrs Worboys now?'

'Right,' she said. 'She was an actress. She never quite made it. Her father was the Manders I told you about just now. The one who had the balance of his mind disturbed.'

His glass continued its upward journey. 'This son ...' he said.

'That's what I was coming to.' She was still hunched forward over the table. 'Nowhere in *any* of the scrapbooks is there any mention of him. Not anywhere.'

But she did remember catching a glimpse of another picture in the child's scrapbook in the moment before it was snatched from her.

'There was this woman,' she said. 'In black, and wearing a veil, coming off a ship. And there was a man coming down behind her. He was in black too – I think.

'He was carrying some kind of box on his shoulder – and he had a top hat, I'm sure it was a top hat. It was only a small box. I think he was an undertaker's man.'

'And the box was a coffin?'

'Right,' she said. 'Baby-sized.'

'And that's why there's no son in any of the scrapbooks?'

'Right,' she said.

He drained his glass. 'Know what, Miss Lindsey?' he said.

'What?'

'I reckon you've missed your vocation,' he said.

She had also done some sums, juggled and jiggled with the dates she'd remembered.

'The New York hospital picture was early 'forty-seven, and the caption said that Greta was ten years old.'

'So?' he said. It was gone ten o'clock now. He was talking around a cheese and pickle roll, Lindsey around a sandwich. He was beginning to like Lindsey. She was smart. Wrong, possibly, but smart nevertheless.

'If I've got the date roughly right – the early winter of 'forty-seven – Greta must have been born some time around early 'thirty-six. Are you with me?'

'No,' he said. 'But don't worry, Miss Lindsey, I'll catch up eventually.'

'So if *she* was born in early 'thirty-six, and her *father*, that's Manders, died in nineteen-thirty-five, he never got to see her, did he?'

'If you say so,' said Roper, still doing his own mental arithmetic.

'Then she married this American, this Schwarz, and he didn't get to see *his* progeny either, did he, because he was burned to death the previous year, wasn't he? What I'm getting to is,' she said, 'that she conceives and her husbands die. You do see what I mean, don't you?'

'Oh, I see what you're driving at, Miss Lindsey,' said Roper amiably, reluctant to dampen her enthusiasm and still dubious about her findings, but nevertheless interested in all that she had told him. 'But some people are born jinxed. An old uncle of mine had three wives in ten years. They all died on him. And the old boy wouldn't have swatted a fly.'

'So you don't believe me?'

'Belief doesn't come into it, Miss Lindsey,' he said patiently. 'It's like I said a while back: all you've got is circumstantial evidence. I mean, this idea of yours about that flying feller, Kilcullen, it didn't come to anything did it? I mean she just wasn't there, was she?'

But then, having delivered himself of that, his hand went inside his jacket and reappeared with a diary and a ballpoint – but not, she noticed, with the official-looking buff-covered notebook that he had been using up in her bedroom yesterday when she'd shown him where she'd last seen Rita Cavallo walking down the garden. That he should be making notes in a mere pocket diary, she concluded, was merely a sop to her self-esteem.

'Can you give me those dates and names again, Miss Lindsey?'

'You sure I'm not boring you?'

'You're not boring me,' he said.

It was almost eleven o'clock. The bell had been rung for last orders at the bar and the potman was wandering around collecting empty glasses. A few customers were already drifting homeward.

'Tell me about the weekend,' he said.

'I already did,' she said. But he made her go over it all again in more detail, her arrival on Friday afternoon, the private film-viewing on Friday night. He seemed more than keenly interested in the doings of Shaw, asked her once if she was absolutely certain that Shaw had been in the army. On Saturday morning she had wandered around the garden looking for suitable places to put a camera, at Saturday lunchtime she had taken the bus to Dorchester, got back around two o'clock in the afternoon. She had gone to bed early. Mentioned that the central heating system had woken her with its creaking some time during the night – the bedrooms, or at least her room, were like igloos. On Sunday there had been the row with Rita over the scrapbook – oh, yes, and the Worboys' son had turned up for breakfast with this girl that George Sheridan called the Walking Dead, with some justification. But they hadn't stayed. She'd heard a car leaving shortly after the row with Mrs Sheridan, and young Worboys and the Walking Dead had not been there at lunchtime.

'So he drives a car, this Worboys lad?'

'Yes,' she said.

Which appeared to have some significance for him because he wrote something in his notebook which was now the buff one he'd been using yesterday.

'What's Mr Sheridan like?'

'A sweetheart,' she said, her tone making it plain that Mr

Sheridan's wife was a sweetheart of nobody's.

'How about Mrs Shaw?'

'The same,' she said. 'She's an absolute love.'

'And this gardener, this Erskine feller ...'

'He's a landscape gardener,' she said, leaping, too quickly in Roper's opinion, to Erskine's defence.

'I see,' he said. He wrote nothing down, just tapped the blunt end of his ballpoint on the table until he thought of something else.

'How about the Worboys? Mr and Mrs?'

'I didn't like him much at first, thought he was a bit snooty. But he's all right. Just a bit coy.'

'How about her?'

'I don't see her much. She seems to be the only one that's really worrying about Rita.'

'I see, Miss,' he said. It was a policeman's 'I see, Miss', dull and heavy as a lead weight. The last time she had heard an 'I see, Miss' which had sounded exactly like that had been the dour response to her feeble excuse for bashing up the M1 at eighty-two miles an hour. The policeman then had been a barn-sized sergeant in a yellow waterproof and with rain dripping off the visor of his cap. That 'I see, Miss' had cost her £25 and an endorsement on her driving licence. Now, as then, she wished she had bitten her tongue off.

'So you're telling me Mr Sheridan's not particularly worried that his wife's gone missing?'

'I didn't say that,' she countered quickly.

'Yes, you did, Miss,' he said.

Despite the hubbub in the bar, the landlord shouting 'last orders gents, please', the clinking of glasses, the raucous laughter, the ringing of the till as people got their last drinks in, she felt herself marooned in a cocoon of silence: a hideous, horrible and pregnant silence. And that was when she decided to make a clean breast of things, things that had been bugging her since Rita had gone missing, things he really ought to know about, things he'd find out eventually anyway. He looked that sort, the stolid, no stones left unturned kind.

'Can I level with you?' she said, and felt better at once for saying it.

'I wish you would, Miss Lindsey,' he said. And he smiled. It was the first time she had seen him do that.

'Can that thing go away?' She meant the notebook.

'All right,' he said. He capped his pen, closed his notebook and pushed it to one side.

'And take your policeman's hat off? Take a tea-break or something?'

'No,' he said. 'sorry. But I do suffer from amnesia from time to time. Depends on the occasion, of course.'

She doubted that very much.

'Look,' she said, 'I don't want you thinking I'm shooting my mouth off.'

'That hadn't occurred to me so far, Miss.'

'And I really like George Sheridan ...'

'But he's not entirely unhappy that Mrs Sheridan's done a runner.'

'Right,' she said. And with that off her chest she felt better still.

He waited patiently while she wrestled with her conscience.

'I'm beginning to wonder if she really has gone missing. It's just that, well, things have changed.'

'Things?'

'People,' she said. 'Like George hasn't had a drop for days. She treated him rotten.'

'Mrs Sheridan?'

'Right,' she said. She dropped her voice. 'Thing is, old George is as happy as a sandboy since Rita went, except when Mr and Mrs Worboys are about. And just before lunchtime today I went into the kitchen. George was washing the crockery and Mrs Shaw was knocking up some pastry. I know it sounds daft, but Mrs Shaw's lost about twenty years as well. Until the Worboys are about. I think they think I haven't noticed.'

'And you think Sheridan and Mrs Shaw are having an affair.'

'I *know* they are,' she said.

101

'Because old George washes up the dishes?'

She shook her head. 'Look,' she said, 'I'm not just talking for the sake of talking, but Rita Cavallo, or whatever she wants to call herself, really is a nasty piece of work, but I hate to think somebody's done her in for it. Nobody's ever that bad.'

'But you know Sheridan and Mrs Shaw are what ... lovers?'

'They're daft about each other,' she said. 'Like a couple of kids. Mrs Shaw's positively bloomed.'

'We are, I presume, talking about the same Mrs Shaw?'

'You haven't seen her the way I've seen her.'

He weighed that. 'And how have you seen her?'

'In George's bedroom. With George.'

'Compromising?'

'Just a bit.'

'How big a bit?'

'A fairly big bit,' she admitted, feeling treacherous. If he'd been writing it all down in his notebook she could never have told him. 'She was massaging his back.'

'I see, Miss,' he said. She had never realised how many ways it was possible to say 'I see, Miss' and mean something subtly different each time. 'I take it we aren't talking about a spot of therapy?'

'No,' she said. 'Hardly.' She hoped he would change the subject. If he hadn't got the picture by now he really ought to have been in a different line of work.

'And you saw all this. How come?'

'You have to go through a dressing-room to get to George's bedroom. He's got a cheval mirror in there. I opened the dressing-room door by mistake – and there they were.'

'In the mirror.'

'Right,' she said. 'And a couple of hours later I was in the kitchen and Mrs Shaw came in, they thought I was out. She looked absolutely gorgeous. Done up to the nines, you know. She told me she'd been to see her gentleman-friend over in Wareham. She said his name was George. She had eye-shadow, lipstick, nail varnish, everything. I can quite

102

see why old George's potty about her.

'And the first night I was there, I was trying to find my room, and I came face to face with George in one of the passages. I didn't think anything of it at the time. But I've got the geography of the house sorted out now, and I know that the way he was going wasn't the way to his bedroom.'

'But it was the way to Mrs Shaw's?'

'Yes,' she said. 'Right.'

'And you reckon they might have put Mrs Sheridan out of the way.'

'God forbid,' she said. 'But it does keep crossing my mind. Could they have, d'you think? They're so damn nice, the two of them.'

The last bell sounded, and the barmaid draped a towel over the beer-pump handles. Someone shouted for twenty Senior Service.

'Put it this way, Miss Lindsey,' he said. 'The Mrs Sheridan I'm looking for is still alive. And if she isn't, I'll be very much surprised.'

She loosed a breath. 'Oh, that's great,' she said. 'You've no idea what a relief that is. Except that I should have kept my damn mouth shut, shouldn't I?'

'About what?' he said.

'About George and Mrs Shaw.'

'George and Mrs Shaw?' he said, looking at her woodenly. He reached out sideways for his ballpoint and notebook and tucked them deep inside his jacket. 'What about 'em?'

NINE

THEY SAT IN ROPER'S DARKENED car on the forecourt of
the Crown and Compass. It was shut now, its doors bolted,
its staff coming out of the side entrance.

'You don't know what time she got back on Saturday
night?'

'I must have been asleep. Sorry.'

'She didn't mention where she might have been all day
Saturday?'

She thought hard, trying to remember if Rita Cavallo
had dropped any hints at Sunday lunchtime, the only time
Kate had seen her to speak to – apart from asking her
where the scrapbooks were and that stupid business in the
study afterwards – since the previous Friday evening.

'No,' she said. 'I don't think so.'

'Anything,' he said, and from the way he spoke it was
obvious that he was as much in the dark as everybody else.

A flash of memory came. 'She'd had her hair done. Cut
and tinted.'

'Ah.' He reached up to switch on the courtesy light. His
hand went inside his raincoat and jacket and came out
again with his buff notebook and the ballpoint pen.

'That's important?' she asked.

'Very,' he said. He uncapped the ballpoint. 'You're sure
she had it done on Saturday? Not before?'

'Certain,' she said. 'On Friday she had grey roots and a
bit of a fringe. She didn't have either on Sunday
lunchtime.'

'Don't happen to know the name of her hairdresser, I
suppose?'

'You're kidding,' she said. 'I hardly know the woman.'

104

He scribbled: 'RS hairdresser Sat(?)'.

'You seemed to have latched on to almost everything else, Miss Lindsey,' he said. 'I thought it was worth a try. Anything else? About Saturday?'

And wearily, exhaustedly, she wrung out her memory like a wet towel for him and went through all of Saturday again, right down to the minutiae, even the creak of the central heating system that had woken her, although that might have been in the wee small hours of Sunday morning. She also mentioned the business of the cheque she had seen pass between Joel Worboys and the Walking Dead out on the terrace and Shaw's obsession with keeping fit.

Of these revelations, however, he made only a note or two in his book. He was clearly fixated on Saturday, and it was to that particular day that he returned.

'And you reckon Shaw was driving her on Saturday?'

'I didn't actually *see* either of them,' she said. 'It was Mr Erskine who told me he'd seen Shaw drive her off in the Jag.'

'Which Jag?'

'George's,' she said. 'His is the black one.'

That, it seemed, was important enough to record in his notebook. 'Any idea what time they both left?'

'He didn't say, just that he saw them driving out on his way in. I think he started work just before nine o'clock.'

That, too, was committed to paper, followed by another bracketted question-mark. The name Shaw, she could not help observing, was underlined, then, on second thoughts, underlined yet again. Which surely had to be significant of something.

'How about a lady called Audrey Blaney? Would that be a name you might have turned up while you've been looking around?'

'No,' she said. 'Sorry.'

Roper dropped her off at the Sheridans' front gates at a few minutes before midnight, and drove on to County still wondering if there really was any meat on the few bones

105

she had thrown to him or if she was simply a young woman with a nose for the bizarre and a talent for embroidery.

That Mrs Sheridan, in her persona of Rita Cavallo, had left a trail of male bodies from the south of France to North America in her youth seemed, on the face of it, improbable.

Certainly improbable was that Rita Cavallo had shot the aviator Angus Kilcullen in his house in Portman Square back in 1930. Perhaps less improbable that the suicide of Mr Manders in 1935 might not have been all that it had seemed. And anybody with a bit of nous could start a fire, which is how Mr Schwarz had died in 1946 in Maine. Or perhaps he had died some other way and the manner of it obscured by the subsequent incineration of his body.

But then, even given that Rita Cavallo was a multiple murderess – and an exceptionally clever one – would she be stupid enough to keep a record of her villainies, albeit under lock and key, in her own house? Well, yes, she might. As a stripling detective constable, and still a little moist behind the ears, Roper had assisted in the investigation and subsequent arrest of a serial murderer who turned out to be a clinically definable psychopath. That gentleman had not only kept newspaper clippings of his misdeeds but a meticulously detailed diary. Had what Lindsey had seen last Sunday morning been a similar record? If she was right, and she probably was, that record had been burned on Sunday afternoon. Which had to beg another question or two.

At half-past midnight, Roper sat in the pool of light from his desk lamp, a cheroot burning in the ashtray and a plastic cup of coffee – cold now – a few inches away from it. On the blotter in front of him was an A4 notepad upon which he had written, with the aid of the notes he had made in his diary, a chronology of Mrs Sheridan's complicated love-life and relationships in the form of a list. It didn't look all that much, or that complicated, once it had been put to paper:

1930 June. Kilcullen, flyer. Suicide. London.
1933 Chester Barclay, actor. Traffic accident. S. France.
1935 Summer (?). Manders, husband. Suicide. (London?).
1936 Greta Worboys, née Manders, born. Daughter of above.
1946 July. Schwarz, husband. Died in house fire. (Maine USA).
1947 January. Son of Schwarz born. And died(?). Possibly shipboard.
1970 Sheridans married. Caxton Hall.
1976 October. Audrey Blaney died.

He crossed out 'died' and substituted 'murdered'. There was certainly no doubt about that.

A knock on the glass panel of the door preceded the entrance of Mower with a cup of coffee in his hand. He looked haggard.

'Thought you'd gone home,' he said.

'Thought you had,' said Roper.

Mower shut the door and sank on to Roper's visitor's chair, took a sip of his coffee. Like Roper, he needed a shave.

Roper sat back and stretched his legs. 'What's new?' he said, tossing down his ballpoint on the pad.

'Not much,' said Mower gloomily.

Nobody who lived in Mrs Blaney's lane had seen or heard anything suspicious last Saturday night. They had either been out enjoying themselves or snuggled up in front of a warm fire with their curtains closed and watching television, blithely unaware that a particularly vicious crime was being committed more or less under their noses. A constable had interviewed Mrs Blaney's milkman, who confirmed that he had called at Mrs Blaney's cottage at some time around 6.45 a.m. on Sunday morning. Pressed harder he was fairly certain that the kitchen light had been switched on. He also confirmed that he had delivered no milk, only taken away an empty bottle and the note that had been stuffed into its neck. DS Morgan had gone across to the village newsagent to enquire about the time he had made his delivery on

107

Sunday morning. With one of his delivery-boys sick, the newsagent had delivered Mrs Blaney's paper himself at 7.30 a.m. – more or less. Mrs Blaney had come in to pay her paper-bill for the previous week late on Saturday afternoon. She had been carrying a couple of carrier bags, so she had probably just come back from doing her weekend shopping, which, according to the newsagent, she did at a supermarket in Yeovil, which she usually travelled to and from on the local bus.

Beyond that there was nothing new. A more thorough search of the cottage had revealed no more than it had the first time, nor had anyone found out yet the whereabouts of Mrs Blaney's son.

'How about you?' asked Mower.

'Been having a chat with that television researcher who's working along at the Sheridans' place.'

'Useful?'

'Could be,' said Roper. He gave Mower the gist of his conversation with Lindsey in the Crown and Compass, to which Mower listened much as Roper himself had, with a mixture of disbelief and ever-growing interest. Like Roper, he found it easier to follow with a chronologically ordered list in his hand.

'Could be a load of happenstance,' said Mower, dropping the pad back on Roper's blotter. 'Could be she had a habit of falling for accident-prone men.'

'True,' agreed Roper.

'And where does it get us?'

'Could be a character reference, though, couldn't it?' said Roper.

'True,' agreed Mower, 'but that Kilcullen's dropped off the list already. Had an alibi for that, didn't she? I don't like being side-tracked, Douglas. And all that's too long ago. We couldn't prove it, any of it.'

And that, too, was true.

'Except Mrs Worboys is standing about handy,' said Roper.

'Don't follow,' said Mower.

'If Schwarz's son was in that coffin ...'

'If it was a coffin ...'

'... Mrs Worboys might know something about it. She was the boy's sister,' Roper added, as Mower's eyebrows came together. Again like Roper, Mower was not at his best in the small hours – well over fifty and fast approaching retirement, Mower was an early starter and had been on his feet since eight o'clock yesterday morning.

'You've got a tortuous mind, Douglas,' he said. Then conceded, 'Bloody right though, aren't you, but where would it get us?'

'Nowhere,' Roper was forced to admit. As Mower had rightly said, it was all too long ago.

'Well, then,' said Mower. 'Anyway, you might upset the woman. She must be worried enough now, without us badgering her about a brother who died when she was a kid.' He took another sip of his coffee.

'Mrs Sheridan's chauffeur was out with her all day last Saturday.'

'I thought we already knew that.'

'We did,' said Roper. 'But it was only a missing person enquiry then, wasn't it?'

'True,' agreed Mower. 'Could be he's worth another tickle, eh?'

'I reckon,' said Roper.

On Thursday morning, the brick wall against which Roper had been banging his head for the last few days started to show signs of cracking. A phone call to Mrs Shaw by Detective Sergeant Morgan had ferreted out the name and telephone number of Mr Anthony, that gentleman being Mrs Sheridan's hairdresser with a salon in Dorchester. Mr Anthony, aka Frederick George Butler, had confirmed what Lindsey had told Roper in the Crown and Compass yesterday evening, namely that Mrs Sheridan had had her hair trimmed, tinted and restyled in his salon last Saturday afternoon.

She had arrived at five past three in the afternoon – her appointment had been for three o'clock but she had been late for it, as she invariably was. She was not, as Mr

Anthony had explained acerbically, a great stickler for time. But she was, however, a good customer and tipped more generously than most, on the last occasion leaving a £5 note to be shared among those of Mr Anthony's junior staff who had, besides himself, attended to her. Whilst her hair had been drying she had also had a manicure. At four o'clock, her chauffeur had come into the shop to explain that the car was causing a minor traffic jam and that the police had asked him to move on, suggesting the car-park behind a nearby supermarket.

'No need to do that,' had said the helpful Mr Anthony. He had sent one of his girls out to the yard behind the salon, where Mr Anthony parked his own car during business hours. The girl had unlocked the gate and Shaw had driven the car in beside Mr Anthony's. Mr Anthony, who had met Shaw on several occasions, was of the private opinion that Mr Shaw was 'a bit of an oddball', but that was by the by. At four-thirty, on the pretext of going to his stockroom, Mr Anthony had retreated to the lavatory to relieve his bladder and have a quiet drag or two on a much-needed cigarette. He noticed that Shaw, who had been sitting in the car, a black Jaguar he recalled, was no longer in it. A few minutes later, however, he heard the wicket-gate, set in the main gate, open, then close again. The next he saw of Shaw was that he was sitting in the car, with the courtesy light on, and reading an evening paper.

Her coiffeur and manicure completed, and having spread her largesse among the staff, Mrs Sheridan had left the salon at a few minutes before five o'clock. She had been wearing, Mr Anthony recalled, a dark brown fur coat – no, he did not know what kind of fur it had been – and a chiffon scarf loosely draped over her new hair-do to protect it from the weather. Mr Anthony had opened the yard gates himself on that occasion and saw Shaw safely out into the traffic. And that was the last he had seen of her.

'What sort of mood was she in?' had asked Morgan.

'Chatty and bright,' Mr Anthony had responded. 'And queening it the way she always did. Nothing unusual.'

It wasn't much, but again it was something. Two hours of Rita Sheridan's Saturday, the day Roper was obstinately certain that Mrs Blaney had been killed, had been accounted for.

It was still only nine-thirty on Thursday morning when Mower trudged back into Roper's office, looking like death, and handed him the photocopy of Weygood's report on his post-mortem examination of Mrs Blaney which had arrived only a few minutes previously. Like Roper and Mower, Weygood had finally signed himself off at one o'clock that morning.

Roper scanned the topmost sheet, the formal First Schedule briefly outlining the probable cause of death: name of deceased; observers present at examination; estimated time of death – Weygood had penned in last Saturday's date, but sensibly hedged his bets by adding Sunday's date in brackets afterwards. There followed then the curtly worded description of Mrs Blaney's external appearance – age, height, weight, state of nourishment – then the most relevant heading: 'Marks of violence etc'.

There had been three. One on the back of Mrs Blaney's right hand, two more on the left hand side of her skull, one of which had been severe enough to fracture the adjacent area into three quite separate fragments. (See annexed sheets, Page 2, para 1.)

Roper turned to Page 2, para 1. If Weygood was right, Mrs Blaney had probably fended off the first blow with her right hand. The next blow had felled her to her knees and the third – Weygood suspected that it was the third because it seemed to have been delivered from above, rather than sideways as the other two had been – was the one that had fractured Mrs Blaney's skull, the one that had finally been the death of her. Around the area of the second blow, Weygood had located a minute pattern, diamond in form, that might have been caused by the knurled barrel of an adjustable spanner, such as might be used by someone like a motor mechanic. Which, as Roper recalled, fitted the weapon that Weygood had guessed at the other morning in Mrs Blaney's cottage – something heavy, something with a long handle, something an assailant could get a good swing with, even a woman ...

The phone rang on Roper's desk. Mower picked it up and grumbled 'Hello,' into it.

... and finally there followed a list of the various parts of Mrs Blaney that had been sent away for further examination: including the débris that Weygood had scraped out from beneath her fingernails. The results of these tests could be expected some time tomorrow.

When Roper glanced up again, Mower was still hunched over the telephone, one hand covering the mouthpiece.

'It's Forensic,' he said. 'You looking for some kind of key?'

'What sort of key?'

'Big old iron thing,' said Mower. 'With green paint on it.'

And that was just another crack in the wall.

TEN

'WHERE WAS IT?' ASKED ROPER.

'It had slipped into the lining of that fur coat the lads found yesterday. There was a hole in one of the pockets. One of the boffins at Forensic found it when he was giving the coat the once-over.'

'Been checked for dabs, has it?'

'Yes. There was nothing they could make anything of.'

There were splashes of green paint on the fretted handle and the lever-end of the key was moist with oil.

'They reckon it's engine-oil,' said Mower.

So did Roper. The key to the garden gate must have been in the lining when he'd taken the coat along to show George Sheridan, but he had not taken it out of the bag at any time for fear of sullying what might be evidence, only giving Sheridan and Mrs Shaw a glimpse of the collar and the lining. What the key did, if it fitted the side gate – and it would, he had no doubt about that – was to tie in the fur coat even more positively with Mrs Sheridan.

'Any blood on the coat?'

'Not yet,' said Mower, 'but they're still looking.'

After a canteen lunch with Mower, Roper collected Morgan and drove back to Milton St Philip's in the depressing greyness of the early afternoon.

'Mr Sheridan's had to go back to London for the day, sir,' said Mrs Shaw, who opened the front door to them. 'The television studio rang him and told him they were getting behind schedule, and could he give them a couple of hours today.'

'The show must go on, eh, Mrs Shaw?'

'Yes, sir,' she said. 'But if there's anything I can do …'

'There is, Mrs Shaw,' said Roper. He took the manilla envelope from his pocket and tipped the key into the palm of his other hand.

She recognised it at once.

'Would you mind if Sergeant Morgan tried it in the gate?'

'No, sir,' she said. 'Of course not.'

They followed her through to the kitchen. Morgan went on out into the garden.

'Would you like a cup of tea, sir?' asked Mrs Shaw.

'No, thank you,' said Roper. A couple of days ago he would have accepted gladly, but things had changed since then. As well as not shaking hands, it was his golden rule never to take fare from anyone who might, even remotely, be up to no good. He might have made few notes in the Crown and Compass last night, but he had absorbed Katherine Lindsey's every gesture and word. As well as being Sheridan's alleged lover, Mrs Shaw was also the mother of the man who had been out with Mrs Sheridan all last Saturday.

'Your son about, is he, Mrs Shaw?' he said.

Her cheerful face stiffened perceptibly. She was, he thought, and not for the first time, a good-looking and well set-up woman. If George Sheridan's married life had taken a turn for the worse, as Lindsey had suggested it had, it was obvious why that gentleman had taken up with her.

'He's upstairs, sir. In his room. It's his afternoon off.'

'D'you think he'd mind if I went up and had a word?' He smiled reassuringly. 'I just need to check on where he drove Mrs Sheridan last Saturday. Nothing important.'

Her face stayed set. If he wasn't mistaken, what he read in it was a sudden anxiety, almost as if she knew something.

'No, sir,' she said hesitantly. 'I'm sure he won't mind. It's out of here, and up the little staircase on your left, as you go towards the hall.'

'Thank you, Mrs Shaw,' he said. 'And if Sergeant

Morgan comes back before I do, tell him to wait here. I won't be long.'

She was not reassured, he could sense it, could almost feel her watching his back as he quit the kitchen.

He found the poky narrow staircase. The little oak door to it was open – when closed it could be easily mistaken for the door of a cupboard set in the panelling. It went up interminably, or so it seemed – from what Roper had seen of it the house was an absolute warren of stairs and passages and alcoves. This staircase was only a few inches wider than he was and he wondered how anyone could possibly get furniture up it. Then, at last, a solitary electric light in a cheap plastic shade illuminated the topmost, windowless landing.

The door immediately in front of him was shut. He rapped lightly on it and bent his ear to it. For a moment or two nothing happened, then the door was opened and Shaw's bespectacled face peered around the edge of it. He was justifiably surprised when he saw who his caller was. From the little Roper could see of him, he was stripped to the waist and an Arctic draught was blowing around Roper's face from the gap in the door.

'Are you looking for someone, sir?' asked Shaw, still keeping most of himself hidden behind the door.

'I'd like a word with you, Mr Shaw. Mind if I come in?'

'If you could wait a moment, sir,' Shaw began to close the door. Roper pressed the flat of his hand against it.

'Now, Mr Shaw,' he insisted, exerting a little more pressure. 'If you're not too busy. It's important, sir.'

Shaw stepped back reluctantly, a reluctance that was as justifiable as his earlier surprise since he was all but naked in his underpants and a pair of leather sandals. The sashed window of the room was wide open, top and bottom, and on a folding baize-topped card-table, its pages slowly turning over in the icy draught, lay a massive, gilt-edged Bible under a reading lamp. The draught diminished as Roper closed the door and stood with his back to it.

'I'd prefer to get dressed, if I may, sir,' said Shaw.

'Do, Mr Shaw,' said Roper. Shaw turned away to a cheap and flimsy plywood wardrobe standing against the wall at the foot of his bed, and took out a shirt and a black suit on a hanger. With his back to Roper, he slipped into the shirt and began to button it.

Roper, gazing around, decided that he had seen prison cells that had looked more comfortable. Shaw slept on a folding, iron camp-bed, a single sheet neatly tucked around its wafer-thin mattress. There was no pillow in evidence, nor any other bedclothes apart from that one undersheet. The rest of the room was as Spartan. There was just the folding table, a single dining chair, the reading lamp, the camp-bed, and the wardrobe – and that looked home-made and probably brought up here in pieces. The floor was covered with well-worn green linoleum, and was without the luxury even of a bedside mat. Fixed to a massive hook-eye in the door-frame was some kind of exercising gadget with chromium-plated springs and blue wooden handles.

'Use this, do you, Mr Shaw?' said Roper.

'I keep myself fit, sir,' said Shaw, buckling his trouser-belt and zipping his fly.

Roper moved to the table where the Bible lay and flipped the pages back to where a leather bookmark was tucked in. It was a handtooled Bible, leather bound with a brass clip, probably printed around the time that the young Victoria had come to the throne. A copper-plate engraving depicted a mob of unfortunates being flogged towards the gates of Hell, where, beyond its towering dark wall, a forest of chimneys belched smoke and flame and demons cavorted in the sky filled with forked lightning and rolling black thunderclouds. If the bookmark was any indication, Shaw – however unlikely it seemed, had been poring, naked in the icy blast, over the Book of Revelations.

'Into all this hell-fire stuff are you, Mr Shaw?'

'Yes, sir,' said Shaw. 'But then we all are, aren't we, sir? Eventually.'

Roper looked across at him, thinking that Shaw might

116

be making some kind of obscure joke. But he wasn't.

'Mind if we have the window closed?'

'No, sir,' said Shaw. 'Not at all.' He closed the window.

Roper drew the solitary chair closer, turned it to face the bed, and sat down on it. Shaw lowered himself to the edge of the bed, his hands clasped primly on his knees.

'Laundry-day, is it?' asked Roper.

'Sir?' said Shaw.

'Your bed looks a bit sparse.'

'It's the way I prefer it, sir,' said Shaw.

Roper looked around again for some kind of domestic comfort, a few books, a radiator, an electric fire. But he had been right the first time. There was none. The old marble fireplace looked as if it hadn't seen a fire in years.

They sat a yard apart, Shaw's tiny eyes unblinking behind his ugly, black-framed spectacles.

'You were out all day last Saturday with Mrs Sheridan,' said Roper.

'Yes, sir,' said Shaw.

'Where d'you both go?'

'We spent most of the day in Dorchester, sir.'

'But not all of it?'

'No, sir,' Shaw agreed. 'Not all of it.'

'What time did you get to Dorchester?'

Shaw thought. 'I can't be sure exactly, sir, but a few minutes before ten, I suppose it would have been.'

'And you left Dorchester when?'

'I don't remember, sir, not exactly.'

'Try,' said Roper. It was raining again. He could hear the drops pattering against the window. Shaw seemed not to notice how cold the room still was.

'I suppose about five-thirty, sir. Thereabouts. I really couldn't make a better guess than that. It might have been earlier, but I'm honestly not certain, sir.'

Shaw had driven Mrs Sheridan straight to Dorchester on Saturday morning. Their first port of call had been Madam's dressmaker – a private house on the outskirts of the town. They had arrived there shortly before ten o'clock. Madam had gone into the house and Shaw had waited outside in the car. After an hour or so, the dressmaker's young daughter had come out to Shaw with a cup of tea and an assortment of biscuits. Shaw had consumed both in the car and the daughter had returned to collect the cup, saucer and plate some twenty minutes afterwards. Shaw had then sat alone until Madam had reappeared at some time around midday. Shaw had then driven her into the centre of Dorchester, where he left the Jaguar in a public car-park while they went to have lunch.

'You lunch together or separately?'

'Together, sir,' said Shaw. 'Madam likes a bit of company while she's eating.'

'Did you talk?'

'No, sir,' said Shaw. 'Not a great deal. Madam did, of course. I merely listened.'

'What did she talk about?'

'Practically everything, sir. But then she usually does. But then they do, sir, don't they?'

'They?'

'Women, sir,' said Shaw, by way of bland explanation. 'Their mouths hardly ever shut, sir. I'm surprised you haven't noticed.'

Roper let that pass. Mr Shaw, who seemed to despise all earthly comforts and sat naked in his ice-cold cell reading his Bible, clearly had little time for women either.

Their meal eaten, Madam had then embarked 'on a bit of shopping', she gazing into shop windows and Shaw trailing along behind her with an ever-growing assortment of carrier-bags. To the best of Shaw's memory, she had bought a paperback novel, a cardigan, a scarf, a new handbag, a pair of shoes and a brooch that had caught her eye in a boutique window. Madam, according to Shaw, had a child's eye when it came to bright trinkets.

They had then briefly parted company, Shaw to pick up the car while Madam waited for him outside the boutique – Mr Anthony's salon was over half a mile away, and *much* too far for Madam to walk. They had arrived at Mr Anthony's shortly after three o'clock – Shaw was able to be more precise about that particular time because Madam had arranged an appointment, and had upbraided him for being too long about fetching the car from the car-park, forgetting that Dorchester on a Saturday afternoon was chock-a-block with traffic.

With Madam in the hairdresser's, Shaw again waited alone in the car until, and once again he was not sure of the time, a young constable rapped on the window and told him to move on, suggesting that he waited in the car-park of a nearby supermarket.

'But when I went in to tell Madam, Mr Anthony told me I could park in the yard behind his shop. So I did that.'

He had left the car for a few minutes, at some time around four-thirty, to buy an evening newspaper and to see how his horses had run.

'Betting man, are you, Mr Shaw?'

'Oh, no, sir,' Shaw protested. 'I've never gone in for that sort of thing – the path to Hell, that is, sir. It's a little game I play with myself, y'see, sir. Quite harmless. I pick out a few horses and see what would happen if I laid a few each-way doubles on them. It's an interesting exercise, sir. But I don't bet.'

Having returned to the yard and the car, Shaw had then checked his racing results. At about five o'clock, in company with Mr Anthony, Madam had returned to the car, and Mr Anthony had opened the gates and seen the Jaguar safely out into the traffic.

'Then?' asked Roper.

'I drove Madam into Sherborne, sir.'

Roper's ears pricked at that. Sherborne was about fifteen miles almost due north of Dorchester. Sherborne lay astride the A30, as did Yeovil, and between Sherborne and Yeovil, on that very same stretch of road, stood the village of East Choately where had lived the late Mrs Audrey Blaney.

'Go there often, did she?' asked Roper. 'Sherborne?'

'No, sir,' said Shaw. 'Not to my knowledge. She certainly never went there with me.'

'What did she do in Sherborne? By the time you got there, the shops would have been shut, wouldn't they?'

'We ate, sir.'

'Again?' said Roper.

'Madam likes her food, sir,' said Shaw. 'Stuffs herself something awful, she does. She had me drive around until we found somewhere that suited her.'

'So she didn't have any particular place in mind?'

'No, sir, I didn't get that impression.'

'And you ate with her?'

'Yes,' said Shaw. 'Unfortunately.'

Having cruised around the town for some time, Shaw thought that they had found the restaurant at some time around six o'clock. Madam had gorged her way through most of the menu while Shaw had picked at a salad. He did not remember the name of the restaurant but only that it was very expensive and situated over a row of shops near a building that might have been the Town Hall. They had left at eight o'clock, after Madam had surprised him by saying that she had an appointment to keep, and did he know the way to Yeovil?

Shaw had said, no, but doubtless the route would be signposted, and, again to his surprise, Madam had joined him in the front of the car.

'She doesn't usually do that?'

'No, sir,' said Shaw. 'Never. She always sits in the back as a rule. She told me she would direct me once we got on to the A30, and we weren't going all the way to Yeovil but to a little village just before we got to it.'

Shaw had soon got on to the westbound A30, and driven for about ten minutes, quite slowly, while Madam watched for landmarks which she obviously recognised.

'And which landmark did you stop at, Mr Shaw?'

'A telephone box, sir,' said Shaw.

ELEVEN

THEY ADJOURNED TO THE DOWNSTAIRS study where
Morgan joined them, because the conversation in Shaw's
bedroom had, at a stroke, become a formal interview.
Shaw sat in the swivel chair in front of the desk, Morgan by
the filing cabinets with his pocket-book on his knees and
Roper at one end of the desk on a chair he had borrowed
from the kitchen. Shaw went through the events of
Saturday again for the benefit of Morgan's pocket book, as
far as eight-fifteen on Saturday night when Mrs Sheridan
had got out of the car, telling his tale so exactly as he had
told it to Roper that Roper was torn between believing him
absolutely and wondering if it was something Shaw had
learned by rote at Mrs Sheridan's knee. Back in Roper's
pocket, in its manilla envelope, was the key to the garden
gate.

'And where was this telephone box, Mr Shaw?' asked
Roper. 'D'you remember?'

'No, sir,' admitted Shaw. 'I've no idea what the place was
even called, but it was on the same side of the road as I was
driving. Madam said stop, and I stopped.'

'Notice anything about the surroundings?'

Shaw considered that. 'I recall a public house,' he said.
'Rather a large one. And there was a signpost, sir, pointing
to Yeovil.'

It felt right, sounded right – Roper himself recalled that
East Choately had not been signposted, at least, not in such a
way as to be obvious – but he taxed Shaw a little harder
nevertheless. The public house had been almost exactly
opposite the telephone box. And beside the public house
had been a small row of shops. One of them, Shaw

121

thought, might have been a Post Office. And when Madam had left the car she had behaved exactly as she had when she had left Mr Buckle's cab. She had walked back in the direction whence Shaw had just driven her.

'How far?'

'I didn't see, sir,' said Shaw. 'Madam told me to drive off and find some grass to walk the dogs on, and to come back for her at nine o'clock. She waited until I drove off.'

So even in the dark, Mrs Sheridan had wanted no one to see where she had been going. Shaw had done as he was told, more or less. He had driven away only far enough to be out of sight, hauled the dogs out of the car and towed them up and down on the footpath until, so he stated, they had done their business, after which he stuffed them back in the rear of the car and settled back in his seat to while away a half-hour's boredom with his newspaper.

At a few minutes to nine o'clock, Shaw was certain of the time because he'd read it off the dashboard clock, he had turned the car and driven back to where he had dropped off Madam, namely the telephone box opposite the public house.

But Madam did not appear at nine o'clock, nor had she at a quarter-past nine.

'Worried about her, were you?' asked Roper.

'No, sir,' said Shaw. 'Not particularly. More irritated, as I recall.'

'So what time did she turn up?'

'About twenty to eleven, sir,' said Shaw. 'And I'd had to walk the dogs again. They'd started whining – their bowels, sir,' he explained distastefully, 'but it's little wonder with all the chocolate and muck she keeps stuffing down them. As I got back to the car, up she popped.'

'Madam?' said Roper.

'Yes, sir,' said Shaw. 'Madam.'

'So she was gone for over two hours?'

'Yes, sir,' said Shaw. He had not seen where Madam had come from, merely that she had suddenly appeared by the car as he had returned to it after walking the dogs that second time.

'Did she say anything?'

'Just, "We'll go home now, Shaw", I don't recall anything else, sir.'

'Did she sound calm? Excited? Upset?'

'I can't really say I noticed, sir,' said Shaw. 'I have to admit to a fit of pique myself, sir. I can't abide unpunctuality, never have. I saw her into the car, and we came back here.'

Roper steered him back to 8.15, when Mrs Sheridan had stepped out of the car at East Choately.

'Was she carrying anything?'

'I can't say I really noticed, sir.'

'Think.'

'Well, I suppose her handbag, sir. She rarely went anywhere without that.'

'But you only suppose?'

Shaw reconsidered. 'I'm sure she did have it, sir. She certainly wouldn't have left it in the car. But I do remember, when she came back, that she had acquired another carrier-bag. A white one, I think it was.'

'It couldn't have been one of those she'd picked up earlier, shopping in Dorchester?'

Shaw thought not. The four carrier-bags she had collected in Dorchester had been stowed in the boot of the Jaguar before Mrs Sheridan had visited the hairdresser's.

'How was she carrying it? Did it look heavy?'

'Sort of under her arm, sir,' said Shaw. 'Like this ...' He tucked one hand under the other armpit.

'So it wasn't loaded up?'

'No, it looked more like a thin parcel, sir, wrapped up in it. I didn't realise it *was* a carrier-bag until she climbed into the car with it.'

'Thin you say?'

'Yes, sir,' said Shaw. 'I got the impression at the time that she might have collected a couple of gramophone records from somebody.'

'And that bag didn't go in the boot with the others?'

'No, sir,' said Shaw. 'I asked her if I should put it in there. She said she'd keep it with her.'

'And then you drove back here?'

'Yes, sir,' said Shaw.

'Did she sit beside you again?'

'No, sir,' said Shaw. 'She sat in the back.'

So, if Shaw was telling the truth, and that was another of life's great uncertainties, it sounded as if Mrs Sheridan had paid another visit to Mrs Blaney's cottage last Saturday night. She had arrived at some time around eight-fifteen and left at some time around ten-forty. When she had returned to the car she had been toting a white carrier-bag that she had not taken with her. Had that bag contained the weapon, the adjustable spanner or wrench, or whatever it had been, folded inside a couple of newspapers perhaps? It was possible. According to the forensic team, traces of blood had been found in the outlet of Mrs Blaney's kitchen sink, as if hands or a weapon had been sluiced clean over it. It was even likely that Mrs Sheridan had taken the weapon with her, perhaps in the pocket of her coat, or even in one of her capacious handbags, but had realized the folly of carrying it away in either of those after she had used it.

Or Shaw was lying in his teeth. Sitting here now, calm and obsequious and chatting away in his precise butler-speak, he was a far-different man from the bully Roper had interrupted last night in the hall. So perhaps Lindsey was right – Shaw did get his jollies from bullying women. How far would he have gone last night? And what part had he actually played on Saturday night, over at East Choately? Had he really walked the dogs and sat in the car watching the time tick by? Or had he taken a more active role?

'D'you carry tools in the cars, Mr Shaw?'

'No, sir,' said Shaw. 'Just a jack and a wheel-brace. I'm not a mechanic, sir. Mr Sheridan has the cars serviced at the garage up in the village.'

'But you've got tools.'

'A few, sir, yes. But I keep them in the garage.'

Shaw switched on the garage light as he led the way in

through the side door. The two Jaguars stood side by side, the black one and the white one, everything glittering and not a speck of dust on either of them.

Roper went further in. Shaw's few tools hung on a square of pegboard behind his workbench. They were mostly household tools, saws, a hammer, pliers, pincers, a purposeful-looking wood-axe with an edge like a razor, a few screwdrivers and an assortment of chisels. And, at the bottom right-hand corner of the board, an adjustable spanner, a foot or so long, lying across two wire hooks. It was spotlessly clean – but then so was everything else.

'Used this spanner lately, Mr Shaw?'

'No, sir,' said Shaw, still at the doorway with Morgan. 'Not lately. Christmas was the last time, as I recall. I used it to release the trap under the sink in the kitchen.'

'Not since?'

'No, sir,' said Shaw.

Roper draped a handkerchief over the shaft of the spanner, lifted it down from its hooks and hefted it in his fist.

'You've got nothing else like this?'

At this juncture Roper had turned and was walking back towards the door, still holding the wrench, and he suddenly felt an ice-cold finger trail up his spine. Because, while his back had been turned, Shaw had taken off his spectacles and was polishing beads of rain off the lenses with a handkerchief, and Roper recalled another rainy day, nearly twenty years ago, when he had been a young PC in the Met. Heathrow at its most dismal, rain hammering down on the roof of the car, and two men walking briskly towards him over an expanse of concrete with umbrellas up, and the man between them, in military khaki, handcuffed to one of them. The memory had dimmed, and Roper had only seen the prisoner's face in his driving-mirror when they'd bundled him into the back of the car – a lot had happened since – but he remembered now when he had last met Mr Shaw.

'D'you mind if I borrow this for a couple of days, Mr Shaw?'

'It isn't my place to say yea or nay, sir,' said Shaw. 'It's Mr Sheridan's property. But I can't see myself using it in the immediate future.' Shaw hooked the wire ends of his spectacles behind his ears again; but the ice-cold finger stayed lodged between Roper's shoulder-blades.

'Mrs Sheridan use her own car on Saturday?'

'No, sir,' said Shaw, tucking his handkerchief up the cuff of his jacket. 'She used Mr Sheridan's.'

'Which is?'

'This one, sir,' said Shaw, nodding at the black Jaguar beside which the three of them were standing.

'Why didn't she use her own?'

'I really couldn't say, sir,' said Shaw. 'A whim, I expect. She has a lot of little whims, does Madam.'

Roper thought otherwise. If Mrs Sheridan had been bent on a spot of villainy last Saturday night, it had been no whim that she had chosen Sheridan's black car. Her own white one, parked in a backwater like East choatley, would have stood out like a gold tooth, even in the dark. More and more it began to seem as if Mrs Sheridan had laid her plans well in advance. And perhaps in concert with Mr Shaw.

'You went quite white there for a minute,' said Morgan.

'I know him,' said Roper. 'Sure as God made little apples.'

Roper and Morgan had returned to Roper's car parked in front of the Sheridans' porch. In a plastic bag on the back seat lay Shaw's adjustable spanner and beside it, in another small bag, two aluminium-capped phials, one containing a sample of oil from the can Shaw kept in the garage, and the other a twist of paper upon which Morgan had managed to blot up a smear of oil from around the lock of the green gate in the garden. Roper had no doubt that the two oil samples would match, but as a matter of private interest he preferred to be certain. It was coming up for three o'clock in the afternoon. Another working day was almost gone.

'Villain, is he?' asked Morgan.

'Was,' said Roper. 'If he's who I think he is.'

'What did he do?'

'It was over in Germany,' mused Roper. 'He killed a

126

young woman. German girl, I think she was. Back in the fifties. I took a car to Heathrow to pick him up off the plane. If it's the same bloke.' He felt around his pockets for his cheroots, lit one, thought a while. 'Get in touch with CRO, Dan,' he said, still staring out through the rain-beaded windscreen. 'Find out all the Gordon Shaws they've got form on.'

'Right,' said Morgan. He, too, thought for a while. 'Think Shaw helped her on Saturday?'

'Might have done,' said Roper. 'Except he doesn't like Madam all that much, does he?'

'She might have made it worth his while. Contract job. She must have known she had a villain on her hands, mustn't she? Unless he'd managed to keep it quiet.'

'He could hardly have kept it quiet from his mother, though, could he?' It occurred to Roper now why Mrs Shaw had looked worried each time he had asked to speak to her son. It had been more than mere maternal interest. George Sheridan must have known about Shaw's background too – if he and Mrs Shaw really were as close as Lindsey thought they were, then surely Mrs Shaw would have at least told him.

'Where is she, Dan?' he said. 'Where the bloody *hell* is she?'

'And who's helping her?' said Morgan. Because somebody had helped her and probably still was. Somebody somewhere was feeding and watering her. Over the last few days Rita Cavallo had become a public face again – she would hardly take the risk of showing it until the fuss of her disappearance had died down. But wherever she was, someone had taken her there.

It was likely that Mrs Sheridan had visited East Choately last Saturday night, but even that wasn't a certainty until Morgan drove Shaw there early tomorrow morning for a positive identification. If Shaw was telling the truth, and he might well not be, Mrs Sheridan had stayed in East Choately for a couple of hours. According to the Misses Murrell, Mrs Sheridan had visited Mrs Blaney on two previous occasions, so it was only likely that on Saturday

Mrs Sheridan had called there again – but it was only likely, it still wasn't a copper-bottomed fact. Weygood had told Roper that whoever had killed Mrs Blaney must have left the house with their clothes splashed with blood. If there had been blood on Mrs Sheridan's fur coat when she had returned to the car, Shaw might not have seen it in the dark – but blood was the kind of stuff that got everywhere once it was spilled and it ought to have stained the car seats. So Roper had taken a good look at the black Jaguar's rear seats and there had been nary a mark on them. According to Shaw all he had done to the interior of the car since Saturday was to run a vacuum cleaner over it.

Roper, guarded, because he was still intent on keeping the possible connection between Mrs Sheridan and Mrs Blaney between himself, Morgan and Mower for the time being, had not mentioned blood to Shaw, but only stains. Shaw had reiterated that he had only used the vacuum cleaner.

So the premise had to be that if Mrs Sheridan had killed Mrs Blaney, then she had done so with her fur coat off. But what had she done with the clothes that she had been wearing underneath the coat?

And what had her motive been? The big why? What was it about Mrs Blaney that had driven Mrs Sheridan to destroy her – if, that is, she had? Mrs Sheridan had visited Mrs Blaney twice before, and on both occasions left her alive. What had happened between the latter of those two occasions and last Saturday night?

'Two cheques,' said Roper, to the middle air beyond the windscreen.

'What two cheques?' said Morgan.

'According to our schoolteachers, Mrs Blaney didn't go out to work,' said Roper.

'She didn't need to,' said Morgan. 'Her old man left her comfortable, so the Murrells said.'

'But how much comfortable?' said Roper, tapping ash from his cheroot on the rim of the dashboard ashtray. 'I doubt that house of hers was painted more than three months ago. How much d'you think that cost?'

'And those carpets were all new,' said Morgan, catching Roper's drift at last.

'And she'd bought a lot of new clothes,' said Roper. 'Lately. And the Misses Murrell reckoned she might have come into a bit more money, didn't they?'

'Lately,' said Morgan.

'Right,' said Roper, reaching for the ignition key.

'Where're we going?' asked Morgan.

'The Misses Murrell,' said Roper. 'Bless 'em.'

At half-past three Roper and Morgan were again comfortably ensconced in the Misses Murrells' front sitting-room and drinking tea from their best set of bone china, while the two ladies fluttered excitedly at finding themselves once again important witnesses, which Roper assured them, and with some justification, that they were. Across the street, number one was still taped off, its newly painted front door open and a uniformed constable standing by the front gate.

The Misses Murrell were presently discussing between their two selves just *when* Mrs Blaney had undergone her transmutation from a relatively poor widow to a relatively wealthy one. Miss Iris was certain it was *very* recently. Two or three months, perhaps.

'The vicar was here.'

'So he was. That was when the men came with the ladders …'

'It was a Monday,' piped up Miss Agnes. 'Whenever Mr Widdowson calls …'

'Mr Widdowson's the vicar,' explained Miss Iris. 'He drops in almost every Monday. In the mornings.'

'Yes, in the mornings,' agreed Miss Agnes. 'That was when the decorators came.'

'To paint the house.'

'Yes, to paint the house.'

'Front and back.'

'And the side.'

'It must have been *very* expensive.'

'We said so at the time, didn't we?'

'How about the new carpets?' asked Roper, breaking in.

'Soon afterwards. A week?'

'About. The red one came first.'

'Then the two green ones.'

'One of those went into the hall.'

'We caught a glimpse.'

'Quite accidentally.'

Gossipy the Misses Murrell might be, but Roper had no doubt that they were reliable. From their tightly enclosed little rock-pool of a world they could only look out, and practically everything they saw through their curtains was in the nature of an event. They had seen the decorators setting up their ladders around Mrs Blaney's, they had seen the new carpets going in, Mrs Blaney's sudden appearance in a new autumn coat. A grey one, Miss Iris thought or, according to Miss Agnes, it was more green than grey; so perhaps it was somewhere in between. Then there was a new handbag. And the boots with the fur tops. And yet another new coat ...

All within the last few months.

'Not that she ever looked raggedy, of course.'

'Most tidy; she always was.'

'But lately; she'd started to look very smart.'

'And there was the silk lampshade we saw her bring back.'

'The one she put in the front bedroom.'

'We couldn't help noticing.'

'When she switched the light on.'

'And the new curtains.'

'Yes, she bought new curtains, too.'

'You said that Mrs Lawson had shown you a photograph once,' said Roper. 'A still photograph from an old film she was in. Can you remember anything about it?'

The question called for a conference.

'It wasn't in colour.'

'No. Black and white.'

'She was standing at the back.'

'Selling ice-creams, from a tray.'

'Like they do in the cinema, during the interval.'

'In a little skirt.'

'And a white pinafore.'

'And two men were fighting.'

And Roper listened, prompting not at all. The only thing the Misses Murrell had wrong was the ice-creams. For the rest, what they described sounded very much like the photograph Lindsey had shown Roper in one of Mrs Sheridan's scrapbooks last night.

They crossed the street to number one. Roper showed his warrant-card and the constable lifted the tape for them to duck underneath.

'Mr Mower about, is he?' asked Roper, to a young officer who was in the sitting-room and rummaging through the contents of Mrs Blaney's bookcase.

'Upstairs, sir. Front room.'

Mower was sitting on the edge of Mrs Blaney's bed, on his knees an old photograph album. A few feet away, another DC was methodically emptying out a chest of drawers full of clothes. Mrs Blaney's life, whatever it had been, had to be turned over now in its every intimate detail.

'Any joy?' asked Mower.

'I think so,' said Roper. 'If the chauffeur was on the up-and-up, he drove Mrs Sheridan over here last Saturday night. She played the same dodge on him as she played with the minicab driver. Got him to stop by the telephone box opposite the pub, then she walked back. Probably to here.'

Mower savoured that. 'Sounds about right.'

'And we picked up an adjustable spanner in Sheridan's garage. A big one. And it's got a diamond pattern machined in the adjusting ring.'

'There're plenty of those about,' said Mower. 'I've got one myself.'

'And Shaw might have some previous. If he's who I think he might be, he killed a young woman once. Over in Germany.'

'Ah,' said Mower. 'That's a bit different.'

'And Dan and I've just been having words with the two

131

old ladies across the street. A photograph that Mrs Lawson showed them once seems to be a dead ringer for one Lindsey showed me in one of Mrs Sheridan's scrapbooks last night. Mrs Lawson *was* Amy Stole and Mrs Sheridan spent the night with her when that flyer-bloke shot himself.'

Mower smiled. It was only a thin smile, but it was rare for him to smile at all. You had to know George Mower for a long time before you found out that his bark was a sight more lethal than his bite.

'Well, I'll be buggered,' he said. 'I said we might meet somewhere in the middle, didn't I?'

'We just have,' said Roper. He tapped the photograph on the open page on Mower's knee. 'That's the same picture.'

TWELVE

ROPER, MOWER AND MORGAN SAT at the table in Mrs Blaney's dining-room. Despite all the activity going on and the occasional murmur of voices, the house still felt empty and depressing. Another premature dusk had brought rain with it again.

There was a general agreement that a lot of changes had taken place in Mrs Blaney's house during the previous couple of months. And that had to mean that Mrs Blaney had spent a lot of money – a lot of money, that is, by Mrs Blaney's standards. According to the Misses Murrell, who had observed these changes for themselves, somebody remarkably like Mrs Sheridan had twice visited Mrs Blaney during that same period. There was the minicab driver's testimony to that too. And now there was Shaw's.

And Roper had seen for himself two cheque stubs, written during that same period, to the tune of £1000, which was only evidence of the most circumstantial kind, but it was a lot of money and Mrs Sheridan had drawn that sum as cash which meant that as soon as it had passed over the counter of her bank it had immediately become untraceable. She had drawn each of those £500 cheques a few days either side of her two first calls on Mrs Blaney. And that had to be more than another coincidence.

And for reasons best known to herself, Mrs Sheridan's visits to Mrs Blaney had been cloaked in secrecy. On two occasions, giving a fake name and ensuring that she was picked up not at her front door but at a nearby bus stop, she had travelled to East Choately by hire-car. Last Saturday night, something had necessitated some urgency and she had to be driven by her own chauffeur to East

Choately. But in her husband's black car, not her own white one. According to Shaw her own had been perfectly serviceable. Why had she chosen to go in George Sheridan's which, according to Shaw, Madam never used unless her own was in for an overhaul?

'How about blackmail?' It was Mower who, tentatively, tossed that idea on to the table and Roper, less tentatively, who picked it up.

'Shaw said she was carrying something flat in a white carrier-bag when she arrived back at the car on Saturday night.'

'So?' said Morgan.

'Supposing it was the scrapbook Lindsey saw?'

'The one she reckons Mrs Sheridan stuffed in the boiler on Sunday?' said Mower.

'Right,' said Roper. 'Say it was Mrs Blaney's ...'

'Or Mrs Blaney's mother's,' proposed Mower. And that, on second thoughts, seemed more likely. If Mrs Blaney had been the blackmailing kind, and had she known something murky about Mrs Sheridan's past, she would have put that knowledge to use years ago.

'Perhaps she did,' said Morgan.

'But let's say it was old Mrs Lawson's scrapbook,' argued Roper. 'We know she knew Mrs Sheridan back in the old days, when she was Amy Stole and Mrs S. was Rita Cavallo. Supposing Lindsey's right, and Rita Cavallo did get up to a bit of no good where her boyfriends and husbands were concerned. And let's say Amy Stole sussed her out, or suspected something, and she happened to be right on the button.'

And over the years had followed with more than usual interest the doings of her one-time friend in the magazines and the newspapers. According to Lindsey, the cuttings in the scrapbook she had seen ranged from 1930 to 1970, so the compiling of all that information had been carried out with resolution, or it might have been a labour of love, of course.

Then this year Mrs Lawson, née Stole, had died. Her daughter, Mrs Audrey Blaney had moved into her mother's house, with her son, so the Misses Murrell had said. Nothing much had happened at first, except that Mrs Blaney's son had soon moved out again, until roughly two months ago, when both Mrs Blaney and her house underwent a sea-change; and, more or less coincidental with that, Mrs Sheridan had paid the first of her visits – and written the first of those £500 cheques for cash. The good and upright Misses Murrell, those keen observers of life beyond their net curtains, who had lived in their house, as old Mrs Lawson opposite had, for twenty years, had only seen Mrs Sheridan visit Number One *after* Mrs Lawson, née Stole, had died. In all the previous twenty years, they had glimpsed her not at all.

And now Audrey Blaney herself was dead. If Weygood was right, and he usually was, that death had occurred some time during last weekend. On Monday morning, just before eight o'clock, Mrs Sheridan had flitted away, in company with her two dogs. She had not been seen since. In the lining of a fur coat – that abandoned fur coat must surely have been hers – had been found the key to Mrs Sheridan's garden gate. Lindsey had seen her going towards that gate from the inside, and Farmer Watcherley had seen her going away from it, a few moments afterwards, on the outside.

And in Mrs Sheridan's garage a tool had been found that could possibly be the weapon that had killed Mrs Blaney, lying along the chauffeur's tool-rack.

'And you reckon this chauffeur-character's got form?' said Mower.

'Not certain yet,' said Roper. 'Dan'll be getting in touch with Records as soon as we get back.'

'It still won't prove anything,' said Mower.

'But he was with Mrs Sheridan last Saturday night,' said Morgan. 'Here in East Choately.'

'Was he?' said Mower. 'Who says so?'

'He did,' said Morgan.

'That's what I mean,' said Mower doggedly. 'According to what Douglas has said, Mr Shaw didn't know where the hell he was, did he? All right, so I'm playing the devil's

135

advocate, but even if he comes here tomorrow to identify the place, where does it get us? And what's it bloody prove?'

'That Mrs Sheridan came here last Saturday night,' said Morgan.

'Or Shaw did,' said Roper.

'Exactly,' said Mower. 'Shaw did. Or they both did. Who's to say? I want that woman, Douglas. Wherever she is. Sharpish.'

Roper drove back to Milton St Philip's and Morgan, in another car, across to County to send the telex requesting information about any Gordon Shaws with whom the Criminal Records Office had done business, also to despatch Shaw's adjustable spanner to the forensic laboratory in the hope, albeit a faint one, that it might be the weapon that had killed Mrs Blaney. When Roper had taken it down from Shaw's tool-rack it had seemed to fit the bill exactly. Now he'd had second thoughts – anybody with their wits about them would have sunk the weapon without trace by now.

He drove through Dorchester in the evening rush-hour and was still a couple of miles out of Milton St Philip's when he glimpsed two winking blue lights in the darkness ahead of him. Thinking it might be a traffic accident, he slowed, but then, as he closed on the lights, he saw that they belonged to a couple of panda cars and that their drivers were out on the grass verge and doing some hard talking to a man and a woman who were standing with their backs to a tall hedge. Only as he passed did he recognise one of the yellow-jacketed and blue-capped drivers as Sergeant Morrison, and he stopped and pulled into the verge a few yards ahead of the scene because Morrison was way off his patch, and he would not have done that unless the other officer, whose beat this probably was, had called for assistance.

Morrison was doing the talking, the other officer keeping his torch on the white faces. They were all standing close to an iron gate set in the hedge; behind the hedge was some kind of dilapidated tin hut.

'Trouble?' said Roper, as he joined them.

136

Morrison stood aside. 'No, sir, not exactly. Sergeant Cloudy here's just found these two dossing down in the old chapel, and they've got a motor parked in the bushes at the back. He reckons they've been here for a couple of days. Chief Inspector Roper, Trevor.'

'Evening, sir,' said Trevor Cloudy, without turning his head, still keeping his torch on the two faces. 'Now I'll ask you again. Your names, or you're nicked, both of you.'

'We haven't done anything,' the young woman retorted. She wore a flimsy black dress down to her ankles and was hugging herself against the cold. The young man was black-shirted, leather-jacketed, leather-trousered and heavily booted. His long fair hair was pony-tailed.

'They were in my patch on Sunday morning,' said Morrison. 'I saw the same car outside the pub.'

'What's your name, son,' asked Roper.

'It's the way she said,' the lad said truculently. 'We haven't done anything.'

'Then you haven't got anything to worry about, have you laddie,' said Cloudy. 'Your name?'

'Worboys,' he admitted. 'And what's it to you?'

'Mind how you go, sir,' warned Morrison. 'Half the floorboards are rotted through.'

The old chapel, a rusting, ramshackle place of corrugated iron, painted green once, was fast being overtaken by the ravages of time. According to the weatherworn sign, bolted to the wall beside the ricketty porch, it still proclaimed itself to be a Free Church Mission Hall where prayer-meetings were held at 7.00 p.m. on Sundays and Wednesdays.

The door would open only half-way, brought up short by the litter of years, so that Morrison, followed by Roper, had to squeeze themselves around the edge of it.

Morrison shone his torch on the crumbling floorboards until Roper was safely in beside him, then slowly around the musty and dusty interior of the hall. Rotting velvet curtains still hung at the windows. The floor was carpeted with dead leaves and old newspapers. A solitary wooden

137

chair, its seat piled high with a ziggurat of mouldering prayer-books, stood in the far, dark corner. A mildewed newspaper under Roper's right foot announced the assassination of John Kennedy back in 1963.

They had been camping down at the far end, the two of them, where two sleeping-bags were unrolled on the floor and the litter was newer. They seemed to have been living on baked beans and pizzas.

'How did you get in on this?' asked Roper.

'Cloudy heard voices in here,' said Morrison. 'And there's a door at the back as well as the one at the front. He thought with two of us they wouldn't be able to scarper off.'

'Has Cloudy checked this place lately?'

'Yes, sir,' said Morrison. 'But only the front door. He didn't go round the back. It hasn't been used since the war, this place.'

'But he knew we were looking for Mrs Sheridan, didn't he?' said Roper tartly.

'Yes, sir,' said Morrison. 'But she's an old lady, sir. She wasn't likely to go breaking in here, sir, was she? And he did try the door yesterday. He thought it was locked. Only someone had shot the bolts on it from the inside.'

'So there's no sign of a break-in?'

'Well, yes, there is,' admitted Morrison reluctantly. 'But Cloudy came up here in the dark, sir, and the place looked the same as it always did.'

They went back to the porch and Morrison shone his torch on the door frame around the lock. There were several marks on the jamb that had clearly been made by a screwdriver, and fairly recently, but they weren't all that obvious unless someone was looking for them. And the lock on the door was a cheap old surface-mounted thing that wouldn't have kept a baby out. So perhaps Cloudy wasn't to blame for not looking hard enough.

The car was parked hard up against the back of the hall and almost obscured by a tangle of brambles. It was a metallic-grey Cortina that had been driven into the ground years ago and was more than ready now for the scrap-heap.

'Anything in the boot?'

'Some kind of disco amplifier and a couple of loudspeakers.'

'Nicked?' asked Roper.

'Could be,' said Morrison. 'We haven't got around to asking that yet.'

'And they've been here since Sunday?'

'Yes, sir,' said Morrison. 'So they say.'

'What time on Sunday?' asked Roper.

'We don't have to tell you anything,' the young woman retorted, a scornful twist to her mouth. She had given her unlikely name as Serena Van Elst, her profession as musician. The shoulders of her flimsy black dress were powdered with dandruff.

'Because we haven't *done* anything.'

'Breaking and entering,' said Roper.

'*That* old place?' she sneered.

'Any old place,' said Roper.

Worboys and the young woman had been taken to Sergeant Morrison's cottage and given the first warm drink they'd had in days. The search-parties had been called in an hour ago at the end of another fruitless day. At the time that Colston had ordered the halt, one of the teams had been only a quarter of a mile from the Mission Hall. But then, like Sergeant Cloudy, Chief Inspector Colston was not endowed with extrasensory perception.

'What were you doing in there, the pair of you?' said Colston, sitting on the corner of Morrison's desk.

'Nowhere else to go.' This was from Joel Worboys, sleepy-eyed, sharp-featured like his mother, and still very sure of himself. He was only about eighteen, grubby and unshaven.

'Heard you lived along at Portsmouth,' said Roper.

'We did,' said Worboys.

'But we got turfed out,' said Van Elst, 'didn't we? Pigs and bulldozers.'

'Pigs?' said Colston.

'Pigs,' repeated Van Elst spitefully, staring Colston out. 'What d'you want? Pictures?'

'Your grandmother gave you a cheque on Sunday morning, Mr Worboys,' said Roper.

'Did she?'

'Cashed it yet?'

Worboys held out his hand towards Van Elst. She unzipped a pocket of the fringed leather jacket she had draped over her bony knees and fished out a crumpled cheque. She handed it to Worboys who passed it to Roper.

'We couldn't cash it,' said Worboys.

'Why not?'

'Because we don't have a bank account, do we?'

The cheque was made out to Joel Warboys, for £250, drawn on the account of Mrs R C Sheridan.

'We thought we just had to take it to a bank,' said Van Elst. 'But they more or less told us to sod off.'

'Can't say I blame 'em,' said Colston trenchantly.

'But it wasn't bloody *fair*, was it,' argued Van Elst. 'They acted as if we'd stolen the bloody thing.'

Tough they might have been, but only on the outside. On the inside they were still untutored in the world's harsher realities – like cashing cheques. When it came to real life they were still little more than children.

It took some time to get their story out of them, and every word of it came grudgingly. They had got back to their squat in Portsmouth late on Saturday night to find the windows and doors newly boarded up with plywood, and a police car outside. During the course of the day, their fellow squatters had been evicted by the bailiffs and police. The property had been scheduled for months for demolition and the owner had finally lost patience and obtained a court-order. On Saturday night Worboys and Van Elst had slept in the Cortina. On Sunday morning with only a few pounds between them, they had descended upon Milton St Philip's with a view to extracting some charity and a temporary roof from Worboy's grandmother, who was usually good for a few shillings, unlike his mother and stepfather.

They had arrived in time for breakfast. Their hopes of a temporary roof were dashed by George Sheridan who declined to shelter them and suggested that perhaps one or the other of them found themselves a 'proper job of bloody work'. Granny, though, had been more sympathetic, but then she usually was, this time to the tune of £250.

Knowing that they could not cash the cheque until Monday, Worboys and Van Elst, with nowhere to go, had driven around the area to find somewhere to camp down until they had cashed the cheque. They had found the Mission Hall, and discovered too that there was a field behind it over which they could drive the Cortina in order to hide it from the eyes of the local law. Neither Worboys nor Van Elst, they made it pithily plain, had much confidence in that organization. Having found a suitable site, they then drove back to Milton St Philip's to stock up on food from the grocer's shop next to the pub, which was fortuitously open on Sunday mornings. That was when Sergeant Morrison had first spotted their car.

After dark on Sunday they had parked the Cortina behind the Mission Hall. Worboys had made his first attempt on the back door but it had refused to give, because it was bolted on the inside as they discovered when they finally gained entrance through the front door. On Monday morning they had driven into Dorchester to cash the cheque, only to have their request declined. They had driven back at once to Milton St Philip's to have words with Granny. But she'd gone out for the day.

'Who told you that?' asked Roper.

'The chauffeur. He told us to come back tomorrow.'

That was new, and Roper was forced to wonder why Shaw had kept that little snippet to himself.

'How about Tuesday?'

'Same again.'

'Shaw told you Mrs Sheridan was out again?'

'Right,' said Worboys. Shaw, on his bicycle, had met Worboys at the gate and turned him away.

'Were you using your car?' asked Roper. Nobody in the house had mentioned hearing a strange car drawing up.

'Couldn't,' said Worboys. By this time, he and Van Elst had been running short of cash; and the petrol-tank of the

Cortina had been almost empty on Sunday morning when they had first arrived here. On both Monday and Tuesday, Joel Worboys had gone to the house on foot. On Tuesday night, listening to their transistor radio, they had heard that Granny had gone missing. They were thus stranded, and down to their last pound note and a few coppers. And in the minutes before Sergeant Cloudy had flushed them out they had been deciding whether or not to call it a day and do the unthinkable: throw themselves on the mercy of either George Sheridan or Julius Worboys.

It all sounded very unlikely, and Roper said so.

'It's the truth,' said Van Elst, who had done most of the talking.

'How about Monday morning,' asked Roper. 'About eight o'clock, say?'

'We were asleep,' said Worboys. 'What time did we get up?'

'About eleven,' said Van Elst, who looked the sort, Roper had to admit, who rarely saw the daylight much before midday.

'You weren't driving your car past your grandmother's house?'

'Eight o'clock?' said Van Elst wearily. '*Do* leave it out.'

Sergeant Morrison, who was hopefully going to negotiate bed and board for them with George Sheridan, at least for tonight, drove the two of them away soon after seven o'clock.

'What did you think of 'em?' said Roper.

'Plausible,' said Colston. 'Just about.'

'I told you not to ring me here, Mags. For Pete's sake …!'

'But it's important. Di Gruber's just called from New York …'

There was a sharp click in the earpiece.

'… it's about that Schwarz man …'

'Mags,' said Kate patiently. 'I'm not alone here. Know what I mean?'

'He was drunk,' said Mags. 'And the entire house went

up … oh, I see,' she said belatedly. 'Sorry. When's the best time?'

'There isn't one,' said Kate. 'I'll give you a ring in the morning. Nine o'clock. At the office.' Without even pausing to say goodnight, she laid the receiver cautiously back on the rest, and there came another distant tinkle from somewhere else in the house.

She went back across the hall towards the stairs, was halfway up then when someone rang the doorbell. She started back down to answer it, as Bill Erskine was going to pick her up around seven, but then Shaw appeared from the sitting room, into which he had pussyfooted – that was the only word to describe the way Shaw was always creeping about – after he had conducted her downstairs to answer the telephone.

But it wasn't Bill Erskine at the door. It was the local bobby, Joel Warboys and the Walking Dead.

THIRTEEN

ROPER FLATTENED THE TELEX ON his blotter with the edge of his hand. He was back in his office at County. It was eight o'clock in the evening.

Gordon Albert Shaw, he read, aged 23, housebreaker, present address Her Majesty's Prisons. Gordon Charles Shaw, 32, doer of grievous bodily harm on too many occasions, again currently living under the grace and wardship of Her Majesty. Gordon Donald Shaw, 33, armed robber, recently released and present whereabouts unknown, even to his probation officer to whom he had reported but the once after being shown the sunlight three months ago. And finally Gordon Winston Shaw, now aged 41. Last known address Milton St Philip's, in the County of Dorset. Released from HMP Parkhurst in August 1974. Indicted for murder April 2, 1957, in Bielefeld, West Germany. Victim: Frieda Anna Warburton. Incident initially investigated by Military Police, later by officers of Kent County Constabulary at request of Deputy Provost-Marshal for the Bielefeld Military District. Senior Investigating Officer: Chief Inspector Charles Longden. Subject guilty. Awarded life imprisonment. Released on grounds of exemplary behaviour after psychiatric and Home Office review. Probation Service also reported behaviour exemplary. Reporting to Probation Service now officially ceased. Nothing else known.

'Right bloke?' said Morgan.

'Got to be,' said Roper.

'And I've tracked down Longden,' said Morgan. 'If you're interested.'

*

144

These days on the pension-list, but albeit hale and still living in Kent, ex-Chief Inspector Longden had not been difficult to trace; and was as keenly interested in the present doings of Gordon Winston Shaw as Roper was when he rang him at eight-thirty.

'Sure he's the same man are we?'

'Bit brawnier than he was then, Mr Longden, but I recognised him. I was driving the car the day you brought him back to Heathrow.'

'Were you b'God,' said Longden reminiscently. 'Long time ago, eh, son? Yes, I remember him well, our Mr Gordon Shaw ... killed his sergeant's wife – a German girl. So he told us.'

To the best of Longden's memory, it was this way: in 1957 Shaw had been a time-serving soldier with the single stripe of a lance-corporal and a record that had been exemplary. On the night in question he had been in charge of the picket-squad detailed to patrol the married quarters attached to the British military barracks at Bielefeld. The squad patrolled in pairs and it had been Shaw's duty to spring up on them from time to time to make sure that they were where they were supposed to be and not having a quiet smoke behind the shrubbery. Lance-Corporal Shaw therefore, had spent most of that tour of duty without anyone being quite sure where he was at any one time.

Sergeant Warburton was Shaw's platoon sergeant, and a man of middle years – he was soon to be pensioned-off into retirement, and had recently taken to his bosom a new young wife, a German girl less than half his age. Within weeks of the marriage it was evident to all but Sergeant Warburton that his wife was, to say the least, prodigal with her affections around the barracks.

By the night of her death, however, Sergeant Warburton had got wind of his wife's possible infidelity. Having told her that he would be spending the evening playing billiards in the sergeants' mess, from which he would return at eleven o'clock, he instead returned home, by a back way, at ten with a view to catching her in the act, as it were.

But, to his chagrin, Sergeant Warburton had gone out

that evening without his doorkeys, so that all he could do was observe. And what he observed, having crept up his back garden in the dark, was Lance-Corporal Shaw, stripped to the waist, sluicing his hands and forearms in Sergeant Warburton's kitchen sink. There were, according to Sergeant Warburton's evidence at the time, no other lights on in the house.

By now an angry and frustrated man, Sergeant Warburton then crept around to the front of his house to lie in wait for Shaw. He had admitted, when Chief Inspector Longden had later interviewed him, that it had been his intention to kill Lance-Corporal Shaw, however unwise that admission might have been.

Shaw had come out some ten minutes afterwards, now back in full uniform, and closed Sergeant Warburton's front door quietly behind him. It was at this juncture that Sergeant Warburton's rage had got the better of him. He had pounced while Shaw was still several yards from him, too soon, time enough for Shaw to swing the night-stick, with which he had been armed for his picket-duty, and floor Warburton with a single blow.

Two squaddies from the picket had heard the scuffle and came running. They found Lance-Corporal Shaw standing over the prone body of Sergeant Warburton in the latter's front garden. He told them what he had later told Longden, that he had not recognized the Sergeant in the dark, and detailed one of them to fetch the guard commander and an ambulance.

As is often the way with the military, the young guard commander, a pink-cheeked subaltern, aroused the orderly sergeant who woke the orderly officer who then rousted out the regiment's adjutant who was the only officer who had access to the master-keys of the married quarters.

They had found the new Mrs Warburton naked on top of her bed, strangled with a military-issue khaki woollen scarf that had been knotted around her neck.

Sergeant Warburton had lain unconscious for nearly twenty-four hours and for two days after that could still remember nothing except that he had been set upon in the dark.

Meanwhile, the Special Investigations Branch of the Military Police had been called in. The evidence against Shaw was damning. His fingerprints were all over the taps in Sergeant Warburton's kitchen and when asked to produce the khaki woollen scarf with which he had been issued, he could not, the only man in the entire battalion who was unable to do so.

It was at this point that the forces of military law handed over the investigation to the Kent police, who, geographically speaking, were the closest to hand, and Chief Inspector Longden and two detective inspectors were flown out to West Germany. Like the officers of the Special Investigations Branch, Longden and his team decided that the evidence was overwhelming. The post-mortem on Mrs Warburton had showed that she had died at some time between 8.00 p.m. and 10.00 p.m. that night, and for those two hours Sergeant Warburton had had an alibi supported by well over a dozen colleagues who had been in the mess with him.

After two days of relentless questioning by Longden, Lance-Corporal Shaw, as Longden succinctly phrased it, finally put his hands up and came over with the goods. Shaw's story was that God had spoken to him and told him to confess. It had been, he swore, an accident. On two previous occasions when he had been on picket-duty, Mrs Warburton had asked him into her house, the first time on the pretext that she believed there was someone lurking in her back garden. She had not, according to Shaw, 'been wearing much'. On the second occasion she had asked him to replace an electric-light bulb that had blown in her bedroom. Over his reward, a cup of coffee laced with schnapps, in the Warburton's kitchen, Mrs Warburton had 'talked dirty' to him and generally 'led him on'. On his way out, in the darkened passage behind the front door, Mrs Warburton had suggested that the two of them became friends – and if he liked they could start now. A few minutes. No one would know. But first she had taken the

147

sash from her dressing robe and told Shaw to put it around her neck. It was something she liked. And so Lance-Corporal Shaw lost his virginity in Mrs Warburton's hallway. Mrs Warburton had asked him to pull the sash very tight.

Which is how, on the third occasion when Shaw had visited the young lady, she had died. Shaw 'had got carried away', so he stated and 'had not realised what he was doing'. Horrified at what he had done he had rushed down to the kitchen to scrub off what he had called his 'sin'.

After a preliminary court-martial hearing, Shaw was handed over to the civilian authorities for trial, and a High Court judge was flown out from the UK. Everyone had spoken highly of Shaw. His commanding officer had testified that he was a fine soldier, respectful, obedient and willing. His platoon commander, who knew Shaw better, had told the court that Shaw was not a man endowed with too much intelligence, and also that he kept himself to himself, not a trait to which Shaw's comrades took kindly, but that otherwise he had no fault to find with him. The padre, too, had vouched for Shaw. Shaw had attended the garrison's church twice every Sunday, and the bible-class which the padre held every Wednesday evening. It had been his impression that Shaw was a devout young Christian man who had fallen foul of a sexual temptation he had been unable to resist.

The jury had deemed otherwise and the judge, not a moderate man, had awarded Shaw life imprisonment. Two weeks after the trial, Sergeant Warburton had shot himself in the regimental armoury.

'But I was never really happy about it all,' said Longden.

'How come, sir?'

'The old gut, son,' said Longden. 'It didn't feel right. Even his confession had holes in it.'

But the weight of evidence had told. Shaw's scarf, Shaw's fingerprints on the taps and the bar of soap he'd used to scrub himself down that night, and that he knew about Mrs Warburton's unusual sexual proclivities. One of

Shaw's fellow corporals had come forward, even at the risk of implicating himself, and privately told Longden that he too had been required to wrap a scarf around Mrs Warburton's throat on the two occasions when he had bedded her. But even that evidence had not helped Shaw, had only damned him more.

Like Roper, ex-Chief Inspector Longden was only too glad that his job had required him to seek justice, not to dispense it.

'I'm surprised this Mrs Warburton fancied Shaw,' said Roper.

'Got the impression she fancied anybody,' said Longden. 'And Shaw was a good-looking lad in those days. Still remember his eyes, one of my DI's reckoned he could drill a hole through a brick wall with them.'

'He wears glasses, these days,' said Roper.

'Ah, well,' said Longden. 'Anno domini. Comes to all of us in the end, eh, son?'

By nine o'clock Mower, too, had read the telex from CRO and dourly heard out what Roper had gleaned from ex-Chief Inspector Longden – which still proved nothing beyond the fact, and Charles Longden himself still entertained doubts that it was a fact, that Gordon Winston Shaw, in the days of his youth, had committed a murder. Statistics showed that few murderers committed a similar crime again, but then statistics weren't always reliable, either.

For the rest, with every passing hour, the trail was getting colder and the only positive development all day had been the reappearance on the scene of Joel Worboys and his girl-friend. Like Roper, Mower was fairly suspicious of that reappearance. Worboys had a car, albeit close to a wreck but it was still a car, and had been fairly close at hand when Mrs Sheridan had made her mysterious exit on Monday morning.

'Know what worries me most?' said Roper.

'What's that?' asked Mower.

'Those two dogs,' said Roper. 'The way she just dumped 'em.'

'She could still be lying dead in a ditch,' said Mower.

'You still believe that?'

Mower continued to stir his coffee with the end of one of Roper's pencils.

'No,' he said. 'Not any more. We ought to keep it in mind though.'

'Say she's not lying in a ditch. Say she got herself picked up by somebody in a car last Monday morning – not Shaw because he was seen in the garden at more or less the same time. It would have to be somebody she knew, wouldn't it? Somebody who wouldn't blow the gaff on her.'

'Family,' said Mower, carefully wiping the pencil on a paper handkerchief. 'It'd have to be family.'

'They were all in the house. So they say.'

'Except young Worboys.'

'So say the lad picked her up. His girl-friend was asleep – and I can at least believe that bit – and he slipped out of that tin chapel without her knowing he'd gone. He collects his granny and the dogs. Granny does a quick-change act in the back of the car, perhaps she was wearing another coat under that fur one. Then she dumps the fur coat, together with the dog-lead in that gritting-bin. But she can hardly dump the dogs in there too, she just lets 'em loose. Or does she know they were let loose?'

'Not following you,' said Mower. 'Yet.'

'Could be she left 'em with young Worboys,' said Roper, and gave Mower a moment or two to mull that over. 'And he let them loose, after he'd let her out of the car, wherever it was. And it could even be him who put the dog-lead into the gritting-bin. Perhaps she asked him to get the dogs back to the house somehow, and he just opened the car door and pushed 'em out once the old lady was gone. And there's another thing.'

'What's that?' asked Mower over his plastic cup.

'Why did she wait until Monday before she did her bunk?'

'Because she didn't have any transport organised,' said Mower.

'Right,' said Roper. 'But then on Sunday morning, the grandson turns up.'

'And she writes him a big cheque.'

'So she does,' said Roper. 'Only when it comes to the point, he finds he can't cash it, and now he and his girl-friend are stuck there. Unless he can get either his stepfather or George Sheridan to divvy up a few bob to get them on their way again.'

The phone rang. Mower, the nearer to it, picked it up, listened then passed it across the desk to Roper. 'Craig,' he said. 'Forensic.'

'Evening, Mr Craig,' said Roper. 'Hope continues to spring eternal.'

'And well it might,' replied the ever-cheerful Craig from the Forensic laboratory. 'Firstly, the fur coat. There's not a useful trace on it anywhere. In fact there's not a sign of very much at all except a lot of fluff in the pockets. That's the bad news.'

'Now the good news?'

'Oh, yes, indeed,' said Craig. 'Although it rather depends upon one's point of view. About an hour ago somebody brought in an adjustable spanner for examination. Suspected weapon. It bears the signature of both yourself and a Sergeant Morgan on the label.'

'It does,' said Roper.

'And it is,' said Craig. 'One of my technicians dismantled it. Had whoever used it as a weapon in the first instance done that, then it's very doubtful I'd be making this phone call now.'

'Because ...' said Roper, drawing a notepad closer.

'Because inside the thread of the adjusting-nut there are blood traces, and one fractured human hair. We'll do a definitive blood test tomorrow, but from the samples we've got here, the hair's a pretty good match with the poor lady who was killed the other day over at East Choately. Can't be certain, of course, hair's notoriously difficult to pin down – if you'll forgive a pun at this late hour – but it's of a similar texture and an identical colour. Oh, yes,' there came a riffling of papers, 'and that lozenge-pattern

151

around the wound. The same spanner could have accounted for it.'

'Odds-on, then,' said Roper.

'More or less,' said Craig.

'How about those oil samples?'

'They match,' said Craig. 'According to our chromatograph, but then one can of motor oil, in this day and age, is identical with several million others. Can't say any better than that. Sorry.'

Katherine Lindsey sat with Bill Erskine in a secluded corner of the Crown and Compass. The subject of conversation was telephones.

'There are telephones everywhere in that house,' said Kate. 'But the only ones that ever ring are in the hall and the study.'

'That's because of George,' said Erskine. 'He hates ringing telephones. So he keeps all the others switched off.'

'Where're the switches?' said Kate.

'Down on the skirting boards. Where the leads come out of the sockets.'

'So if you just reach down and flip the switch, you can make the phone work?'

'Look,' he said. 'What's this all about exactly?'

'I think someone in the house is listening to me on the telephone.'

'Oh, come on …'

'No,' she said. 'I'm serious …'

FOURTEEN

'And you recognized this place, did you, Mr Shaw?'

'Yes, sir,' said Shaw. It was nine-thirty on Friday morning, the venue Sergeant Morrison's back office. Shaw had just returned from East Choately with Detective Sergeant Morgan.

'Thanks for your help, Mr Shaw,' said Roper.

'You're most welcome, sir,' said Shaw.

'There is one more thing.'

'Yes, sir?' said Shaw.

'None of my business, I know, sir, but does Mr Sheridan know all he needs to know about you?'

'I'm not quite sure what you mean, sir,' said Shaw. But his jaw had stiffened and his eyes had narrowed.

'I think you do, Mr Shaw,' said Roper. 'I know about it, I just want to know if Mr Sheridan does.'

'Yes, sir.' Shaw plucked off his spectacles and began to clean them with a paper handkerchief he drew from his cuff. 'That unfortunate affair is over and done with.' He continued to polish vigorously at one lens, held it up to the light, then polished the other. 'And Mr Sheridan is a very kind and understanding gentleman. The salt of the earth, as they say, sir.'

'And Mrs Sheridan?'

'Yes, sir,' said Shaw. 'I've made no secret of it.' He replaced his spectacles and stuffed his handkerchief back in his cuff.

'I borrowed an adjustable spanner from your tool-rack yesterday.'

'Yes, sir,' said Shaw. 'I remember that.'

'We've reason to suspect it could be a weapon we're looking for.'

'Really, sir?'

'Yes, sir. Really, sir.'

'I see, sir,' said Shaw.

'A lady over at East Choately. Last Saturday evening. She was murdered, Mr Shaw.'

Roper waited for some kind of reaction. This time there was none.

'I know absolutely nothing about that, sir. I've never killed anyone in my life, sir. It's not my way.'

'Tell us about last Saturday, Mr Shaw.'

'Again, sir?' said Shaw.

'Again, sir,' said Roper.

Shaw was still word-perfect. He sat on Morrison's chair, a mug of Mrs Morrison's tea in his hand.

'Reckon anybody saw you walking the dogs?'

'I recall several people passing by, sir. But I doubt they'd remember me. I certainly don't remember them.'

'And you didn't go into this lady's house?'

'I've already told you,' said Shaw. 'I did not go into any house, sir.'

'But you've already told one lie, Mr Shaw,' Roper pointed out to him. 'Why should we believe you now?'

'I've told no lies, sir,' Shaw insisted, still unruffled. 'As God is my witness.'

'How about Mrs Warburton?'

'I did not kill Mrs Warburton, sir,' Shaw retorted quietly. 'Sergeant Warburton did that.'

'You confessed, Mr Shaw.'

'It was the best way, sir,' said Shaw. He took a prim sip of his tea. 'I couldn't get clean, you see, sir. However hard I scrubbed myself I could never get rid of her. I chose prison as a way of absolution, if you see my point, sir. It still didn't take away all the dirt, but it helped.'

'Dirt?' said Roper, still uncomprehending.

'From Mrs Warburton, sir,' explained Shaw patiently. 'She led me into temptation. As she had led many others before me. I was tempted and I fell, and I have not been clean since. There are even times, now, when I fancy I can still smell the scent she was wearing.'

'The perfume she was wearing when you killed her?' asked Roper.

'No, sir,' said Shaw. 'The last time – the second time she called me into her house – I never went back there again until after she was dead.'

'Sergeant Warburton saw you in his kitchen, Mr Shaw,' Roper reminded him. 'You were stripped to the waist and having a wash. Mrs Warburton was dead then.'

'Yes, sir, she was,' agreed Shaw. 'And I was the one who found her. I thought she was dead, you see, sir, but I had to be sure, so I forced myself to touch her – to feel for a pulse. That's why I was washing, sir. To get the taint of her off me. You can have no idea, sir, what it cost me to touch her – that second time.'

'Then you clubbed Sergeant Warburton with your night-stick,' said Roper.

'Yes, sir,' agreed Shaw again. 'But I panicked, sir. I was already in something of a state. Sergeant Warburton leapt on me and accused me of killing his wife. I thought he was going to kill me, so I drew my stick – in desperation really, sir – and struck him.'

'Hang on, Mr Shaw,' said Roper, quick to spot the flaw between Longden's version of the story and the one he was presently hearing. 'Sergeant Warburton pounced on you in the front garden. As you came out.'

'Yes, sir,' said Shaw.

'And Sergeant Warburton hadn't been into his house?'

'No, sir,' said Shaw. 'It was very quiet; I would have heard him.'

'If Sergeant Warburton hadn't been into his house, then how did he know his wife was dead?'

Shaw's expression stayed inscrutable. 'Yes, sir,' he agreed. 'Quite. That's why I'm certain Sergeant Warburton killed Mrs Warburton himself.'

'But Warburton spent the evening in the sergeants' mess. He had witnesses.'

'Who's to say, sir,' countered Shaw. 'It was only a minute or two's walk from the mess to the married quarters. He could have left and been back again in less than ten minutes. A visit to the toilet could easily have covered that. And the toilet windows were easily climbed out of, sir. And it was quite dark, of course. So it was really rather simple, you see.'

Roper disagreed. It did not sound simple at all.

'But you were there, Mr Shaw,' he persisted. 'At one and the same time as Sergeant Warburton turned up – and your scarf was around Mrs Warburton's neck. How come?'

'You must remember that we are talking of a military establishment, sir,' said Shaw. 'Everything is done by rote and numbers. As the NCO in charge of the picket it was my personal duty to patrol the sergeants' married block, which I was detailed to do every hour, on the hour. Sergeant Warburton would have known that, sir. And that I would not have passed an open front door without investigating the reason for it.'

'You're saying Sergeant Warburton's front door was open?' Roper broke in as he recognized another flaw. 'Hadn't you checked it previously that evening?'

'Yes, sir,' said Shaw. 'I'd shone my torch over it from the street. It had looked firmly shut.'

'But then it wasn't?'

'Yes, sir,' said Shaw. 'There had been a spate of thefts, you see, sir, and we'd had special instructions to keep an eye open for interlopers. I believe the thief was eventually caught, sir, a German civilian, he was, one of the cooks in the officers' mess. So you see, sir, Sergeant Warburton would have known *exactly* where I was likely to be, and the fact that he saw me washing myself in his kitchen was merely a little gilt on his gingerbread – if I may coin a phrase, sir.'

'And the scarf Mrs Warburton was strangled with,' said Roper. 'That was another fortuitous coincidence, was it, Mr Shaw? I suppose you're going to tell me you'd lost it a couple of days before all this happened?'

'No, not a couple of days,' said Shaw. 'It was that very

morning, in fact, sir. Have you been perhaps an army man yourself, sir?'

'Drafted,' said Roper. 'Unfortunately.'

'Well, then, you'd know what a kit inspection was, wouldn't you, sir?'

According to Shaw, his entire billet had been due for a kit inspection that very morning and, to that end, had risen early in order to lay out their kit on their beds in the prescribed pattern and to arrange their spare clothing in their metal lockers in such a manner that it could all be seen and counted. Shaw's khaki scarf had been put on show on the top shelf of his locker and the locker doors left open. Shaw, in common with the rest of his company, had then assembled for breakfast parade and morning roll-call, both conducted by Sergeant Warburton. The company had then been marched off, under the aegis of the senior corporal, to the lower-ranks' mess, while Sergeant Warburton and the other sergeants had gone into the billets to make sure that everything was in order for the company commander's kit-inspection at eight-forty-five.

When Lance-Corporal Shaw had returned from his breakfast, the scarf had gone from his locker.

'And you reported it missing?'

'Yes, sir,' said Shaw. 'I could hardly do otherwise with the kit-inspection so imminent.'

'Who did you report it to?'

'Sergeant Warburton, sir.'

'Who was nosing around the billet while the rest of the lads were at breakfast.'

'Yes, sir,' said Shaw. 'Exactly. And Sergeant Warburton very kindly lent me his scarf to put in my locker – he liked to run a tidy ship, sir, if I may coin another phrase, and it would be to his credit if the kit inspection in our room passed off without unfavourable comment from the company commander.'

'You couldn't have drawn another scarf from stores? Before this kit inspection?'

'No, sir,' said Shaw. 'As I recall, the day was a Friday and the clothing stores only opened on Monday mornings, from eleven hundred hours to twelve hundred hours. Not a minute sooner or later. You know how it is in the army, sir.'

And Roper, for whom his two years of National Service was a sharp if not always joyous memory, did know that that was how things were arranged in the army. And like everything else that Shaw had told him in the last half-hour it had a ring of copper-bottomed authenticity that was not easily dismissed.

'What happened to Sergeant Warburton's scarf?'

'He took it back, sir,' said Shaw. 'After the kit inspection. And do you know, sir, I thought at the time he was doing me a kindness.'

Instead of which, if Shaw was telling anything remotely close to the truth, Sergeant Warburton had been setting him up.

'Who d'you think opened Sergeant Warburton's front door that night?'

'I think Sergeant Warburton did, sir,' said Shaw.

'So he must have nipped out of the sergeants' mess when nobody was looking.'

'Yes, sir,' agreed Shaw. 'I'd say that was highly likely.'

'And how about when you went into the house, did you leave the door open?' Because, if Shaw had, Sergeant Warburton would not have needed the door keys he had left at home that night, he could simply have crept in after Shaw.

'No, sir,' said Shaw. 'I closed it, sir, and shot the bolts behind me. I had it in mind to apprehend whoever might have been in there. I was a keen soldier, sir. Very conscious of my duty.'

'So why didn't you tell Inspector Longden all this, Mr Shaw? Treat you rough, did he?'

'No, sir, indeed not,' protested Shaw. 'I found him a singularly courteous and patient man, sir. Rather like yourself. In fact my conscience pricked me for a long time afterwards because I had to lie to him. I had been brought up not to tell lies, you see, sir. But it seemed to me at the

158

time I was as guilty as Sergeant Warburton – perhaps even more so. I am sure, sir, in your line of work, that you are not unfamiliar with the ways of sin. Well, I had sinned, sir, and I sought earthly punishment for it – the alternative was too much for me to consider.'

'The alternative?'

'Eternal Hellfire, sir,' explained Shaw. 'If I could refer you to the Gospels, sir. Saint Matthew, sir, Chapter Nine. "If thine eye offend thee— ..." '

'No need for quotes, Mr Shaw. We get the point.'

'Then that's really all I have to say, sir,' said Shaw. 'If Sergeant Warburton chose to face his Maker – as he subsequently did, with the murder of his wife on his hands – then that was his business. That I had been tempted into carnal knowledge of another man's wife – well, sir, that was mine. And when I drop to my knees on the Day of Judgement I shall be able to tell my Maker, with justification, that I have striven earnestly to punish myself in all the years since for that trespass here on earth, and that I have never sunk to such hideous depths since.'

'You could still get some kind of redress, Mr Shaw,' said Morgan.

'Oh, no, sir,' protested Shaw. 'If that's what you think, then you have misunderstood me entirely. I merely related the story to acquaint you with my true past. I have never even touched a woman since that night, sir, let alone killed one – which is what I believe this other gentleman is suggesting. In fact I *could* not touch one, sir. To be honest, I can't abide them, and that's a fact.'

'I saw you raise your hand to Miss Lindsey the other night, Mr Shaw,' said Roper.

'It was my intention to put a stop to her private activities, sir,' said Shaw. 'She is taking advantage of Madam's absence. I know for a fact that she is prying into Madam's private affairs. I saw it as my duty to put an end to it once and for all. In my opinion, sir, Miss Lindsey is a dangerous young woman. I also know for a fact that she has already begun to lead Mr Erskine down the stony path, sir. They're all the same, sir, the pretty ones. Deep down inside they are riddled with corruption. But I would not have struck Miss Lindsey – for the reasons I explained earlier. I intended only to take Madam's book from her and frighten her into minding her own business.'

'Frighten her, Mr Shaw?'

'It's the only way, sir,' said Shaw solemnly. He might have been talking about training dogs. 'I have found women, as a general rule, do not respond readily to reasoned argument. But I say again, I had no intention of striking Miss Lindsey.'

'I'm surprised you didn't report her to Mr Sheridan.'

'I have, sir. On several occasions since Madam went away. But Mr Sheridan told me that Miss Lindsey was there to do a job of work and that she was probably doing it – in short, sir, that it was none of my business. It's all down to sex again, you see, sir, and the myth that women can do no wrong. Sugar and spice and all things nice, that's what little girls are made of. You might remember that, sir? A nursery rhyme, which I strongly suspect was written by a bitter woman. It's propaganda, sir, of the most insidious kind, and it's usually drummed into us by yet another woman. Indeed, sir, I can say quite truthfully that learning *that* calumny is one of my earliest memories. I had an aunt—...'

'Perhaps we could get back to that spanner of yours, Mr Shaw,' Roper broke in, before Shaw digressed any further from the real matter at hand, however interesting and revelatory Shaw's own matter was – if it was true. 'Did you notice it on your tool-rack before you took Mrs Sheridan out on Saturday morning? Or notice it missing when you put the car away afterwards?'

'No, sir,' said Shaw. 'Frankly, I didn't.'

'Did you burn anything in the boiler-room on Sunday afternoon, Mr Shaw?' asked Roper.

'I never put rubbish in the furnace, sir.'

'Who said it was rubbish?'

'I inferred, sir,' said Shaw. 'The way you spoke ...'

'You didn't burn any paper in the furnace on Sunday afternoon?'

'Indeed not, sir,' said Shaw. 'I went nowhere near the boiler-room on Sunday afternoon.' He stoked the furnace twice a day, at seven o'clock in the morning and seven o'clock at night, and if the weather was very cold he sometimes topped it up with a shovelful of coke before he went to bed.

'And you didn't notice any ashes that might have been burned paper when you looked at the furnace on Sunday night?'

'No, sir,' said Shaw. 'That was in the morning. Sunday morning.'

'What was?' said Roper.

'The ashes, sir. I had to relight the furnace. I must have left the damper open the night before – after I'd come back with Madam. I don't remember doing that, but I suppose I must have. With the damper open the furnace burns out very quickly, sir,' he explained. 'The water was cold on Sunday morning. Madam gave me a right proper coating over that.'

And then it was that Roper recalled what Lindsey had told him twice, and what Julius Worboys had told him as if some kind of miracle had occurred. At some time in the small hours of Sunday morning, both had been awakened by the creak of the central heating pipes.

'Tell me about these ashes, the ones you found on Sunday morning.'

'They were just ashes, sir, spread over the clinker.' At the time, Shaw had thought nothing of them, his greater need had been to get the boiler relighted as quickly as possible, before Madam came breathing down his neck again.

'What did you do with these ashes?'

'They went into the dustbin, sir.'

But the dustmen had called on Monday, and the bins had been emptied and their contents disposed of on the county rubbish-tip. Which was a very great pity, because ashes, in this technological age, could often tell a story or two. And those ashes might have told a particularly interesting story because they might have consisted of

161

several items of bloodstained clothing that had needed to be incinerated with the utmost urgency. And not too long after Mrs Blaney had been bludgeoned to death over at East Choately last Saturday night.

'There is something else, sir,' said Shaw, hesitantly. 'Something that happened last Friday. My mother happened to mention that you'd gone through Madam's handbag. On Tuesday afternoon, that was, sir, if you remember. And that you didn't find much money in it. I was wondering about that Miss Lindsey, sir, her being a stranger, if you know what I mean.'

'No, Mr Shaw,' said Roper, wondering what new event was about to unfold. 'I don't see what you mean.'

'Only, Madam asked me to drive her into Dorchester last Friday morning, sir. To the bank. She asked me to go in with her and wait by the door – I think she was afraid of being robbed, you see, sir. She cashed a cheque, sir. For a lot of money. Five-pound notes they were, sir. In bundles, with paper bands round them. She had quite a job stuffing them all into her handbag. What I'm really saying, sir, is that Madam didn't spend *that* much money on Saturday. And on Sunday she didn't leave the house.'

But on Monday she had. And perhaps with that same money. And Roper recalled then the blank stub he had seen in Mrs Sheridan's cheque book, immediately before the cheque she had written for Joel Worboys. Perhaps she had left that stub blank deliberately, perhaps because she didn't want her husband to know that she had drawn that much money.

'Would you like Sergeant Morgan to give you a lift back to the house?'

'No, sir, thank you,' said Shaw, seemingly disappointed that Roper hadn't taken up his accusation against Katherine Lindsey. 'I can easily walk, sir.'

Morgan stood aside and went to usher Shaw out; but as Shaw reached the door, Roper said to his back: 'There is one more thing, Mr Shaw.'

'And what might that be, sir?' enquired Shaw, slowly turning.

'Young Mr Worboys and his lady friend,' said Roper. 'You didn't tell me you'd turned them away from the house twice this week.'

'You didn't ask me, sir,' said Shaw.

'Did you tell Mr Sheridan they'd called?'

'No, sir,' said Shaw. 'They toil not neither do they spin, those two, sir. Layabouts, Mr Sheridan calls them. He gave me strict orders not to let them into the house, and that's what I did, sir.'

'How about last night? Did they get a bed?'

'Mr Worboys prevailed upon him, sir. It took him some time.'

'Thank you, Mr Shaw,' said Roper.

'And thank you, too, sir,' said Shaw. 'Good-day, sir.'

'Good-day, Mr Shaw.'

Roper and Morgan stood side by side at Morrison's barred front window and watched Shaw march off so briskly that Roper wondered if his refusal of a lift was yet another penance.

'Head-case, d'you reckon?' said Morgan.

'Who's to say?' said Roper, his hands stuffed into his trouser-pockets, still gazing at the spot where Shaw had gone from sight. But if Shaw was right, Mrs Sheridan could have left Milton St Philip's last Monday morning with enough cash to keep her for several months.

One other doubt was resolved when Craig from the forensic laboratory phoned a few minutes after ten o'clock. The burning of some midnight oil last night had allowed his biologist to ascertain that Shaw's adjustable spanner, or, more accurately, George Sheridan's adjustable spanner, was the weapon that had killed Mrs Blaney.

The fragment of human hair trapped around the nut-thread was of a colour and texture that matched Mrs Blaney's. And the diluted blood that had seeped under the nut was definitely of Group B, a type that was shared by only some ten per cent of the population – which made it comparatively rare. Of itself, neither find was incontravertible evidence, but their sum made it nigh on a certainty

163

that the spanner was the weapon. Of fingerprints on the handle, though, there were none, which could only be further evidence that the spanner had been thoroughly cleaned after it had been last used, and nobody went to that much trouble to clean a spanner without good reason.

'If you've finished with it, I'll have it back this afternoon, Mr Craig.'

'Will do,' said Craig.

'Got the right spanner, have we?' said Morgan, as Roper laid the phone back on the cradle and it started to ring again before his hand had left it.

'I reckon,' said Roper. 'Police, Milton St Philip's …'

'That you, Douglas?' The voice was Superintendent Mower's. He was speaking from County. There had been a development over at East Choately.

A few minutes ago, Mrs Blaney's son had turned up at his mother's house, and to the constable keeping an eye on the place had fallen the unpleasant task of informing that young man that his mother had been dead for nearly a week, and that that lady had died in suspicious circumstances.

Which was hardly, in Roper's opinion, the most exciting development he could think of at the moment.

'I haven't got to it yet, Douglas,' said Mower testily. 'The bobby had the wit to ask the lad if he knew if a Mrs Rita Sheridan had ever called on his mother.

'And did he?'

'No,' said Mower. 'But he knows about her.'

'And what does he know about her?' asked Roper.

'He says Mrs Sheridan could be his granny,' said Mower. 'You still there, Douglas?'

FIFTEEN

BY TEN-THIRTY THEY HAD all assembled in Mrs Blaney's cramped little sitting-room, Peter Blaney in one armchair, a young woman he had brought with him in the other, and Mower, Roper and DS Morgan on three hard chairs borrowed from the dining-room.

One thing was obvious from the start. Somewhere along the line, Joel Worboys and Peter Blaney had been doled out with a remarkably similar set of genes. Even though Blaney was as dark as Worboys was fair, the rest of them was uncannily alike, their builds short and stocky, their faces struck from almost identical moulds. Their voices differed, but then Worboys had probably had the kind of education that Mr and Mrs Blaney could never have afforded. Blaney was, perhaps, three or four years older than Joel Warboys. Both he and the young woman wore motor-cycle leathers, both looked shaken by the turn of events, and both were drinking cups of tea from what Roper recognised as the best bone-china from across the street.

'We only got back in the country an hour ago.'

'From?' said Mower.

'France,' said Blaney. 'We caught the early ferry to Weymouth out of Cherbourg. We've just come back from honeymoon, Lisa and me.'

'We got married last Saturday,' explained the new Mrs Blaney, a plump, pink-cheeked young woman with closely cropped dark hair and too much lipstick.

'Your mother come to the wedding, Mr Blaney?' asked Roper.

Blaney shook his head. 'That's why we called in here this

165

morning. We were going to tell her.'

'We should have told her before,' Lisa Blaney complained, 'I did say we ought to, didn't I?'

'Things were different then, weren't they?' he snapped back at her. 'We didn't know this was going to happen, did we?'

Mower and Roper waited for them to settle again.

'When did you last see your mother, Mr Blaney?' asked Mower.

'Months ago,' said Blaney.

'July,' said Lisa Blaney. 'It was July.'

'Not since?' asked Mower.

Blaney shook his head again. 'We didn't get on. Hadn't for a long time.'

'Care to tell us about it?' asked Mower.

'No,' said Blaney. 'Don't really want to talk about it.'

'It might help us, son,' said Roper. 'We don't have a lot to go on at the moment.'

'You really *ought* to tell them,' said Lisa Blaney. 'I mean it's all so stupid really, isn't it?'

'Yeah,' he agreed with a sigh. 'I suppose it is really. But it won't help any.'

When he had fallen out with his mother, back in July, it had not been over a girl, as the Misses Murrell had thought, but over his father's garage business of which his mother was the nominal owner. After his father had died his mother, on the advice of her solicitor, had rented the business out, with a view to bringing herself in a small but steady income. When that decision had been made, Peter Blaney had been a child. Now he was, and had been for some time, a man with a mind and skills of his own and he wanted the garage for himself. Mrs Blaney, however, as is often the way with mothers and their offspring, had declined to let him have it on the grounds of what she thought was his youth and inexperience. They had finally parted company, as the Misses Murrell had said, last July, and Peter Blaney had gone off to live with his girl-friend and her parents. In the few months since, Blaney had started up a small motor-servicing business of his own. It was beginning to thrive, and now he had married. It was with a view to imparting this news to his mother that he had called at her house this morning.

'We hadn't got along all that well for a long time,' he admitted. 'She was a bit spiky, especially since the old lady died – my old granny, that is. Only apparently she wasn't my granny. Although we didn't know that until she died. Mind you, I still reckon it was a load of old nonsense.'

'Your grandmother left this information in her will, did she?' asked Roper.

Blaney lifted his face – he really was incredibly like Joel Worboys. 'No,' he said. 'The old lady had written a letter. Her solicitor gave it to Mum after he'd sorted out the will. She'd written it a couple of years before. And Mum developed a sort of obsession about it.'

'Did you, personally, ever see this letter, Mr Blaney?' asked Mower.

'Yes, I read it,' said Blaney. 'Once. And I reckoned it was a bit of a fairy story. The old lady was great on stories. She used to make 'em up for me when I was a kid. She had a lot of imagination, my old granny.'

'Do you know where that letter might be now?' asked Roper.

Blaney shook his head. 'It's somewhere about, I expect, but I wouldn't know where.'

'My old granny was an actress,' said Blaney. 'I know that much was true. And she was in some movies too, but only bit-parts and walk-ons. I don't know the ins and outs exactly, except that she joined some travelling repertory company. It got as far as North Wales – Colwyn Bay, I think it was – and it went broke, or the bloke who ran it did a bunk with the week's takings. Whichever it was, none of the company got paid. Gran hadn't even got her fare back to London and she still owed her landlady for her week's lodgings. So she had to stay up in Wales and get herself a job – in a tobacconist's it was.'

'Any idea what year that was, Mr Blaney?' asked Roper.

'God knows,' said Blaney. 'About nineteen-thirty, I suppose. Mum was born in nineteen-thirty-one, so it had to be before that.'

Blaney could not remember his grandmother's maiden name, only her married name, which was Lawson. She married the tobacconist, a man much older than herself, who had died within a few weeks of the wedding and left her with a business of which she knew nothing and debts of several hundred pounds – or so the family fable had had it. She had also been, according to that same fable, newly pregnant with the child who was later to become Mrs Blaney of East Choately.

Beset by her late husband's creditors, the fable then had it that Granny Lawson had sold the shop, and to her surprise received more than she had ever dreamed it was worth, enough in fact to set herself up with a small boarding-house near the sea-front at Worthing, on the Sussex Coast.

The fable ended with Granny Lawson's death, and the letter she had written to her daughter.

Granny Lawson had lived a lie for the previous forty-odd years, which had troubled her greatly. Audrey Blaney was not her natural child. She had been paid to adopt her. Several thousand pounds. A Colwyn Bay doctor had been bribed to keep his mouth shut, and Granny Lawson had registered the birth as if it had been her own.

The child's natural mother, so the letter said, had been Rita Cavallo.

Peter Blaney couldn't remember the whole story, but from what he recalled from his one reading of the letter, his granny and Rita Cavallo had been childhood friends and both had run away from home together to go on the stage. Rita Cavallo had made a moderate success of it, and Granny Lawson had fallen by the wayside and finished up in the travelling repertory company which finally took her to North Wales and left her stranded there. Granny Lawson and Rita Cavallo, however, had kept in touch, and one day, when Granny Lawson had reached her lowest financial ebb, the day before she had contracted to sell the shop and was due to move and felt that her world had collapsed about her, Rita Cavallo turned up in the shop. She needed a favour. Desperately. And there would be money in it. She had just had a child, a girl, there in Colwyn Bay, and had to farm it out. Discreetly. The father was heir to a lot of money, the child an inconvenience to both of them.

The young, inexperienced and fraught Mrs Lawson had scarcely needed to think about it. She was up to her neck in her late husband's debts, and the money Rita Cavallo was offering was more than she had ever seen in one piece in all her life, or was ever likely to, the answer to all her prayers. Armed with the doctor's fake certificate with her own name on it. Granny Lawson had registered the birth of the child as her own. And promptly fled Colwyn Bay, well aware that she had broken the law and to live in dread of it for the rest of her days.

'Did the letter say who your mother's real father was, Mr Blaney?' asked Roper.

'I don't remember,' said Blaney. 'Except that he was some kind of flyer.'

'A bit earlier, you said your mother had developed an obsession about all this, Mr Blaney,' said Mower. 'D'you mind expanding on that?'

Over the weeks succeeding his grandmother's death, Peter Blaney had watched his mother sink into bitterness – yes, he repeated to Mower, his mother had got bitter, she felt she'd been cheated out of something, so much so that she'd hired a private detective to track down the family of her real father. The detective's services had cost her £30 for a week, which she could ill afford. He had come up with nothing except that the family was now extinct, the father's only brother having been killed in North Africa during the war and his entire estate handed over to the Crown, as is the way with property which no longer has neither an owner nor a claimant, and that the aforementioned property had been in Portman Square, and was now part of an hotel.

Mrs Blaney had then turned her attention to finding her natural mother, and this she did on her own account, scouring all the local libraries for any mention of Rita Cavallo and then, one of the library assistants mentioning to her that she thought Rita Cavallo had married the actor George Sheridan, she switched her attention to finding him, which was only a question of looking up his entry in *Who's Who* and establishing that his home was in Dorset. She had then tried to find his telephone number, but it was ex-directory. Mrs Blaney had then spent some days back in the public libraries, this time searching the electoral registers, where eventually she found George Sheridan's name and address.

'She was determined,' said Blaney. 'I told her to pack it in, there wasn't any point, she was getting herself all worked up over nothing, but she wouldn't listen. They owed her, she said. In the end, I stopped talking to her about it and let her get on with it. It was all history, I told her.'

'D'you know what your mother did when she found Mrs Sheridan's address?' asked Roper.

'She wrote.'

'She get a reply?'

'Not the first time,' said Blaney.

'How about next time?'

'I don't know,' said Blaney. 'I'd got so fed up with her, the way she was, I'd left home by then.'

'This letter your grandmother left for your mother, Mr Blaney, d'you think your mother might have destroyed it?'

'Hardly,' said Blaney, with a disgusted twist of his mouth. 'I told you, she was obsessed with it. If she read it once, she read it a dozen times – I used to catch her at it.'

'Was there anything else, Mr Blaney?' asked Roper. 'Anything else your grandmother might have left behind? Besides this letter?'

'There was a scrapbook the old lady used to paste bits and pieces into,' said Blaney, totally unaware of Roper's sudden glance at Mower and Mower's sudden glance at Roper.

'D'you ever look at it? This scrapbook?'

'Once,' said Blaney, shrugging. 'I wasn't all that interested. You make your own way in life, don't you? Where you've come from isn't all that important, is it?'

'But your mother didn't think that way?' said Roper.

Blaney shook his head, which so far as Roper was concerned was answer enough. Mrs Blaney, having lived more than half her expected span in the sure knowledge that Amy Lawson had been her mother, had then discovered that she was not even remotely related to her. It would have been a blow. Shock would have come first, then, in Mrs Blaney's case, anger and a need, perhaps, for some kind of restitution. She had written once to her natural mother and received no reply. What would her mood have been thus?

'Can you recall what this scrapbook looked like, Mr Blaney?'

'Tatty,' he said. 'With fairies and toadstools on the cover.' He smiled with fond reminiscence. 'Granny had me believing in fairies for years.'

'A personal question, Mr Blaney,' said Mower. 'Did your mother have any other source of income, other than rent from your late father's garage?'

'None,' said Blaney. 'Until Granny died, she was thinking of finding herself a job. It was getting to the stage when she was having trouble paying the rent.'

'So your father didn't leave her with a house she could sell?'

'No,' said Blaney. 'Dad couldn't afford a mortgage; he kept ploughing all his money back into the garage. He'd just broken even when he died.'

'D'you know how much this garage paid your mother each month?' asked Roper.

'I don't know exactly,' said Blaney. 'She was always a bit close when it came to talking about money, but I reckon the going rate'd be about a hundred and fifty a month. The place didn't have any living accommodation. It was just a workshop and a couple of pumps.'

Roper did some quick mental arithmetic. If Blaney was

right, then his mother's income was something around £35 pounds a week, certainly enough to live on without her having to scrape, but a long way from luxury.

'Did you notice your mother had had the house painted, Mr Blaney?' asked Mower.

No, Blaney had not. After talking to the constable at the gates he had been in no mood to examine paintwork. The front door had always been yellow and that it had been a newer and glossier yellow this dull and miserable morning had passed him by. And *new* carpets? *And* wallpaper?

'She couldn't afford it,' said Blaney. 'She was only just getting by. Where did she get that kind of money from?'

Both Roper and Mower had already guessed the answer to that, but neither, for the moment, were prepared to enlighten him.

Roper and Mower were alone again. It was eleven o'clock and Peter Blaney had gone and left Roper and Mower with a free hand to search his mother's house however they wished. The house held no fond memories for him – his mother had become bitter here and he himself had left it in anger. As soon as the law permitted, he intended to sell it. Mrs Blaney's son was a pragmatist. He had a living to earn and a new wife and nothing was going to bring his mother back. Just so long as Roper and Mower found out who had killed her. That had been his parting shot. Again, neither enlightened him that they were ninety per cent certain that they already had.

'Feels right, eh Douglas?' said Mower.

Roper agreed. It felt right. With Shaw's earlier confirmation they were sure now that Mrs Sheridan had indeed been to East Choately last Saturday night. Mrs Blaney's natural father, if it wasn't part of yet another fable, had been an aviator. Angus Kilcullen, victim of his own service revolver and of his own hand all those years ago, had been an aviator. Kilcullen had shot himself in the late summer of 1930. Audrey Blaney, née Lawson, had first seen the light of day in March 1931. From date to date just covered the obligatory term of gestation. Angus

Kilcullen had had a brother, the last of the Kilcullen line, who might, just might, have felt bound to pay his late brother's mistress a substantial sum of money to rid herself of a child that might have threatened yet another scandal – for it would certainly have been a scandal back in 1931. Mrs Sheridan had somehow come into possession of the scrapbook that had once been the property of Mrs Amy Lawson, adoptive mother of Mrs Audrey Blaney. Upon discovering that she was not who she thought she was, Mrs Blaney had written to her natural mother, perhaps with a view to reconciliation but more likely in spite. Having received no reply, she had written again. To what end?

Highest on the list of probabilities had to be blackmail in some guise or other. Soon after making contact with her mother, Mrs Blaney's financial resources had been given a boost. Mrs Sheridan had written two fat cheques at about the same time. As Mower said, it all slotted together – if you pushed the pieces hard enough.

The Bone of Contention tugged impatiently at Bill Erskine's trouser leg. 'It's true, Daddy, it's true! Come and see!'

He crouched in front of the child and affectionately re-adjusted her muffler and tucked the ends of it into her little grey duffle coat.

'One minute, Sausage,' he promised, holding up one finger. 'Then I'll come and see your froggies.'

'Promise?'

'Promise.'

The child pelted off happily in her shiny red wellingtons across the wet grass and went back to the footbridge, where she arranged herself on the planks with her legs straddling one of the uprights and her feet dangling over the water.

'So that's Janey,' said Kate sourly, when the little girl had settled again and was watching the water.

'Yes,' he said, 'that's Janey.' She waited for an apology, although what he should apologise for she was not quite certain. She was feeling particularly small-minded this morning. He had sprung the child on her last night in the Crown and Compass. They had finally got down to the subject of their divorces, the hows and the whys and the tackiness of it all. He had come home one evening to find a letter on the bed. The letter had purported to explain everything but in fact had explained nothing. His wife had simply found what she wanted with another man.

'Me too,' Kate had confessed. Although in her case her ex-husband had at least had the guts to tell her to her face.

'Any kids?'

'No,' she said. And then he'd dropped his blockbuster. He'd got this little girl. She was four, nearly.

'You didn't mention that before.'

'I didn't want you thinking I was looking for a surrogate mother.'

'You haven't exactly sent out any clues about what you're looking for,' she'd retorted. 'Yet.' It was true. He had made no physical advances. Even when he leaned across to open the door of the Mini for her, he was careful not to touch her. A friendly peck would have been something, and even a moderate show of lust would not have come amiss. But there had been nothing. They were just good friends, and had looked as if they were going to stay that way.

'You've kept her well under wraps.'

'Wouldn't you have?'

'No,' she'd said. But then qualified herself. 'Not for a whole week.'

'I told you,' he said. 'I'm not looking for another mother.' They were back in the here and now again and the child was flesh and not just an image in a mind that wouldn't go to sleep last night.

'Don't worry,' she said. 'You're not getting one.'

'That was a lousy proposal,' he confessed.

'You've got that in one,' she said, only just realizing that it was a proposal and it was probably the best one she'd had in years and that she was in imminent danger of passing it up. 'I'm not even sure you bloody like me.'

'*Like* you?' he said angrily. 'I've been lying awake nights trying to work out how to tell you all this.'

174

'Daddy, come and see,' the small voice shrilled from the bridge. It was ignored.

'I'm supposed to be a mind reader?' said Kate.

'I was in a cleft stick, wasn't I?' he argued. 'I couldn't make a move without telling you about Janey, and if I'd told you about Janey first you might have slammed the door in my face. Which you have.'

'Dead right,' said Kate. 'I have.'

'Where're you going?' he called after her, as she turned and strode off.

'The village,' she called back over her shoulder.

'You coming back?'

'I don't know,' she said, and left it at that. She walked faster and almost relished the luxury of being unreasonable. She felt angry and cheated, and if he'd brought the child up here this morning in the hope of her going all gooey-eyed over it, then he had another think coming. It wasn't that she disliked children, merely that she preferred them to be other people's.

It was only as she drew closer to the house and searched her soul more deeply, and more honestly, that it occurred to her that the emotion boiling up inside her was not anger, but something nastier and far more potent. She was jealous of a three-year-old child.

The thought came like a slap in the face, and she almost turned back – then decided not to because it wasn't going to work anyway. And, come to that, it had never really got started, had it? Cold, hard thinking told her that they were poles apart. What she knew about gardening could be engraved on a thumbnail.

She heard the raised voices as she went in through the kitchen door. They were somewhere out in the hall, their voices echoing from the high ceiling.

'You think I haven't *seen*!' A woman's shrill voice: Greta Worboys'.

'I don't give a damn if you have,' George Sheridan's, softer but no less angry.

'You don't *care* that Mother's gone missing! You're *glad*!'

'Look, Greta. I'm not *glad*. I'm as concerned as you

175

bloody well are …'

'Liar!' she hissed back. 'You're glad. I almost wonder if you're hoping something terrible's happened to her. And that *wretched* woman you've taken up with.'

'Taken up with?' Sheridan retorted scornfully. 'I took up with your mother, for Christ's sake, or rather she took up with me. The way you took up with Julius, and hung that jackanapes of a son of yours around his neck. And mine.'

'I love Julius,' she flung back at him. 'He's kind. Not like you.'

'So why d'you sleep in separate bloody rooms?'

'That's none of your damn business. I shall have to tell Mother. I *shall* tell her, you know.'

'She knows,' said Sheridan. 'It keeps me out of her bed. She approves of that.'

'That's *disgusting*! You're an *old* man!'

'My dear,' said Sheridan patiently, 'I love that dear lady, and that's the end of it. She gives me something your mother never has.'

'Sex!'

'No,' said Sheridan, his voice soft once more, almost menacing. 'Peace. A word your mother's never heard of.'

Kate turned and crept out again before she heard any more.

Sanity and reason came in the village 'phone box with the sound of Mags Biggs on the telephone from London.

'You're going to want a brand-new notebook and a powerful lot of pencils,' said Mags. 'You ready?'

SIXTEEN

AT HALF-PAST ELEVEN THE same morning, Roper and Morgan were back in Milton St Philip's and talking with George Sheridan in his drawing-room. It was obvious from the way the conversation was going that Shaw had confided in no one as to why he'd gone with Sergeant Morgan to East Choately this morning.

Roper said, 'The other day, sir, I asked you if you'd ever heard of a lady called Audrey Blaney, or Audrey Lawson.'

'Yes, I remember,' said Sheridan.

'You had any more thoughts about it, sir?'

Sheridan shook his head. 'No,' he said. 'As I told you at the time, I've never heard of the lady. Do you think I should have?'

'It was just a chance, sir,' said Roper. 'We know your wife visited her a couple of times. She went in a hire car, but when she booked the car she gave her name as Mrs Manders.'

'Her name *was* Manders, once,' said Sheridan, beginning to look bewildered again.

'Yes, sir, I know,' said Roper. 'That's why we're fairly certain the lady who called on Mrs Blaney was your wife.'

'Perhaps I should call on this lady,' Sheridan said hopefully. 'Perhaps she knows where Rita is.'

'Mrs Blaney's dead, sir,' said Roper, watching carefully for Sheridan's immediate reaction, not forgetting for a moment that Sheridan was an accomplished actor.

'Ah,' murmured Sheridan, frowning as he looked down at the carpet between his slippers. 'A pity. Then she can't help us, can she?'

'It may very well be that this Mrs Blaney was your wife's

daughter, sir,' said Roper, after a pause. Sheridan's first reaction might have been measured, this one was not.

'What?' he said, glancing up sharply and with his bushy silver eyebrows beetled together. 'My wife only has one daughter ... surely.'

'Perhaps not, sir,' said Roper. 'We're not completely certain ourselves yet, there's still a lot of loose ends to tie up, but I spoke to Mrs Blaney's son earlier this morning and he seems to think his mother might have been adopted, not altogether officially. The lad's story could have been a fabrication, of course.'

'But you doubt it?' said Sheridan. 'You think he was telling the truth?'

'I think he might have been, Mr Sheridan,' said Roper. 'It wasn't as if he stood to gain anything.'

'No,' said Sheridan. 'Quite. So what are you getting at exactly? You think this lady – this daughter – might have had something to do with my wife's disappearance?'

'We think, sir,' Roper ventured carefully, still watching, still measuring, 'that Mrs Sheridan visited Mrs Blaney late last Saturday evening. If she did – and I stress that "if " – then Mrs Sheridan had to be one of the last people to see Mrs Blaney alive.'

Sheridan, by the very nature of his profession, was a man practised in listening for nuances, and he plainly heard Roper's and recognized what it might signify.

'So this Mrs Blaney didn't just die?'

'No, sir,' said Roper. 'All the evidence points to foul play.'

'And you think my wife might possibly be a witness?'

And that was only the least of it, thought Roper. 'Yes, sir,' he said.

'And that might be why she's disappeared?'

'It could very well be, sir.'

'Whoever did whatever was done knew my wife could speak against them – they've taken her somewhere to keep her quiet? Is that what you're saying?'

'No, sir, not exactly,' said Roper, and deftly changed the subject. 'What do you know about your chauffeur, sir?'

178

'Gordon?' said Sheridan. 'What about him?'

'Exactly when did you employ him, sir?'

'About eighteen months ago,' said Sheridan.

'Did you know that he'd just been released from prison?'

'I did,' said Sheridan. 'The first time he came to see me, his probation officer was with him. I had to sign papers, more or less consigning him into my custody.'

'And d'you know why he was committed, sir?'

'I do,' said Sheridan.

'And it didn't bother you?'

'Yes,' said Sheridan. 'Initially.'

'But you still took him on.'

'I did,' said Sheridan.

And of course, thought Roper, he would have, with Shaw's mother in the more immediate offing.

'Been behaving himself, has he, sir?'

'It was all a long time ago,' said Sheridan on a rising note of irritability. 'People change. I have absolutely no fault to find with the man.'

'It doesn't worry you that he drives your wife about?'

'Not at all,' said Sheridan.

'He was with your wife all day last Saturday, sir, and when she went to East Choately to see that Mrs Blaney I was telling you about.'

'The lady who was murdered,' said Sheridan, still seemingly missing the point.

'Yes, sir, that lady,' said Roper.

But Sheridan had not, after all, missed the point. 'What rubbish – with respect, Inspector. The man spends practically every spare minute reading what he believes to be the word of God. He's a deeply religious man.'

Roper left a pause hanging. In the silence, he could hear the soft hiss of gas from the fireplace.

'I borrowed a spanner from your garage tool-rack yesterday afternoon, sir,' he said. 'It had been cleaned recently. But when the people at the forensic laboratory dismantled it, they found blood traces and human hair wrapped around a thread. The blood group and the hair matched with samples the pathologist took from Mrs

179

Blaney. If you take my point, sir. It means we have the weapon, you see, sir. And it was here, on your premises. I really don't think there's any mistake.'

'I see,' said Sheridan. 'And you think that either Gordon Shaw, or my wife, may have used it?'

'I don't think anything, sir,' said Roper. 'Yet.'

'Oh, but that's preposterous,' protested Mrs Worboys. 'I never had a sister. I'd have known.'

'It was a long time ago, Mrs Worboys,' said Roper. The news had plainly knocked the poor woman sideways. She sat where George Sheridan had been sitting a few minutes ago. 'Nineteen-thirty-one. Your mother had her adopted.'

She shook her head, still incredulous. 'No. I'd have known. She would have told me. She *would* have told me.'

'But you did have a brother.'

She didn't reply at once, and when she did her voice was wistful and far away, scarcely more than a whisper.

'Yes,' she said. 'I had a brother. He died. An accident. So stupid.'

Roper waited, hoping she would go on. She was very pale suddenly, very drawn. She looked like a woman who was never far from the brink of hysteria.

'So very stupid.' She fumbled out a handkerchief. Roper thought she was going to burst into tears, as she had the last time he had spoken to her, but the handkerchief was only to occupy her hands. 'We were coming back from America. Mother left a cigarette burning in the ashtray. Gregory was in there. When we came back ...' a shudder of horror shook her, '... the cabin was full of smoke. All alight.' She broke off, screwing and unscrewing the handkerchief between her hands, her knuckles the colour of ivory. 'All alight.'

'We don't have to talk about it if it distresses you, Mrs Worboys.'

'Oh, it does,' she said. 'It distresses me.' She had lifted her head, she was like, really very like, Audrey Blaney. Her huge eyes were bright, but not with distress. What showed in her face now was anger. 'She blamed me, you

180

see. She had to blame somebody, so she blamed me. No, I need to tell someone,' she insisted when Roper tried to stop her again, because she had started to shiver under the strain of her emotions and had become even more deathly pale. 'I've never told anyone. All my life, I've never told. She made me promise. Made me lie. It was easier for her, you see.' Her mouth for a moment was a thin, tight line. 'Oh, I realize now that that was the way it had to be. *Her* way, it was a tragedy. I was only a child, you see, and children have accidents, don't they?'

The story came out rambling, piecemeal, zigzagging and backtracking, the way stories do when painful memories have to be dredged up after being buried for most of a lifetime. The year had been 1947, January, and the fire had taken place aboard the liner SS *Andromeda*, two days out of New York and bound for Liverpool. Aboard had been the widowed Mrs Schwarz, her daughter Greta and baby Gregory. They had travelled in style, in a suite with two bedrooms and a sitting room. On the evening of the second day, Mrs Schwarz had found herself out of cigarettes.

'She asked me if I'd like to go for a walk, I said yes. She wrapped me up. Coat, scarf, gloves, everything. I can remember going up some stairs and along the boat-deck and leaning into the wind and thinking what fun it was. Can you imagine?'

'I take it you'd left your brother in the cabin?' said Roper.

'Yes, we did. Asleep. He slept in Mother's cabin. They'd put a little cot in there for him. We weren't going to be gone long, you see. Just a few minutes. Mother left me outside the bar while she went in for her cigarettes. She was gone for ages. Then she came back. And we started back to our cabin, but then she met somebody on the way and got talking. And I stood there holding her hand and freezing to death. I remember asking her for the cabin key so that I could go back on my own. She kept saying she wouldn't be a moment, she wouldn't be a moment.'

And then, at last, they had gone on their way to the

181

cabin, Mrs Worboys thought that some twenty minutes had passed since they had left it.

'Oh, I can't be certain, of course – children have no real idea of time, do they? Anyway, we got to the cabin. And Mother unlocked the door. And there was smoke. *So* much smoke.' Into Mrs Worboys eyes the tears sprang at last. 'We couldn't get in, couldn't see. A steward came. Mother was screaming, and the steward broke the glass on the fire-alarm and all the bells started clanging. The steward pulled the back of his jacket over his head – I remember that particularly – and went into the smoke. And men were there with fire-extinguishers, then some more men with hoses, and the steward had had to come back out again – his jacket was alight and they had to hose him down, and his hands were burned. Then somebody took me away. The doctor put a needle into my arm.'

She had woken next morning, in her nightclothes and in another, smaller cabin. There was no baby Gregory.

The inquest was held in Liverpool a few days after the SS *Andromeda* had docked – the verdict, one of accidental death. The Liverpool police, who had investigated the fire, drew the conclusion that a burning cigarette, left in a glass ashtray on Mrs Schwarz's bed, must have fallen from the edge of the ashtray and ignited the bedclothes.

'She told me to say that I'd been playing with the ashtray before we went out, that I'd taken it from the dressing table, and left it on the bed.'

'But you think your mother left it on the bed?'

'Yes,' she said. 'I know I wouldn't have touched it – I can't bear even the *smell* of cigarettes, even as a child I hated them. But *I* took the blame, you see. It was easier for her. It made people feel sorry for her – she couldn't afford to be seen as a bad mother, not in her position. And of course I was only a child, so the press was kept out of the inquest, and that suited Mother too ...'

And Mrs Worboys' reward had been a doll, after the inquest.

'It walked, talked, everything. I'd seen one like it in New

182

York. I was absolutely *desperate* for a doll like that.'

'D'you think your mother bought the doll in New York, Mrs Worboys?' asked Morgan, whose thinking was obviously on the same set of rails as Roper's.

'Yes,' said Mrs Worboys. 'She must have. You couldn't buy that sort of thing in England until *years* after the war.'

Which sounded to Roper like more premeditation on Mrs Sheridan's part, the doll a bribe, purchased well before the deed. Mr Schwarz, too, had died in a fire.

'But gradually, over the years, I came to understand her motives, and I realized that I could have done the same thing if the need had ever arisen. I'm not saying I *would* have, but I *could* have, faced with a similar set of circumstances. I mean, what do you do? You make a mistake and your child dies because of it, and you earn your living in the public eye. It must have been a terrible decision for her to have to make.'

Her voice had softened, her posture had relaxed, and the handkerchief now lay loosely between her hands. Whatever had happened all those years ago, Mrs Worboys had come to terms with it and her sympathy clearly lay with her mother.

Events began to gather momentum in the early afternoon. And one of them, at least, provided the first faint glimmer at the end of the tunnel.

The first sight of Mower was his hand, with a pound-note in it, that stretched between Roper and Morgan as they sat on high stools at the counter of the Crown and Compass.

'Thought I'd find you here,' he said. 'What's your poison?'

'Depends what we're celebrating,' said Roper, for Superintendent Mower's wallet was renowned for seeing the daylight but rarely.

'Mrs Lawson's letter.'

'Scotch,' said Roper.

'The same,' said Morgan.

They adjourned to a more secluded corner at the other

end of the bar, where Mower opened his briefcase and took out a transparent evidence bag with a several-times folded envelope inside it. He slid it across the wooden table.

'Where d'you find it?' asked Roper, taking it up and shaking the envelope into his hand.

'In Mrs Blaney's kitchen,' said Mower. 'In her rice tin.'

Roper beaked his fingers into the long manilla envelope – it was addressed to Mrs Audrey Blaney, care of a solicitor in Yeovil – and extracted the folded wad of cheap and grubby blue notepaper that was folded inside it.

The handwriting was shaky, the letter dated the 2nd of July, 1974, two years, roughly, before Granny Lawson had died. Roper started to read:

My dear Daughter,

I am writing this for you to read after I have gone. I do so because one day I intended to tell you who your real mother was and so that you would know all about her. I was never able to find the courage to do that.

What I could never tell you – and how I have agonized over telling you even now – is that your real mother was Rita Cavallo the actress and your father was a man called Angus Kilcullen. He died before you were born but I believe that Rita Cavallo is still alive, although I lost touch with her many years ago.

The full story of your mother's life is laid out in a scrapbook that I have made (you will find it in the little brown attaché case on top of my wardrobe with all my insurance policies and things). I began it as a record of your mother's life with the idea that one day I would show it to you. Only as time went on did I realise that I was putting together a record of evil, although I should have known from the very beginning …

The next few pages described the events that Peter Blaney had talked of this morning, Granny Lawson stranded in Colwyn Bay with nothing but debts, the visit of Rita Cavallo in the tobacconist's shop with her offer of money. Granny Lawson's flight to Worthing and the boarding-house near the sea-front with the baby she had illegally adopted in exchange for a new life. The letter continued:

What followed you will be able to see in the book. I hope you can read my writing. All that I have written there, I am sure, is true. I even wonder sometimes if she killed that first husband of hers, Sidney Manders, and that little baby she had in America – poor little thing. It would take a terrible woman to kill her own child wouldn't it, but it wouldn't surprise me if she had, really it wouldn't.

What the book will not tell you – and how I still wonder whether I should tell you – is that I am sure that Rita killed Mr Kilcullen. You see, she was not with me the night he committed suicide and I only told the police that she was because I believed that she was in some other kind of trouble – and I was also young and not very wise and thought I was helping a friend – although as soon as the inquest was over I guessed the truth. But by then it was too late and I was too frightened to tell them that I had been alone that night because I believed I had committed perjury and might go to prison.

The rest you know – except for one thing. She promised to pay for your keep until you were 21. She never did. Once when I was very down at the beginning of the war I wrote to her and asked her to help me. In her reply she denied all knowledge of you. I never pressed the matter because I feared hurting you if the truth ever came out.

That I took her money for adopting you I hope you have by now forgiven me. Even though I realized by then that she had used me I was so desperately in need of money that I took you in. It seemed such an easy way out at the time – and such a lot of money that it pushed all other considerations aside. But never doubt that I grew to love you and devoted my life to you.

I swear, my dear, that all I have written is true.

All my love

Mother – for I hope that is what I became.

'If that isn't a blackmail lever,' said Mower, over his scotch. 'I don't know what is.'

And Roper agreed.

It would seem, if it were all true, that Granny Lawson

had kept a log of Rita Cavallo's lifetime of evil doings and subsequently, at the end of her days, she had passed that log and this letter over to her daughter, like a legacy.

Was that why Rita Cavallo, in the persona of Mrs Manders, had gone thrice to East Choately? And had she not merely visited, but been summoned? To make some kind of recompense, which finally she had not been prepared to pay?

The Bone of Contention gave a tug to the tops of each of her shiny red wellingtons, then extended her plump little legs.

'Daddy bought me these,' she confided solemnly. 'Last week.'

'They're nice,' said Kate. 'Daddy buys all your things, does he?'

'Yes,' the child said. 'He buys me lots.'

The two of them sat on the oak bench a few yards beyond the green gate set in the wall. The sun was shining brightly for the first time in days.

'Have you got a mummy?' the child asked.

'No,' said Kate. 'I haven't.'

'I haven't either,' the child said. She spoke without rancour, swinging her crossed ankles. 'Does your daddy look after you, too?'

'Sort of,' said Kate, trying to stifle the lump that was rising in her throat. 'You don't come up here with your Daddy every day?'

'No. I stay with Granny Erskine. She's got a dog. Muffin. Daddy calls it Allsorts.'

'But you're not staying with her today?'

'She's gone to the hospital. She's got veins.'

Kate forebore to smile in the face of such gravity. 'Can I ask you something, Janey? Did your Daddy send you down here to talk to me?'

'No,' said Janey. 'He told me not to bovver you.' She extended her legs and contemplated the twin reflections in the toes of her wellingtons. 'But I got bored. I get bored a lot.'

Then Bill Erskine's silhouette appeared at the top of the slope, and he bawled, 'Janey! Lunch!' and the child slipped off the bench and raced pell-mell up the grass to join him. They went off holding hands. Neither of them looked backward once, and the hard oak bench suddenly felt like the loneliest place in the world.

SEVENTEEN

ROPER LAID THE ADJUSTABLE SPANNER, recently returned from Forensic and still in its polythene evidence bag, across Shaw's open hands.

'Take a closer look, Mr Shaw.'

'I don't need to, sir,' insisted Shaw. 'I've never seen it before.'

'I took it off your tool-rack myself, Mr Shaw. You saw me do it.'

Shaw tried to hand it back. Roper declined to take it.

'So you're denying it's yours?'

'Yes, sir,' said Shaw.

'And you're denying that I took it down from your rack, even though you saw me do it? And Sergeant Morgan here saw me do it?'

'No, sir,' said Shaw. 'I didn't say that. I agree you took a spanner from the rack in the garage, sir. But it wasn't this one.'

'It was that one, Mr Shaw,' insisted Morgan. 'Mr Roper asked you when you'd last used it, and you told him it was to release the sink-trap in the kitchen. At Christmas.'

'So I did, sir,' agreed Shaw. 'But I was clearly mistaken.'

'You identified it.'

'I assumed, sir,' said Shaw. 'I saw this other gentleman take it down from the rack. If you recall, sir, I was standing with you by the door. We were some distance away.'

'And when I came back you were cleaning your glasses,' said Roper.

'Yes, sir,' agreed Shaw. 'I do believe I was.'

'How far can you see without your glasses?'

'About a foot, sir, in a good light.'

'If you're messing us about, Mr Shaw ...' said Morgan.

'Oh, indeed I'm not, sir,' protested Shaw. 'I wouldn't dream of doing that, sir, and that's the truth. I agree that this does *look* like the one that was in the garage, but if you examine it closely, sir, this one was made in Germany. The one I'm used to using, I'm sure, was made in England. It also doesn't feel right, sir. The handle seems to be fractionally longer.'

'You've got a leather coat, Mr Shaw,' said Roper, chancing his arm as far as he dared. The Forensic Laboratory had at last identified the predominant débris under Mrs Blaney's fingernails. It had been leather, dyed black. 'We'd like to see it, please.'

'I don't have such a thing, sir,' said Shaw. 'I couldn't possibly afford one, not on my wages. And, anyway, I wouldn't go in for that sort of thing, sir. It smatters of personal vanity.'

'So you wouldn't mind if we looked in your wardrobe?'

'Sir,' said Shaw. 'You may look wherever you wish. I've told you before, sir: I have nothing to hide and nothing to explain.'

They looked in Shaw's wardrobe. Apart from his shoes and a couple of trouser belts, there had been nothing in there made of leather; and when Sheridan took them up to his wife's more extensive wardrobe, neither did she seem to possess any kind of leather coat unless, as Morgan suggested, that lady was currently wearing it, wherever she happened to be. Which left Joel Worboys and his girlfriend – both of whom, as Roper recalled, had had leather jackets, with, in Worboys' case, leather trousers too – and, however far-fetched the idea sounded, Mrs Blaney's son and his new wife, both of whom, when Roper had seen them, had been clad in black leather from head to foot. Except that young Mr and Mrs Blaney had spent last weekend in France – or so they had said. And now Joel Worboys and Serena Van Elst were gone. According to Mrs Shaw, George Sheridan had sent the pair of them packing soon after breakfast this morning.

'Reckon we ought to be chasing after 'em?' asked Morgan.

'Don't know yet,' said Roper. He and Morgan sat in the bright autumn sunshine on an oak bench a few yards beyond the green gate set in the wall. Further down the path, a child Roper hadn't seen before was playing with a beach-ball that was almost as large as herself.

'My missus'd give her eye-teeth for a place like this,' said Morgan.

'Bet she wouldn't,' said Roper. 'Think of the work.'

They fell to silence for a while. The little girl moved closer with her ball.

'Know what's bothering me?' said Roper, to the trees in the middle distance.

'What's that?' said Morgan.

'I've just thought of something: say Mrs Sheridan did burn something in the boiler furnace during last Saturday night – why didn't she burn the scrapbook at the same time?'

'We don't know she burned anything yet.'

'Somebody did,' said Roper. 'Somebody came down in the wee small hours and burned something in the furnace, they left the flue-damper open and Shaw found the ashes in the morning. Then Lindsey finds a scrapbook and Mrs Sheridan gets very uptight about it. On the same afternoon, Lindsey notices the scrapbook's gone from where it was, and she's also pretty certain she saw black ashes floating out of the chimney. And Mrs Lawson kept a scrapbook, just like the one Lindsey saw.'

'So what are you getting at exactly?'

'I don't know,' said Roper. 'Yet.' And nor at the moment did he, but his ramshackle rationale would, he knew, get somewhere eventually. Two burnings in the furnace, twelve or so hours apart. Why twelve or so hours apart? Why had the burnings not been simultaneous? The scrapbook, if it had been evidence – and he was sure it had been – had not been destroyed until Sunday afternoon. Had whatever had been burned on Saturday night/Sunday morning been evidence too – bloodstained clothing, perhaps?

The beach-ball came scudding by. Morgan stopped it with the side of his shoe and tapped it back.

The child approached. 'Thank you,' she said, and scooped up the ball. Hugging it close, she manoeuvred herself up on to the bench between Roper and Morgan. She regarded them frankly, and settled for Roper.

'I'm Jane,' she said. 'What's your name?'

'Douglas, my love,' said Roper, as gravely. 'And it's very nice to meet you, but hasn't your mummie told you not to talk to people you don't know?'

'I haven't got a mummie,' she said. 'But Daddy says you're policemen, so that's all right, isn't it? He's up there.' A woolly-mittened finger pointed up the slope. 'Working. Will you play ball with me? For a minute?'

'I will,' said Morgan. 'Let's go further down the path, shall we?'

They went off down the path, kicking the ball between them. Morgan was an old hand at that. He had two children of his own.

Alone for a few minutes, Roper lit a cheroot and sat hunched over it, his hands clasped loosely between his knees and his face staring back at him from a small puddle that was drying as he watched it between his feet.

Two burnings. Two different times.

Two separate sets of circumstances.

Two different people, perhaps? That thought hadn't occurred to him before. Two different people with something important to incinerate. Not one person, but two. With quite separate motives.

And Mrs Sheridan had stayed on here until Monday, hadn't she? She'd killed somebody – her daughter – on Saturday, and yet all day last Sunday she had gone nowhere. She had slept, eaten and conversed, all in the bosom of her family. And yet on *Monday* morning she had taken flight, but not until Monday.

Smoke from his cheroot drifted up past his cheeks. Further along the path the child – it could only be Erskine's – had discovered a new game. If she kicked the ball up the slope, instead of along the path, it rolled only slowly down to Morgan and neither she nor he knew quite where it was going to finish up. She was a pretty child.

Cheroot ash hissed to extinction in the puddle.

Why had Mrs Sheridan stayed until Monday? And who had picked up her and the two dogs out there in the lane?

Who, and why?

Footfalls sounded along the path to his right, from the direction of the house. It was Katherine Lindsey, in a smart grey suit, with a rollneck red pullover under the jacket. She moved slowly, but not casually, her eyes already fixed on him from some distance away so that he knew that he was her ultimate destination.

He rose as she came closer. She stopped a couple of paces away, her hands stuffed into the pockets of her open jacket.

'I saw you from my bedroom window,' she said. 'I wondered if it was all right if I left today. I mean, do you have any more questions to ask me?'

'No, I don't think so, Miss Lindsey,' he said. He put out his hand. Hers was icy cold. 'I thought you were staying over until tomorrow.'

'No,' she said. 'I've changed my mind.'

'You've been a great help,' he said. 'I really do mean that. Shaw driving you to the station?'

'No,' she said, smiling. 'Not likely. I'm hiring a car. Mrs Shaw's fixing that for me now.'

Behind Roper came the hollow thud of the ball and a gurgle of child's laughter.

'I was wrong, you know,' she said.

'About what?'

'Her. Rita Cavallo. She didn't kill anybody. I really thought she had, you know.'

'Perhaps she did,' said Roper.

She shook her head. 'That actor, Chester Barclay, died in a car crash in Nice. She was over here making a film. And Mr Manders chucked himself off Tower Bridge, there were a dozen witnesses. And Mr Schwarz's fire happened when Rita was miles away at a party. He was dead drunk, apparently, the only people in the house with

192

him were the housekeeper and the daughter.' She shrugged. 'So I got it all wrong, didn't I?'

'Not entirely, Miss Lindsey,' he said. 'You were right about the undertaker's man and the child's coffin. The son died on board ship, when Mrs Sheridan and the daughter were coming back from the States. There was some kind of fire in their cabin.'

'That makes three fires,' she said. 'But then they do say history has a habit of repeating itself, don't they?'

'How come three?' asked Roper.

'That's how Mrs Worboys first husband died. He died in a fire, too. Hampstead. Nineteen-sixty-eight. My friend turned that one up by accident.'

The child joined them, flushed and breathless after her romp with Morgan.

'Why are you dressed like that?' she said to Lindsey.

'I'm going home, Janey. Back to London.'

The child's face fell. She was obviously about to lose another playmate. Lindsey didn't look all that happy, either.

'You must come and say goodbye to the froggies first. You must, you *really* must.' She reached up and grasped Lindsey's hand firmly and started to tug her away.

Roper and Morgan watched them go, Roper still thoughtfully digesting what Lindsey had just told him.

'That,' accused Erskine, 'sounds like a bad line from a bad movie.'

'I know,' she said. 'But it's true. I really do have to get back to London.'

'And you can't wait to get away.'

'It isn't like that at all,' she said, although it was. 'I could have just walked out of the front door, you know. I didn't have to come out here.'

'Look,' he said. 'I'm sorry about this morning, but I really didn't bring Janey along here to soften you up. My mother usually looks after her, but she's had to go along to the hospital.'

'I know,' she said. 'She told me. Your mother's got veins.'

'Yes,' he said. 'That sounds like Janey. She's a bit like a parrot.'

'You've done a good job,' she said. 'She's a lovely kid.'

He stabbed his fork into the grass between them and thrust it in deeper with the sole of his boot. 'I don't suppose,' he said, leaning on it, and looking only a shade less miserable than she felt, 'that there's anything I can possibly say to you that'll persuade you to stop over until tomorrow?'

'What's so special about tomorrow?'

'I could drive you back to London – I've got to go to Harrow to make up my mind about that garden centre. And Harrow's not a million miles from Hammersmith, is it?'

'What about Janey?'

'My mother'll look after her for the day.'

The child came running excitedly from the wooden bridge. 'They're back again! They really are. Come and see.'

'But she was only a child,' said Morgan. He and Roper sat side by side on the bench by the gate. The subject of the conversation was Mrs Worboys. 'How old would she have been? Eight? Nine?'

'She only had to strike a couple of matches,' said Roper. 'How old were you when you first started playing with matches?'

'About five,' said Morgan. 'And I got a bloody good clip round the ear.'

'So did I,' said Roper. 'But she was eight or nine. And according to the inquest on Schwarz he was drunk at the time, which was probably why Mrs Schwarz went to that party on her own. She goes out, and the stepdaughter creeps to wherever her stepfather's sleeping it off and strikes a few strategic matches. And it could be Mrs Worboys was lying to me yesterday about what happened to her baby brother on that ship. Supposing she put a match to the bedclothes, before she and her mother went along to the ship's bar to get those cigarettes?'

194

'She was still only a kid,' said Morgan. 'She would have to have been a bit bloody evil, wouldn't she?'

'Perhaps she still is,' said Roper. 'I haven't told you the best part yet.' Roper rose, so did Morgan who fell in beside him as he started back for the house. 'According to Lindsey, Mrs Worboys' first husband died in a fire, too. Up in Hampstead, in sixty-eight.'

'Could still all be coincidence,' said Morgan. 'Anyway, what's all that got to do with Mrs Sheridan scarpering – and Mrs Blaney?'

'Perhaps it hasn't,' said Roper. 'But I keep asking myself why Mrs Sheridan hung about here until Monday morning. Or if she did.'

'We know she did,' said Morgan. 'Lindsey saw her, Farmer Watcherley saw her.' He jerked a thumb over his shoulder. 'She went out through that gate.'

'Somebody put something in that furnace on Saturday night,' said Roper. 'And somebody burned something else in it on Sunday afternoon. Supposing it was two different somebodies? And suppose it was the other somebody that Lindsey and Watcherley saw walking the dogs last Monday morning? They never saw her face, did they? Just a fur coat and a couple of dogs that they thought they recognised. It could have been anybody. And what about those two dogs? Why did she bother to take 'em with her when she knew she wasn't coming back?'

They walked a few paces more. A snatch of conversation Roper had had with George Sheridan last Tuesday afternoon surfaced briefly ...

'I want you to make a 'phone call, Dan, from Sergeant Morrison's place.'

They parted company by the steps down to the boiler-room, Roper to go into the house and Morgan to drive along to Morrison's cottage to make the 'phone call. The kitchen was empty, although a couple of cups and saucers were set out on a tray on the table and the electric kettle was just beginning to murmur. Roper all but bumped into Mrs Shaw as they met in the doorway out to the passage.

195

'Mrs Worboys about, is she, Mrs Shaw?' he asked stepping back and aside.

'Yes, sir. She and Mr Worboys have just come back from Dorchester. I think she's in the drawing-room with Mr Sheridan.'

Roper heard their two voices raised through the open doorway of the drawing-room as he reached the end of the passage.

'Look, Greta,' Sheridan was saying. 'I'm deeply sorry that I'm not more concerned. I know I ought to be, but I'm not.'

Over on Roper's left, down the narrower of the two staircases, Shaw appeared carrying a heavy suitcase in each hand. He set them down on the coconut mat while he opened the front door, then carried them down the steps to a black Jaguar that was drawn up outside with its boot open. It looked as if the Worboys were leaving, and with a haste that was almost indecent.

'You were always a selfish man, George.'

'So your mother's always telling me.'

Roper drew back into the passage as Shaw returned and closed the front door again. As he went up the stairs, so was Julius Worboys descending them.

'There are two more to come down,' mumbled Worboys, as they passed each other. 'Know where my wife is, by any chance?'

'The drawing-room, sir,' said Shaw. 'I think she's saying goodbye to Mr Sheridan.'

Roper watched Worboys tread ponderously towards the drawing-room.

'Hallo, Julius.' Sheridan's voice again, ironically cheerful. 'Ready for the off, are we?'

'Almost,' said Worboys, his hand on the drawing-room doorknob. 'You seem to be missing a coat.'

'I've packed it,' his wife's voice replied. 'I thought I'd go home in this one.'

Worboys turned and started back across the hall. Shaw was on the stairs again with two more suitcases.

'Could I have a word, Mr Worboys?' said Roper, coming

196

out of the passage and catching up with Worboys as he reached the foot of the stairs. 'And you can leave those two cases here if you would, Mr Shaw, and bring back the rest of Mr Worboys' luggage from the car.'

Worboys stopped in his tracks, and Roper distinctly saw his shoulders brace before he slowly turned round and looked Roper straight in the eye.

'This is very high-handed of you, old chap,' he complained loftily. 'Aren't you exceeding your authority a little?'

'Possibly, sir,' said Roper. 'You and your wife leaving, are you, sir?'

'We are,' said Worboys. 'Is there some reason why we shouldn't?'

'No, sir, not particularly. Does your wife own a leather coat, sir?'

'She does,' said Worboys. Despite his show of dignity, a lot of the watchfulness went out of his eyes, almost as if he had expected to be questioned about something more serious.

'May I see it, sir.'

'Well, yes, I suppose so. I take it there's some point to all this?'

Shaw came back with the two suitcases he had taken out earlier and stood them beside the two he had just brought down.

'Do you mind opening them, sir,' said Roper.

Worboys knelt clumsily, tipping one of the cases on to its bottom and snapping open the catches. His hands were decidedly unsteady.

Footsteps sounded on the tiles behind Roper. They were Mrs Worboys', her bony face thrust forward on her thin neck and her eyes glittering with anger.

'What the hell's going on?' she raged. 'What *are* you doing?'

'He only wants to see your coat, dear,' said Worboys, still on his knees, his tone placatory. 'That's all.'

'Your leather coat, Mrs Worboys,' said Roper, slowly and carefully drawing his hands out of his raincoat pockets. Worboys might not make any trouble but his wife looked downright dangerous. Crazy dangerous.

'I haven't a leather coat,' she spat. 'What leather coat?' Her gaze flashed from Roper to her husband, to Shaw, back again to Roper, her huge eyes crafty and wary.

'Yours, dear,' said a befuddled-looking Worboys, clutching the newel-post in his struggle to regain his feet. 'The one you wore down here.'

'I didn't,' she said, staring hard at him. 'I wore *this* one.'

'No, dear,' said Worboys. 'I'm sure you didn't.'

Sheridan was in the hall now, come to see what the commotion was about.

What happened next was so swift that it caught Roper unawares, and if Shaw hadn't been standing between her and the front door Mrs Worboys might have chosen to make her break that way.

Roper thought she was turning to complain to Sheridan, but after taking a couple of paces towards him, she suddenly lurched off at a splay-footed run towards the passage to the kitchen. Roper leapt a suitcase and chased after her, almost caught her, but she'd snatched the passage door shut after her and while he was still wrenching at the doorknob he heard the key turn in the lock and fall to the floor on the other side, then more running footsteps, and he realised how stupid he'd been to send Morgan away.

'How many ways out of this place?'

'Only the two side ways,' said Sheridan.

Roper walked back quickly to the front door. 'You go left and I'll go right, Mr Shaw. That all right with you?'

'Yes, sir,' said Shaw, not looking all that keen. 'I don't have to physically restrain her, do I, sir?'

'Just cut her off,' said Roper impatiently. 'And grab her if you have to. All right?' He hauled the front door open and hurried down the steps. Shaw followed him out, going the other way, walking at first, then breaking reluctantly into a run.

'You all right, dear?' asked Mrs Shaw, as Kate rushed in

198

from the garden carrying Janey Erskine.

'Tell you later,' Kate said breathlessly, swinging the bemused child on to one of the kitchen chairs. 'Keep an eye on her, will you, Mrs Shaw? Those two policemen still about?'

'Yes, dear, one of them's out in the hall. But there's a terrible commotion going on out there—'

There was a reverberating crash, running footsteps, then Mrs Worboys erupted into the kitchen, white and staring, eyes everywhere at once, working out quickly that both her ways around the table were barred and that the lesser of the two evils was probably Mrs Shaw who was still standing by the cooker with her mouth open, and that on the draining board was a clutter of wet knives. She swiftly snatched one up in the same moment that Kate darted forward and gathered up Janey Erskine, because Mrs Worboys' crazy eyes had taken her in, and bundled the child behind her as Mrs Worboys came around the table.

'Give her to me!'

'Not on your bloody life,' said Kate, the rush of adrenalin making her legs completely useless – the knife was a bread-knife – blunt ended, but no less fearsome as Mrs Worboys waved it about. Then Mrs Worboys sprang, pushing the knife up into Kate's face while her other hand tried to make a grab for the child's wrist. Then bedlam, the child screaming, Kate struggling to fend the woman off, Mrs Shaw coming round the table to help, then a man, Shaw – Kate had never ever thought she'd thank God for the sight of Shaw – she thought he'd pinion Mrs Worboys, but all the stupid man did was to wrap his hands around the saw-toothed blade of the bread-knife, and twist it and twist it, the two of them struggling in silence, until Shaw's blood came, running down the blade of the knife and the handle and Mrs Worboys' hand. And then another man was there and Mrs Worboys was struggling and kicking, and there was a click of metal and then another, and Mrs Worboys was flat on her face on the floor with her hands behind her back. The detective was straddling her and holding her down like a movie cowboy on a bucking

199

bronco, telling her to behave her bloody self or she was going to get hurt and that he was arresting her on suspicion of murdering Mrs Audrey Blaney in East Choately last Saturday night and that anything she said was going to be taken down and used in evidence, so she'd better put up or shut up – which Kate thought was definitely not gentlemanly but was admirably controlled of him in the circumstances because if she'd been him she'd have beaten the living daylights out of her.

Only then did Shaw go to the sink and let the knife he was holding fall into it and turn on the cold tap.

'You all right, Mr Shaw?' asked the detective, still pinning down the writhing and swearing Mrs Worboys.

'Yes, sir, thank you, sir,' said Shaw, and Kate's stomach curdled as she saw how red the rush of water was after it had run over Shaw's outstretched hand.

The detective struggled breathlessly to his feet, hauling up Mrs Worboys by the scruff of her coat-collar. The kitchen was full now – Bill Erskine, George Sheridan, the other detective, the village bobby and a big beefy woman with three stripes on her blue sleeve who wasn't going to stand any nonsense from anybody and to whom Mrs Worboys, still with death in her eyes, was handed over. Kate was relieved to see that she was securely handcuffed behind her back.

'Take her to your place, Sergeant,' the detective said to Morrison. 'Caution her again, and if she cuts up nasty lock her up. She's bloody dangerous.'

Mrs Worboys was bundled outside, silent now. There was blood all over the front of the detective's raincoat and one of its buttons was missing. He straightened his crooked tie.

'Can somebody get Mr Shaw along to a hospital?' he said.

'I will,' said Erskine.

'That's very kind of you, sir,' said Shaw calmly, his hand now wrapped in a towel.

'Janey all right?' asked Erskine.

The child sidled out from behind Kate's skirt. 'They

were fighting,' she proclaimed proudly. '*Proper* fighting.'

'She's all right,' said Kate.

'You told the Inspector about the other business yet?'

Kate shook her head. 'Didn't get a chance.'

'What other business is that, Miss?' said Roper.

'Mr Erskine's found Mrs Sheridan,' she said.

EIGHTEEN

JULIUS WORBOYS WAS SITTING AT the foot of the stairs, still surrounded by his suitcases, his head in his hands, as huddled a picture of abject despair as Roper had seen in many a long year.

'I need to talk to you, sir,' said Roper. 'D'you feel up to it?'

Worboys nodded miserably in his hands.

'We've just had to take your wife into custody, sir. I'm sorry.'

Worboys' face slowly lifted, his eyes lingering momentarily on the front of Roper's raincoat and widening.

'Is that blood?' he asked anxiously.

'Yes, sir,' said Roper.

'My wife …?'

'She's fine, sir. Mr Shaw cut himself.'

Worboys struggled to his feet, hanging on to the newel-post, broken, his jowls white, all dignity gone.

'You'll be cautioning me, I take it?'

'Do I need to, sir?' asked Roper.

Worboys nodded, his eyes cast down. 'Yes,' he whispered softly. 'Oh, yes. I helped her, you see. So foolish. So very, *very* foolish.'

The house was quiet again. Up by the lake a half-a-dozen cadets were filling sandbags with soil and two more were carrying a petrol-driven pump across the lawn. Weygood the pathologist was there too, together with his assistant and the Coroner's Officer and a couple of technicians from the Forensic laboratory, wearing fisherman's waders, who could do nothing yet except stand about and have a quiet smoke until all the sandbags were filled and put in place.

'It was about one o'clock,' continued Worboys, hunched over the dining-room table. 'Monday morning. She came into my room. And woke me. And told me that her mother was dead. In the bath. I told her we'd better get a doctor. She told me not to be stupid. Her mother was dead.' He passed a hand across his broad forehead, struggling to marshal his facts into their right and proper order. 'I got into my dressing-gown and went with her. Rita was in the bath. Quite dead. Her eyes open. So horrible. There was no water. The plug was hanging from a tap. Greta, my wife, shut the bathroom door.'

Roper waited. Morgan turned another page of his notebook.

'She told me that she'd *had* to do it. I didn't understand. "Do what?" I said. "Kill her," she said. Initially, I didn't believe her. Couldn't believe her. I love her, you see. But she had. She showed me the marks on Rita's neck where she'd pushed her head under the water. And the scratches on her own arms and wrists. Evidence, you see. The police would know it was murder. I had to help her, she said.'

'And did you?' asked Roper. 'Did you help her, sir?'

Worboys nodded miserably, 'I love her, you see. And there was so much at stake. My work. My wife would go to prison. And I couldn't have born that. Not prison. Not for her. And, God help me, I never liked Rita. A cold, mean woman. Always was. Poor old George. How on earth that dear man ever put up with her for so long …

'We dried her. Terrible job. I could hardly bring myself to touch her. We took a blanket from her bed, put her in it, like a hammock. I took the head and my wife took the feet. I'd got dressed by then, or have I told you that? Not that it matters really, does it, whether I was dressed or not?

'We used the back stairs. We thought we'd bury her in one of the flower beds, then it occurred to me that we'd have to bury her deeply or there would be a chance of poor Erskine digging her up again, and that was too terrible to contemplate. Then I thought of the pond that Erskine was making. He'd lined the inside and the next day, so he'd told me, he was going to start filling it. The pond was the only place in the garden that wasn't likely to be dug up again. And we'd only have to bury her deep enough to cover her. It seemed by far the quickest way, you see. And Erskine's spoil heap wasn't far away, and he'd left his tools and wheelbarrow in the old greenhouse. He wasn't likely to notice a few more inches of earth scattered over the heap.'

Worboys had dug and his wife had wheeled away the spoil from the hole and spread it over the heap that Erskine had made further up the garden. It had taken them the best part of two hours before the hole was long enough and deep enough.

'We put her in, covered her, Greta trod the soil in – I couldn't – then folded the polythene sheeting back over the place. Greta swept it, and I put the bricks back. When I shone the torch over it, it looked just the way it had before.'

The two of them had then returned to the house, dried the damp blanket in front of the electric fire in Mrs Sheridan's bedroom. There had been a few grass stains on it but they were not immediately obvious. The blanket was returned to the bed, the bed made tidy, then rumpled again to make it look as if someone had slept in it. The time was almost four o'clock in the morning.

'I couldn't sleep,' said Worboys. 'Afterwards. Not at all. So terribly exhausted.' He drew a finger and thumb together wearily across his eyebrows. 'Then I heard the rain. So much rain. And I knew – I thought – that everything was going to be all right.'

But of course it had not been. The rain had not been able to cleanse Worboys' conscience.

The fraud case that he had been defending in Dorchester had finished earlier that afternoon. 'My wife wanted to stay on here for a few more days, to make everything appear normal, but I couldn't. Not with all that behind us.'

'Tell us about last Monday morning, sir,' said Roper.

'Monday?' said Worboys, blinking vaguely. 'Oh, yes, Monday. We couldn't bring them back to the house, you see. So we had to let them go.'

'Them, sir?' said Morgan.

'The dogs,' explained Worboys. 'We couldn't bring them back.'

'Why did you take them in the first place, sir?' asked Roper.

'For verisimilitude,' said Worboys. 'My wife is much taller and thinner than Rita. She thought the dogs would lend credence.'

'In the event that someone saw her?' said Roper.

'Oh, someone *had* to see her,' said Worboys. 'That was the very essence of the idea. If she hadn't been seen, there was no point.'

'Supposing she'd come face to face with somebody?'

Worboys lifted his shoulders. 'It was a risk, wasn't it? Personally, I was absolutely terrified that it would all go wrong.' He sighed massively. 'I almost wish now that it had.'

It had been Worboys who had been waiting out on the road and driven off as soon as his wife had bundled the dogs and herself into the car. The sighting of the roadside gritting-bin had been fortuitous. Worboys had pulled in beside it, and, as soon as there was a gap in the traffic, Mrs Worboys had stuffed in both her mother's fur coat and the bifurcated dog-lead. Neither had realised at the time that they had thrown away the gate key, too. The dogs had been let loose at the same time. Worboys had driven on until he found a suitable spot to turn the car, then driven back to the house. His wife had gone in, as if she had just been for a walk – as Roper had suspected, she had been wearing another coat under her mother's fur – and using her mother's doorkey. Worboys had then driven on to the village and bought a newspaper. Back at the house again, he parked a few yards beyond the bus stop and returned to the house on foot – his excuse, if anyone saw him, that he had strolled up to the village to buy a newspaper. But his wife had been watching for his return and let him into the house. No one, it appeared, had even noticed they had been out.

'What about the boots your wife was wearing, Mr Worboys?' asked Roper. 'What happened to those?'

Because the one thing, or, rather, the pair of things that Mrs Worboys had not thrown into the gritting-bin had been her mother's old boots.

'We forgot about those,' admitted Worboys. 'We had to dispose of them later on our way into Dorchester. A litter-bin. They're probably still there,' he added helpfully.

'Who put the oil on the gate-hinges and the lock?'

'I did,' confessed Worboys. 'After we'd buried her. After we'd decided what to do in the morning. We experimented with the key. It wouldn't turn. Rust, you see. And I was frightened the hinges might have seized too. Greta found a can of oil in the garage.'

'She was able to get into the garage?'

'The key,' said Worboys. 'It hangs on a board by the kitchen door.'

Roper gave him only a brief pause.

'Now tell us about Saturday, sir.'

'Saturday?' Worboys repeated dully. 'What about Saturday?'

'Your drive down from London, sir,' said Roper. 'On Saturday evening.'

Worboys looked genuinely puzzled. 'I'm not following you,' he said.

'You told Mr Sheridan you'd been held up by a traffic accident on the A31. That's why you arrived late.'

'Yes,' agreed Worboys, after a moment or two. 'We did tell him that.'

'My sergeant checked with the Hampshire Traffic Division a while back, sir,' said Roper. 'There was no traffic accident reported on the A31 anywhere near Ringwood between half-past four on Saturday afternoon and a quarter to midnight.'

'It was a little story we made up to tell George,' said Worboys. 'My wife did. And once we'd told it, we had to keep it up. I wouldn't offend old George for the world.'

'Story, sir?' said Roper. 'Why did you need a story?'

Because neither Worboys nor his wife liked coming to this house, and driving down here on Saturday night Mrs Worboys had suddenly suggested that they looked for somewhere to have a meal to keep them away a little longer.

'But we told them we'd be there by eight o'clock,' had said Worboys.

'Oh, we'll think up a story to tell them,' his wife had reassured him.

'So what *did* you do, Mr Worboys?' asked Morgan.

'We found a restaurant,' said Worboys. 'Eventually.'

'Eventually, sir?'

It had taken them some time to find one. They had passed several but Mrs Worboys had not liked the look of any of them. The one they had finally settled for had been beside the A30. It had been on the first floor of a public house.

'Between Sherborne and Yeovil, Mr Worboys?' asked Roper.

'Yes,' said Worboys. 'I do believe it was.' But he could not be absolutely certain because his wife had been driving and, of course, it had been dark.

'So your wife chose this particular place?'

'Yes,' said Worboys. 'She did.' He still looked honestly puzzled at the new line the questions were taking.

'What time did you arrive, sir?' asked Morgan. 'At this pub.'

'I suppose about eight-forty-five,' said Worboys. 'Perhaps a little afterwards.'

He had taken a drink in the bar, and reserved a table in the restaurant upstairs for as near nine o'clock as possible, while his wife went off to make the belated 'phone call to her mother to explain their lateness. She was gone for some time. She returned, the call still unmade because the public telephone in the lounge-bar lobby had seemed to be out of order. She had spotted a 'phone booth across the road, but there was someone using it and two more people waiting outside. She would try again later.

She attempted to make the call again between dinner and dessert – Worboys thought the time then would have been somewhere around ten o'clock. On that occasion his wife was gone for only a few minutes. The phone box across the road was still occupied. At this juncture, the anxious Worboys had suggested that they had better forego the dessert and be on their way, Rita and George were likely to be getting worried by now.

But Mrs Worboys had insisted upon leisurely finishing her meal, complete with coffee and a liqueur for herself and a brandy for her husband. And another brandy when he had downed the first one.

'What sort of mood was your wife in, sir?' asked Roper.

'The way she used to be,' said Worboys. He spoke wistfully, as if the way his wife had once been was infinitely more preferable to the way she was now. It was the woman who she used to be with whom he had fallen in love. Things had clearly changed since then.

'And how was that, sir?'

'Bright, sparkling,' said Worboys fondly. 'Amusing. We talked of things we hadn't talked of in years.'

Roper gave him another pause, almost felt some sympathy for the man.

'Did your wife eventually get around to phoning her mother, Mr Worboys?'

'Yes,' said Worboys. He was less certain now about the time. He had, he admitted, by then consumed yet another brandy and his wife had suggested that he indulged in a cigar. A special treat. Mrs Worboys did not smoke herself and disliked, as a general rule, even the smell of tobacco.

'It might have been about a quarter to eleven,' said Worboys.

Roper suspected it might have been a few minutes earlier. Some time around ten-forty, which was when Shaw had said Madam had finally reappeared at the car and told him to drive her home. Whether or not the public telephone in the pub had been working last Saturday night could easily be established later. What was more important were the times Mrs Worboys had chosen to try and make those 'phone calls to her mother.

How frustrated she must have been, on the first two occasions, to have seen a black Jaguar parked near the telephone box and with its driver sitting in it – perhaps even recognized the car and known to whom it belonged – from which she would have deduced that either George Sheridan, or her mother, were paying a call on her recently discovered half-sister. The last thing Mrs Worboys had needed last Saturday night had been witnesses, especially witnesses who would recognize her at a single glance.

On the final occasion, Mrs Worboys had finally got through to Milton St Philip's. Her mother was out and she had spoken to George, which was when, on the spur of the moment, she had cooked up the story about herself and Worboys being witnesses to an accident on the A31. Leaving Worboys happily with his cigar, Mrs Worboys had been away for a long time. Some quarter of an hour, Worboys thought. There had again been somebody occupying the telephone box and she'd had to wait. By the time his wife had returned, Worboys had gone downstairs to settle the bill and was waiting for her, as they had arranged, in their Jaguar in the car-park at the rear of the pub.

'What sort of mood was your wife in, sir?' asked Roper. 'When she came back?'

'Angry,' said Worboys. Mrs Worboys had returned to the car with her coat and boots drenched all up her front. Some idiot in a car had driven through a puddle as she'd been about to cross the road, and doused her with spray. And that thought Roper, was yet another improbable story. Mrs Worboys' coat and boots were more than likely soaked because she'd had to scrub blood off them.

'Your wife had to change out of her coat and boots, I suppose?'

'Yes, she did,' said Worboys. 'She was very upset.'

'What did she do with them, sir?'

'She put them in the boot,' said Worboys, still innocently, and with good reason because he was, in Roper's considered opinion, in this instance, little more than an innocent bystander. Whatever he might have done over the course of last Sunday night he knew nothing of what had occurred on Saturday night at Mrs Blaney's.

'In a bag?'

'Yes,' said Worboys, 'in a bag. They were soaking wet.'

'This pub, sir,' broke in Morgan. 'D'you know where it was exactly?'

'No,' said Worboys. 'Not exactly.' Nor, if he had ever known it, could he recall the establishment's name. All he remembered was a road sign pointing to Yeovil – he had noticed that as his wife had turned into the public house's car-park, and that beside the pub, as they had driven out, he had observed a row of shops, one of which had had a post office sign hanging from its fascia board. Which might have been a description of any one of a dozen little villages in the county, but Shaw's description of East Choately had been much the same, and so would Roper's have been had he not developed a more vested interest in the place.

But hard proof was at hand, and Roper reached down into his briefcase and drew it out and laid it on the table in front of Worboys.

'Recognise this, do you, Mr Worboys?'

Worboys fished out a spectacle case from inside his jacket and put on a pair of reading-glasses. The plastic evidence-bag crackled as he turned the adjustable spanner slowly over and over between his hands.

'Yes, I think I do,' said Worboys. 'It looks like the one I keep in the back of the car.'

'You only think, sir?' said Roper.

'No,' said Worboys, lifting his gaze from the spanner and regarding Roper candidly. 'I'm fairly certain. May I ask how you come to have it?'

'It was used to kill your wife's half-sister, sir,' said Roper. 'Near where you and your wife had your meal last Saturday night.'

'Oh, my God,' whispered Worboys, his face slowly blanching. 'You mean my wife did that, as well?'

Roper didn't answer him. There was no need.

He stood with Mower on the grass by the lake, for Mower had arrived now, and two of the detective constables who had been working with him in his team over at East Choately.

The earth-filled sandbags had been used to build a circular dam around the area of the lake under which the body had been buried. From the caisson thus made the water had been pumped, not entirely, but sufficiently for the two forensic technicians to slosh about and do their work. For the moment the pump was just about holding its own against the water still dribbling through the sandbags.

It was easy now to see how it had been done. The bed of the lake had been lined with overlapping runs of heavyweight polythene sheeting, the overlaps weighted down with housebricks. A few bricks had been removed, the join peeled open and the body buried beneath it. After a topping of earth, the polythene and the bricks had been replaced. Then had come the rain, early on Monday morning.

But nothing is ever perfect. Because corpses putrefy and in putrefying give off gasses and those gasses will out – one way or the other. What Janey Erskine had thought were bubbles rising from a 'frog's nest' had been gasses seeping from the overlapping joint between two sheets of polythene. It had been Erskine who had first smelt the peculiar odour the bubbles were giving off and guessed what might be the cause of it. Grubbing about in the mud under one of the joins, his fingers had found a human face.

There came a sucking squelch from within the sandbag caisson.

'Jesus,' somebody swore softly.

'Recognise her, do you, Mr Erskine?' asked the Coroner's Officer.

'Yes,' said Erskine. 'That's her.'

Worboys reached tenderly for his wife's hands. 'My dear,' he insisted gently. 'I've told them everything. There's nothing left to hide.'

'Everything?' she sneered contemptuously, snatching her hands away. 'You? You know *nothing*!'

'They know you killed your sister. I know too.' Worboys reached for her hands again and this time held them

211

tightly. 'My dear, you simply have to tell me.'

'She was *my* mother. Not hers. How dare she!'

'How dare she what?' asked Worboys softly. 'Tell Jumbo.'

'She asked for money. Asked mother for money. *And* me.'

'But why should she ask you for money?' Worboys' voice was soft and lulling.

'Because she knew – guessed. She was going to tell the newspapers. That's what she said.'

'What was she going to tell the newspapers? Something bad?'

Mrs Worboys nodded. There was something about her now that was almost childlike.

'Yes,' she said. 'Bad. About Gregory. And Daddy Schwarz. But she *never* knew about Donald.'

'Who's Donald, sir?' asked Roper, quietly, from behind Mrs Worboys' back.

'Her first husband,' explained Worboys. His wife seemed not to hear as he fondled her hands.

They all sat in Morrison's back office. The Worboys, Mower and Roper, Morgan, the WPS from County, the area police surgeon in whose opinion Mrs Worboys was unfit to be formally questioned and might not be for several months, and then only with psychiatric treatment.

'You did something bad to them?'

She nodded. 'Burned. All burned. Didn't like them.'

'Ask her about Gregory,' said Roper. 'Her brother, sir,' he explained, when Worboys didn't seem to know what he was talking about.

'Burned,' she said, when her husband asked her. 'I set fire to him. Mummy loved him more than me. Mummy said let's go walkies. I went back for my pennies, to buy chocolate. Made a fire.'

Worboys eyes shut tightly and his hands stilled. Roper had to prompt him twice before he could continue.

'Tell me about Daddy Schwarz.'

'Hated him.' Her nose wrinkled and her mouth twisted. 'Nasty man. Horrid.'

'Why was he horrid?'

'He took Mummy away from me. I burned him. Because he took Mummy away.'

'And Donald?'

'I burned him too. Burned him *all* up. He was going away. Didn't love me any more. So I burned him.' Her vacuous gaze lifted. 'You won't go away, will you, Jumbo?'

'No my darling,' said Worboys. 'I shan't go away. I promise. Never.'

She smiled inanely at him. 'Silly old Jumbo,' she said. She played absently with his fingers. 'I told Mummy she didn't have to worry any more. I'd polished her off. She said she was my sister. Said Mummy had given her money. She wanted *our* money too, Jumbo. Said she knew all about us. Said our Mummy had killed her Daddy, that's what she said. And Baby Gregory and Daddy Schwarz. Wasn't that silly? She didn't know about Donald though. I was *very* clever with Donald.

'I went to see her, you know. After the first letter. I told her I was taking a poll of housewives to see what soap they used in their stupid washing machines. She was such a *common* little woman. And it was such a common little house. Jumbo wouldn't have liked it at all.'

'And you went back on Saturday, didn't you?' said Worboys.

'Took Jumbo's spanner,' she said. 'But Shaw was there in George's car. But I went back. I could see she didn't remember me. I'm Greta, I said, and you're Audrey, aren't you? I'm sure we can make an arrangement.'

'An arrangement about what, my darling?' said Worboys.

'The book,' she said. 'In the letter she said she had a book. All about Baby Gregory and Daddy Schwarz – and her own Daddy, the one she said Mummy killed. But she wouldn't let me have it. Mummy had it now. Mummy had given her a lot of money for it. She showed me the money. It was in a paper bag. She took it out and waved it at me.

'But she hadn't finished with Mummy yet, *or* me. She'd got something else and it was going to cost Mummy even

213

more. Lots and lots. And me too, because Jumbo was a big man. Jumbo could afford it. She was going to write to you next, Jumbo.

'So I polished her off. Hit her and hit her and hit her. And she was all blood. I was all blood too. And it wouldn't come off. I washed it and washed it, but it wouldn't come off.' She spoke earnestly, still like a child. 'I had to burn them to make them clean again. My nice coat ... and everything.

'I thought Mummy would be pleased. But she wasn't. She was in the bath. When I was little we always had our secret talks in the bathroom. I told her about the letters. She told me she'd had letters too. But it was all over now, that's what she said. There'd be no more letters, that's what she said. She'd bought the book. It was safe. She'd burned it all up in the boiler.

'I said it wasn't true. That common little woman had something else and she wouldn't let me have it, so I'd polished her off. And d'you know what she said, Jumbo, what Mummy said to me?

'She said I was mad, Jumbo. Since always and always. Said she'd spent her life protecting me. I'd killed Baby Gregory, hadn't I? And I'd killed Donald too. And Daddy Schwarz, and she said she should have had me locked up years ago, Jumbo. She said she'd have to tell the police. And I told her not to be stupid because I knew *she'd* killed my half-sister's Daddy, because that common little woman had told me so. And she told me she hadn't, Mummy did, but I knew she was lying. You know how her eyes go all funny when she's telling lies, don't you, Jumbo?

'And I told her how I'd brought her bag of money back from that woman, Jumbo. And she told me she didn't want it. Money wasn't important any more. She was going to have to tell the police, and you, Jumbo. Get out, she said, get out! She'd *never* talked to me like that before. And she was going to hurt us, Jumbo. You and me. So I pushed her under the water. And she *hit* me, Jumbo. She hurt me. And then I came to you, didn't I, Jumbo. And we put her away, didn't we? For ever and ever. And they'll blame

Shaw for killing that common little woman, Jumbo, so you don't have to worry. I changed Jumbo's spanner for George's. Because everybody knows about Shaw and how he killed that German woman, don't they? They'll blame him, won't they. Won't they, Jumbo? Mm?' A child herself, she spoke to her husband now as if he too were one. 'And now we have to go home before that *wicked* girl makes any more phone calls. She's dangerous, that girl, Jumbo. She *knows* things. I heard her talking about Daddy Schwarz on the telephone. We don't want her to know too, do we? So *can* we go home now, Jumbo? Please? Pretty please?'

NINETEEN

ROPER TOOK UP THE PHOTOCOPIES of Lindsey's and
Erskine's statements and stapled them together – an act
more prophetically symbolic than he probably realised,
and tucked them into the folder labelled WITNESSES.
Which folder he then slipped into a file labelled
SHERIDAN, MRS R.C., which in turn he laid atop another file
labelled BLANEY, MRS A.E., which he then gratefully
pushed aside to join the two identical piles ranged at the
end of his desk. Like fleas on a mangy dog, there was
nowhere like County HQ for breeding paperwork.

He sat back then, a cup of coffee in one hand, a cheroot
in the other, and his legs stretched out under his desk.
There was still more paperwork to do, but it could wait
until tomorrow. Somewhere outside in the dark, a
patrol-car took off with its siren howling, doubtless in
pursuit of yet more skulduggery.

Weygood's assistant had rung in an hour ago. Mrs
Sheridan's lungs had been awash with soapy water, and
under several of her fingernails was débris that Weygood
had already identified as human skin. The formal medical
examination of Mrs Worboys had revealed several deep
and savage scratches on her forearms. A bio-match would
be carried out at the laboratory tomorrow, but no one
doubted that the particles scraped from Mrs Sheridan's
fingernails had come from her daughter. Mrs Worboys
had still to be charged, and whether she would ever come
to trial or not was still in doubt. Of the two, Roper felt
sorrier for Julius Worboys. His wife had at least found
some kind of refuge in a disordered mind.

For the rest, Shaw had identified the adjustable spanner

that had been in the boot of Worboys' Jaguar as the one that had hung on his tool-rack in the garage. However clever Mrs Worboys thought she had been in swapping them over, that had been her greatest mistake. And Lindsey, Roper suspected, had been right about Sheridan and Mrs Shaw. When he had called at the house earlier this evening, Sheridan had ostensibly been alone in the drawing-room, but Roper had not failed to notice the ball of red wool and the two needles and the strip of knitting peeking out from under a cushion beside him.

'Miss Lindsey still about, is she, Mrs Shaw?' he'd asked, as he'd passed her in the hall on his way out.

'She left a couple of hours ago,' had replied a smiling Mrs Shaw, omitting the 'sir' to which she had treated him unfailingly hitherto. 'But if you need her particularly,' she added helpfully, 'she's staying over at Mr Erskine's till tomorrow. I think he's driving her back to London.'

Which, in Roper's considered opinion, was a very shrewd move on the part of Mr Erskine.

There was only one loose end, and that was lost now in the mists of history. He would have liked to know for certain why Rita Cavallo had asked Amy Stole to alibi for her on the night Angus Kilcullen had died, all those years ago. But nothing ever got tied up that neatly, and perhaps the loose end was better left dangling.

A shadow fell over the glass panel of the door, a set of knuckles rapped and Mower's trilby-hatted head appeared.

'If you fancy a bevvy,' he said. 'I'll meet you down at the Swan. My shout.'

'Ten minutes,' said Roper. 'I've just got a phone call to make.'

'Right,' said Mower. 'See you there,' and backed out again.

Roper wedged open his pocket book with an ashtray and picked up the telephone. 'Outside line, please, old son ... no, log it as a personal call. Many thanks.'

He dialled the number he'd copied the other day from Morgan's pocket-book, and while he waited for the connection he opened the top drawer of his desk and took out the telex from CRO concerning Gordon Winston Shaw – the fastidiously misogynistic Mr Shaw who, today, for reasons best known to himself, had chosen to grapple with the blade of a knife rather than touch the woman who had wielded it and had needed eight stitches across his hand for his trouble. With the receiver trapped between his ear and his shoulder, Roper tore the telex into shreds and dropped them into his waste-basket.

He swung his legs back under his desk as the ringing tone stopped and a rich Kentish voice sounded in his ear.

'Good evening, Mr Longden,' he said. 'Douglas Roper, sir .... We were talking the other day about Gordon Shaw .... No, sir, he wasn't our man. And I think you were right ... he wasn't yours, either.'